JOHN BARBER

A TALE OF TWO TIMES

JAMES BARRETT GRUBBS

Paperback ISBN: 979-8-218-26584-7

Ebook ISBN: 979-8-9893022-0-8

Dedicated to
Nancy Barrett

Written and Edited by Human Beings:

Theodora Bryant, Authors' HQ,
Developmental Editor

Jennifer C. Deaton, Focus Features, MPG, Story Analyst

John David Kudrick, Authors' HQ, Proofreader

PART 1

ONE

FEBRUARY 9, 2222

It took a miracle to get here, and only luck will save me now, I thought as the door slid open to my last sanctuary. I knew Death was racing to finish its task. Fear ripped at my soul and sweat covered my palms as I glanced around the dark room.

"Crystal on," I said, trying to sound strong and determined. I rubbed my right hand through my hair, collecting my thoughts. Fear, my constant companion, pulled at my breath as the words crossed my lips.

I turned to face the far wall and watched a speck of pure white light appear in front of me, levitating in the center of the room. The dot of light pulsated, then filled the room with bright, floating, three-dimensional colors and objects. The objects came together and formed several viewing screens the size of French patio doors. My last refuge was now lit by a pale-amber light. My words appeared several feet in front of me, floating in midair:

CRYSTAL ON

Instantly, several more holographic images appeared, displaying memories of my once-gifted and now-shattered life.

The room I stood in was buried deep in an isolated New Mexico mountain and like no other on Earth, a marvelous mixture of the nineteenth and twenty-second centuries. Three-dimensional holographic portals floated about, flashing real-time images of Earth and the known universe.

By a simple request, the Security Windows—as they were called—could display any activity, odor, and sound to the curious or professional voyeur. There were no mysteries or secrets left on Earth. The only unknown: my XP-LiDAR Mosquitoes, which could create a perfect-looking holographic object and transport me to watch something anywhere as an invisible hologram.

Fear ripped at me again as I watched the lifeless armada of Security warships speed toward me. *Soon nothing will save me.*

After a moment, I moved to the center of the room and stood behind a small wooden chair facing the holographic images. I took several deep breaths, leaned forward, rested my hands on the top of the chair, and pressed down on the back of it to ready myself to fight. A sudden chill shook my shoulders as I felt my perspiration-drenched shirt press against my skin.

Driven by the possible horror of dying with my story untold, I looked down on the chair and saw my tattered Caltech cap on the seat. I picked it up and held it; the old relic gave me comfort and strength.

"Open John Barber, February ninth, two thousand twenty-two."

I rubbed my right hand through my hair, still thick and jet-black, a nervous habit that has always calmed me.

I walked around the chair, sat down, and put the cap in

my lap. Then I leaned back against the cold hardwood and looked up at the ceiling, sweat dripping into my eyes. I used the cap to wipe the perspiration off my face. I looked at the fear-spawned sweat on the hat with a look of resignation.

"My name is John W. Barber. I was born February seventh, nineteen eighty-eight. My secret life and home will soon be destroyed."

That said, I took a deep breath. "It's far better for me to die than to let my discovery loose on a vanishing human race. I can't do that. Too many loving souls have died building humanity's history for me to give a soulless creation the gift of eternal human life."

I rubbed my right hand through my hair and again looked down at the cap in my lap. I tightened my lips, and my jaw twitched as memories of failure flashed through my mind's eye.

"They're close. I can almost hear their collective hearts pounding with anticipation. They won't fail a second time. My annihilation is their solution, but I fear Death. How will God punish me for discovering his guarded secret? Adam and Eve were driven from Eden. How much greater is my violation? My only grace is that I did not kill the baby."

I rubbed my hand through my hair.

"My ever-patient companion, Death, can no longer offer sanctuary. The Security Servers have perfected the transfer of human memory from the dead. Every vision, love, fantasy, and regret of a once-exclusive mind will forever be archived and put on exhibit for all to see and hear."

I stood and walked closer to the hologram displaying the flying armada of Death Ships. I clenched my jaw and narrowed my eyes, filling myself with rage.

"It is *time*"—I heard my voice getting stronger with each word—"to tell the story and build a plan."

I turned and took several steps to the door to leave. As the door silently slid open, I added, "And survive."

TWO

OCTOBER 2035

Tyler "Ty" Leggett was late for his 9:00 p.m. meeting with the president of the United States. His tires screeched as he stopped at the White House rear security gate. He flashed his security pass through the open window of his gray, government-issued, electric F-150.

After a quick glance at Ty and the blue-and-gold plastic badge, the young Secret Service agent aimed the silver biometric iris scanner, shined the blue light into Ty's eyes, looked at the results, and backed away from the vehicle with a salute as the gate opened.

Ty tapped his long, dark fingers impatiently on the steering wheel as the gate slid by. With only inches to spare, he punched the accelerator and raced to his parking spot, which faced the back of the White House.

As he prepared to park, a wry smile flashed on his lean, handsome face. Only the president's chief of staff had a parking spot closer to the White House back door. *Symbolism is everything, and the White House is at the top of the food chain,* Ty thought. *Not bad for someone born in nineteen sixty-five Alabama.*

Ty had clerked for Justice Thurgood Marshall in his last year at Howard University School of Law. Justice Marshall liked Ty and often gave him advice. He would say, "Always have a plan, look the part, never show emotion, and keep both eyes on your friends."

The day Ty passed the bar exam, Justice Marshall sent him a simple note: "Join the FBI. Those boys need changing."

Ty swung the truck into his parking spot, popped the door open, and jumped out as he brought the vehicle to a jerking stop. He moved with the energy and grace of a much younger man as he strutted toward his Homeland Security meeting with the president.

He reached the cobblestone walkway that led into the White House with a few graceful strides, and as usual, he hopped over the small hedge lining the path. The action reminded him of his track and field days. *Not bad for seventy either.*

At six-two, 190 pounds, with the chest of a gymnast, Ty Leggett looked flawless, as usual, in his custom-tailored suit.

He effortlessly maneuvered through the maze of hallways and security posts leading to the Oval Office. He smiled as he passed through the last metal detector, his security badge pinned to his coat pocket. He was well known and liked among the White House staff for his pleasant demeanor.

It was always impossible to tell if it was day or night in the White House. The building was perpetually cold, and while the president was in residence, the hallways stayed alive with dedicated staff.

A Secret Service agent stood at attention with a dour expression in every hallway. The obsessive call to duty made the White House even colder, and one could not help feeling intimidated. Someone wanted to know who you were and where you were going at every turn. Only gossip could come and go unchallenged.

Ty checked his Rolex as he reached the mahogany door guarding the White House's inner sanctum.

Three minutes late. I'll catch shit.

He opened the door for the Oval Office waiting room and was greeted with a look of disappointment from the president's personal assistant, Mrs. Oland. She had met Ty long ago while she worked in the then-senator's office. She was now standing next to the Oval Office door holding a blue clipboard with a piece of paper held on by a gold-colored clasp. On the paper were the names of the night's invited attendees, all but one crossed out.

"Jesus, Ty. Late." Her warm brown eyes softened the rebuke. "He's in a foul mood. Had to cancel a duck-hunting trip."

Ty raised his rich eyebrows, smiled, and whispered, "Thanks for the heads-up."

She started to open the door to the Oval Office.

"No, I'll get it." It was little moments like this that reminded him how many doors others had to open for him to reach his position as director of the FBI.

Ty held the door handle for a moment, took a breath, shot a quick smile, pulled the door open, slid in, leaned back against the door while still holding the handle, then gently closed it. He stepped to the right side of the door and pressed his broad shoulders against the cold plaster wall. It would only be moments before there would be a lull in the conversation and he could join the seated group.

He glanced around the room, and it struck him how small

the Oval Office was and how insignificant it made him feel. Conversations were stilted, jokes were funnier, and everything was important.

Ty knew more than he wanted about the group assembled before him, all experts in their fields and longtime survivors of Washington DC gossip. Ty had learned to force a smile when frustrated or uncomfortable. *Never show emotion*, he thought. He hated being late. *Damn divorce lawyers.* As he stood there, he glanced at each person seated around the antique Victorian coffee table.

President Ralph Rodda sat at one end, his back to the fireplace, his right foot pressed against the edge of the freshly oiled table. He rocked comfortably back and forth in his handmade rocking chair.

Rodda, an avid hunter, every so often glanced down at the tip of his handmade, soft-leather boot and squeezed his left eye closed.

Bang! Another duck gets it, Ty thought.

Rodda was in his first term and relished the trappings of political power and never missed a trick. He was wearing a tailored, white silk shirt, oversized, gold American eagle cuff links, a hand-painted Egyptian tie, and a gold Rolex, which fit loosely on his left wrist.

Rodda never removed his suit jacket while sitting, and his silk Italian slacks had a perfect crease down the center. To complete the picture, he was strategically seated under a portrait of Abraham Lincoln.

For Ty, it never got old seeing Rodda framed by Lincoln's portrait. Rodda's roots and fortune were deeply embedded in antebellum Georgia society, and he hated Abraham Lincoln.

A Southerner himself, Ty admired Lincoln for his courage and blamed John Wilkes Booth, the ignorant fool, for what followed the Civil War. Lincoln would never have allowed for the persecution of the victims of slavery.

Seated to the president's right was fifty-five-year-old Chief of Staff Eric Berg, a fastidiously organized person whose only ambition was to protect the president from self-inflicted wounds. Berg was a founding member of the FBI's Cyber Security Committee, and it was there he and Ty had become friends.

To Berg's right was sixty-five-year-old CIA Director Robert Pensky, an avid jogger and semiprofessional bridge player. Ty liked Pensky; unfortunately, Pensky did not understand Ty's sarcasm, which led to occasional misunderstandings. One time, Ty mentioned an ex-wife who had wanted a new car and had said to Pensky, "I told her, 'Of course. I'm rich on my government salary.'" Pensky thought Ty was bragging.

Next to Pensky was seventy-two-year-old Secretary of Defense Jordan Turner, a collector of Western art and a man consumed with defeating the Chinese Communist Party. Turner's mother had been a Red Cross nurse stationed at the "Hanoi Hilton" during the Vietnam War, and she relayed countless stories of how the Chinese were innately sneaky, obsessively racist, and should never be trusted. It had stuck with Turner.

This was Turner's second term as DOD secretary, and he was determined to disrupt the CCP's hundred-year plan. Having been appointed once before in a lame duck president's term, he did not have time to establish any meaningful initiatives against the Chinese then. He felt this time was perfect: Rodda was popular, and no one was happy with the Chinese.

The most down-to-earth person sitting around the coffee

table was Health and Human Services Secretary Carol Hallett, and it struck Ty: *Why is Carol at this meeting?*

Carol Hallett was without a doubt the smartest person in the room too; anyone who worked with her understood if she said something, it was not only correct, but also true. She'd graduated first in her class at George Washington School of Medicine and first at Stanford Law School. Rodda had met her while serving as Georgia's US senator, and they'd become trusted friends. One of Carol's many gifts was she made everyone feel like they were her best friend.

Her career came with a price. Carol had never had time to create a social life, she was single, and she had overcome breast cancer. Her only nonwork passion was supporting Food for Kids, a weekend food program for underprivileged elementary school children. The men in the room never gave a thought to how different their personal lives were from hers.

Seeing his moment to join the group, Ty took a quick breath, smelled the cool air of fresh paint and cleaned carpets, and purposefully walked to his chair.

CIA Director Pensky was about to speak.

With a quick glance, Ty and the president's eyes met. Ty sat down, and Rodda, a nut on punctuality, shot a glare.

"I expect people to be on time," Rodda said, looking at no one. "Y'all had plenty of notice to be on time."

Ty showed no reaction.

Rodda continued, "Before we begin, Homeland Security is not represented here tonight because Michelson resigned for medical reasons earlier this evening. He's learned he has stage-four lung cancer. Which is very sad. He's an old friend and hunting buddy. My prayers are with him and Nancy."

Rodda then turned and looked at CIA Director Pensky and gave him a nod to continue.

"Mr. President," Pensky said in his deep voice, "according to a recent report from our in-country assets and confirmed by our Five Eyes partners, the Chinese government has reopened the Wuhan laboratory and is allowing the Iranians to conduct gain-of-function research. The—"

Rodda interrupted, almost angry: "Are we funding any part of that program?"

"No, Mr. President. All federal agencies are adhering to the Dual Use Research of Concern polices and are following the UN security resolution banning gain-of-function research into pathogens to increase human morbidity and transmission."

"They never quit," Hallett whispered to herself.

DOD Secretary Turner's eyes glassed over for a moment while he tapped his pen against his lower lip and mumbled, "No surprise here."

Not seeing any connection to the FBI. Why am I here? Ty wondered.

The group fell silent, waiting for Rodda to react.

"This is how it starts," Rodda said in his relaxed Southern style. "Fear, a half-truth, followed by an overreaction. The Chinese lost more people to Covid than anyone. Why would they do this?"

"We believe it's part of their second hundred-year plan," Pensky said.

"This doesn't follow their history. That's why they built the damn wall, to keep everyone out," Rodda said.

"That is true, Mr. President, and it doesn't change a thing," Pensky said. "They want to survive the next pandemic, and this follows their modus operandi: Let someone else do the work and they get the results. They're after world domination, not like Nazi Germany—no urgency or bombs. Their weapon is time. They are following their plan."

"Why the genocide of the Uyghur Muslim population in Xinjiang?" Rodda asked.

"Purification. The Peoples Republic of China officially recognizes fifty-six ethnic groups, and the Uyghurs are not one of them." He hesitated, then looked at the president, not wanting to appear he was giving a speech.

Rodda nodded for Pensky to continue.

"Everything they do is geared toward the future. There're over one point four billion people in China, and the Chinese government wants more babies. Why? Why more babies? Why a new state-of-the-art gain-of-function lab?"

Carol whispered under her breath, "Filling the gap."

"They learned something eye-opening from Covid: They're vulnerable. Which is why they let it infect the world. They knew if it was contained inside China, no one would come to the rescue. And they had no way of stopping it." Pensky hesitated to dramatize the moment.

"To the Chinese, the world is a tool, nothing more. Everything they've done since the communist takeover in nineteen forty-nine has followed two principles: plan long-term and use greed against capitalism. To quote Karl Marx, 'The last capitalist will sell us the rope to hang him.'" He glanced around the room. "Mr. President, we have got to act." He looked down and removed a five-inch-round holographic projector from the security satchel lying on his lap and placed it on the middle of the table.

"I have two critical national security information statements. The first is Doctor Robert Royer's, our most prominent genetic scientist. May I initiate his image?"

"Yes," Rodda said.

Pensky tapped the hockey-puck-sized device, and a six-inch-tall miniature human appeared standing on top of the table. "Mr. President," Doctor Royer said, "we are at the cusp of the quantum-computing age. If we fail to join this evolution in the study of human biology, and if others succeed, this will portend our elimination."

Pensky looked at the president. "Do you have any questions?"

"No," Rodda said.

Pensky looked at Doctor Royer. "Thank you for your time, Doctor." He then tapped the holographic camera, and the image disappeared.

Feeling he had not yet convinced Rodda of the threat, Pensky said, "Once Taiwan is fully assimilated and transformed like Hong Kong, and the Japanese military is neutered, we believe Chinese expansion will be over. Our concern is: What happens after that? What happens when they or another nation needs food? What's the cleanest and fastest way to eliminate competition without bombs or machines? A virus *and* those Chinese babies? Insurance, Mr. President. They know if the Iranians are successful, they'll use it against the Israelis, and they don't want to be a casualty. They have begun storing food, and they control most if not all of the world's shipping lanes."

"A sick strategy," Rodda mumbled.

"We learned a lot from the last pandemic," DOD Secretary Turner interjected. "Our bio-med technology is still the best in the world. Vaccines are a short-term Band-Aid. The Chinese gain-of-function strategy is wrong; vaccines are not the answer. Mr. President, we need a much different approach. We do not want to race our enemies to hell, looking for a silver bullet cure next time a virus attacks. It's too dangerous."

Pensky jumped back in with, "Doctor Victoria van Dyke, director of US National Institute of Infectious Disease, would like to address this meeting. May I initiate her image?"

"Yes," Rodda said.

Pensky tapped the holographic projector. Instantly, another six-inch-tall person appeared standing on the table.

"Gentlemen, the key to surviving any future plague or pandemic is housed inside the human body. The only permanent solution to overcoming said disease will be found by adjusting our DNA and the human genetic code. I believe a genetic approach will take the teeth out of an artificially enhanced gain-of-function-created virus. And with this approach, we have the advantage: Regardless of what virus is created, once we see the DNA, we'll be able to kill it and, if necessary, modify our DNA to survive."

"Do you have any questions of Doctor van Dyke?" Pensky asked.

"No," Rodda said.

"Thank you for your time, Doctor van Dyke."

Pensky tapped the holographic projector, and the image disappeared. He picked up the projector, turned it off, and placed it back in his secure satchel.

Rodda spoke. "Congratulations, gentleman and lady, you've scared the hell out of me and saved the world. Instead of mutually assured destruction with bombs, it's now MAD viruses. Are you suggesting we modify everyone's DNA?"

"No," Secretary Turner answered. "We want to create a genetic database to address any pathogen and create a kill switch through its DNA."

"What makes you think genetic modifications will work?" Rodda asked.

"It already has on certain environmental cancers. We can't be one hundred percent sure until we study the approach," Turner said.

"And in the short term," CIA Director Pensky said, "our agents could—"

"Call Doctor No," Ty interrupted in his raspy voice, with a slight sarcastic laugh.

HHS Secretary Hallett breathed a sigh of relief under her breath. It was clear she liked Ty; they shared many of the same challenges and humor.

Rodda smiled, welcoming the break in tension.

Pensky stared blankly at Ty, not understanding his quip, and Turner showed no reaction.

Rodda turned to HHS Secretary Hallett and asked, "Carol, you're the only doctor here. What's your opinion?"

"It's true that vaccines are too specific to be effective against fast-moving variants. Gene therapy is a possible solution. It's a worthy study, and it could buy us time to survive."

Rodda turned his attention back to DOD Secretary Turner. "What's the proposal?"

"We recommend Defense and the CIA join together and develop an offline facility."

"Why?" Hallett interrupted. "There are plenty of private labs working the genome."

"That's true, and every one of them is an open door to a Chinese spy. We need a closed facility," Turner said.

"Government facilities don't exactly have a solid history," Carol replied. "Maybe we should ask ourselves: Would you place your survival on a government lab or a private enterprise?"

"I agree with both of you; an accommodation is necessary," Rodda said. "Carol, do you believe HHS can lead a program to create a genetic defense against viruses?"

Carol took a moment before answering, "Yes, we can manage such a program. The DNA mapping is done with AI technology and massive computing speed, which we have, so I believe we could undertake such an effort. No guarantees. Success depends on accruing the elite experts, and—" she glanced at Turner—"all meddling comes to me first."

Rodda smiled as the room fell silent.

"This needs tight reins," Rodda muttered to himself. After a moment, he looked at Ty. "Since this is basically a domestic operation, I want you to co-chair with Carol."

"For a moment, I was hoping the FBI didn't have a pony in this race," Ty said with a smile.

"They don't. *You* do," Rodda said quickly, lifting his eyebrows.

"Mr. President," Turner jumped in, "DOD must—"

"Mr. President," Hallett interrupted. "To save time and a lot of money, the facility we'll use is in the Nevada desert. The people we hire must commit to moving to Reno, which is a long way from DC. Our biggest competitor for talent will be Big Pharma, and they're throwing ungodly amounts of money at graduate students. For us to recruit microbiologists, geneticists, data analytics scientists, and AI programmers like those at Roadrunner, they must believe they are working for the common good of humanity and their discoveries will not be used as weapons."

The room fell silent again as Rodda rocked back in his chair, setting his eyes out the window at the Washington Monument.

"Three years," Rodda whispered. After what seemed like

minutes, he turned his eyes away from the window and looked at Hallett. "If given everything you need for three years, what would this project cost to develop and manage?"

"Why three years?" she asked.

"Because I'm not convinced this will work and I don't want a boondoggle."

Hallett tapped her fingers on the armrest. "An educated estimate," she said, her gaze fixed on the president's eyes, making sure he understood it was not a hard number.

She waited.

Rodda nodded.

"I'd say three hundred billion, and that's if we use the Nevada facility."

"Mr. President," Turner said matter-of-factly, "Defense and HHS can cover that with discretionary funds."

"A hundred billion a year," Rodda mumbled, then asked, "What's it buy?"

"AI computing and associated algorithms, cataloged results of AlphaFold, a state-of-the-art supercomputer, a fully staffed and equipped three-story research facility led by industry-leading computational biologists, geneticists, and programmers, all dedicated to one purpose: creating a database and genetic solution to killing viruses. I must add, the only caveat to our budget is if we need to get Clement Corporation's Syntopicon Q_1 computing system."

"How long to set up?" Rodda asked.

"Staffing will be the issue. Knowing that, plus getting the facility prepared, nine to ten months."

"Okay, then HHS will be the lead agency. Ty will co-chair, and Defense will be the assisting authority." Rodda leaned forward slightly, looking over his bifocals at Turner. "I dislike the CCP as much as you do; however, if any problems are created by DOD on this, I'll pull the pin."

Surprised, Turner nodded.

"Carol, you have three years' operation time," Rodda said, looking at her. "Berg will chair future meetings, select the CEO, and receive all updates." He looked around the table. "All right then." He stood and left the room.

As the others were leaving, Ty waited patiently to speak to Chief of Staff Eric Berg. As Berg was about to go into his private office, Ty touched him on the shoulder and asked, "Why wasn't Fenton from DHS here? He's number two over there."

"There've been too many leaks coming out of Homeland Security. The president is uncomfortable with Fenton and his staff. After we select a new director and things settle down, I'll bring them along."

Ty smiled and started to leave.

"Oh, by way," Berg said, touching Ty's shoulder, "I want you and Carol to choose who leads the research, and I hope John Barber's in the running."

THREE

Frustrated with the rain and apparent meeting no-show, German Assistant Federal Minister of Finance Gerhard Klaus glanced at the dashboard clock in his Mercedes EQS several times as he started his third trip around the block along one of the narrow streets in Bonn, Germany.

He turned right at the next corner, and standing ahead in the street was a thin person wearing a tailored raincoat. The person's hands were pressed deep into the pockets, and the coat collar was pulled up, obscuring the face. Klaus slowed as he approached. When he got alongside, the person turned to face the oncoming car.

Klaus recognized the man, rolled to a stop, and Peter Gysin opened the car door and jumped in. Gysin was a man in his early thirties, of average height and a slight build, with his wet auburn hair matted to his head. His distinguishing feature was how naturally feminine he looked. Some would say pretty.

"Drive toward Am Hof, and where's my fucking money?" Gysin hissed softly in German with an American accent.

Klaus squeezed the steering wheel with his oversized hands several times before he spoke. "It was wired to your bank at two p.m. today." Klaus reached into his shirt pocket and removed a banknote, tossing it at Gysin. "That's the confirmation. There will be four additional payments of a million American wired to the Bern Freya account every December."

Gysin wiped the rainwater from his face with his left hand as he snatched the paper off his chest before studying its every detail. His happy green eyes and thin-lipped smile betrayed his joy.

"You're out of the drug?" Klaus snapped.

Gysin continued to look at the paper and did not intend to answer.

"Right?" Klaus asked in his heavy German accent, his voice building in volume and anger.

There was no reply.

Klaus was not the person to push. He shot out his massive right hand, grabbed Gysin by the collar, and smashed Gysin's face onto the dashboard with a muffled thud. A small drop of blood dripped out of Gysin's nose.

"Answer me, prick," Klaus growled through clenched teeth.

With every moment of silence, Klaus pressed Gysin's face harder against the hand-oiled leather.

"It's over," Gysin grunted, trying to push Klaus' arm away.

Klaus released his grip, and Gysin sat upright, fixing his collar and wiping off the blood with the top of his left coat sleeve.

"Which US agency are you targeting?" Klaus asked.

"You'll get what you want. Did you get my sister into the American university?"

"Yes," Klaus grunted, then reached down, popped open the armrest, and removed a government-issued #10 envelope. After a quick glance, he tossed it at Gysin. "It's all in there. She's set."

Gysin ripped open the flap of the envelope with his index finger, almost tearing the enclosed paper too, and pulled out the letter. With the letter in his left hand, he glanced at it: "George Washington University—University Chair granted to Doctor Gloria Gysin, Molecular Biology."

Gysin smiled as he saw the letterhead. With a quick glance at the body of the letter, he folded the paper in half and put it into his coat pocket. He then flicked the empty envelope toward Klaus' lap.

Klaus again squeezed the steering wheel.

"Too perfect," Gysin whispered to himself as he looked out the passenger window. "Drop me off at the next corner," he ordered. "We're done."

Klaus squeezed the steering wheel harder with his right hand. He pulled the car over and stopped at the end of the next block. Gysin touched the door release and started to turn. As the door popped opened, Klaus reached out, grabbed Gysin by the hair, and twisted his head so the two men were facing each other. Gysin's bloody nose was almost touching Klaus' pockmarked face.

Klaus' hot cigar breath was thick and moist. "I've had enough of you," he growled, almost spitting the words. "If you screw with me, your sister will wear your balls for earrings."

Gysin's eyes were wide with fear as adrenaline flushed his face. He feebly struggled to free himself. Klaus' grip was too strong and painful. Helpless, Gysin relaxed and stared into Klaus' bulging, bloodshot eyes.

After a moment, and with a disdainful grunt, Klaus shoved Gysin out of the car into the flooded gutter. As Gysin got to his feet, Klaus punched the accelerator and shot down the street.

"I'll kill you, you fat pig!" Gysin screamed as his fear turned into bravado. He got onto the sidewalk, fixed his coat, and brushed the gutter mess off his pant legs. Finished, he glanced up to see Klaus turn down the next block and disappear toward the Kennedy Bridge.

Gysin moved over to a storefront window and looked at his reflection. After a few moments of fixing his hair and coat, he turned and walked halfway up the street to a nondescript two-story office building. He glanced over his shoulder as he pushed the glass-and-metal door open.

He looked around, standing in the empty foyer. The damp carpet and musty smell filled the small room with a pungent odor. He crinkled his upper lip and again wiped the remaining blood from his nose on his left coat sleeve.

He saw that the iron-and-glass elevator cage was empty and then glanced at the stairs. With only a second's hesitation, he walked to the elevator, pushed the call button, and waited for the cage to return to the ground floor.

The elevator door opened. He moved toward the side of the black cage, turned, and pushed the second-floor button, leaning back and pressing his shoulders against the bars. As the elevator bounced its way up to the second floor, he reached into his coat pocket and fingered Klaus' letter.

"Too perfect," he whispered again, shaking his head from side to side with a tight-lipped smirk.

Before the elevator door even opened, Gysin impatiently

stepped closer and waited. He exited and walked quickly down the tattered carpeted hallway, looking at the door nameplates. With only two doors remaining, he found what he was looking for: "Doctor William Dougdale, Plastic Surgeon." He grabbed hold and twisted the small brass doorknob and pushed on the cut-rate wooden door. It opened into a small, cheaply decorated reception area.

On the side walls hung ten-by-ten photographs of successful cosmetic surgeries. A well-used, cracked, fake-leather couch and several cloth chairs lined the back wall facing the reception counter. Unfinished wooden end tables filled the remaining space. The room did not inspire confidence or success. People came to Doctor Dougdale to fix a problem or hide one. Like some of his patients, Doctor William Dougdale had gotten greedy and destroyed a successful public career. Now he worked alone and in the shadows.

With a quick glance around the room, Gysin moved to the front counter. Not seeing anyone, he pressed the silver-plated push bell sitting on the center ledge in front of the closed, opaque sliding-glass window.

After a moment, a man appeared at the window and slid it open. He was tall and obese, likely in his late fifties. His lab coat was pristine, his fingernails manicured, and his full head of hair tightly combed. He held his large frame with an air of ascendancy.

The man leaned forward. His breath smelled of mints, and his Krigler Topaze Imperiale cologne completed the picture of someone who was sophisticated with refined taste.

"Where's Dougdale?" Gysin snapped.

"I'm Doctor Dougdale," the man answered in a warm, compassionate voice.

"I'm Gysin."

"Come with me," Dougdale said, his demeanor suddenly cold.

An hour later, the examination complete, Gysin exited Dougdale's building. It was dusk. He walked to the street corner, waved down a taxi, and, with a fulfilled grin on his face, waited to be picked up.

"Too perfect," he muttered as the tan Mercedes taxi pulled to the curb. He jerked the door open with his left hand and slid into the car, closing the door on his raincoat.

"Bonn University administration building."

Several minutes later, the taxi stopped across the street from a massive, baroque, stone-faced fortress. Gysin glanced at the meter, threw the fare money at the bearded driver's face, opened the door, and slid out without closing the door.

He followed the dirty cement walkway to the imposing university administration building. Up ahead, three students were walking toward him, focused on their cell phones. As they approached, he purposely bumped into one girl, knocking her out of the way.

"Jerk," she said in German.

Unfazed by her comment, he glanced at his gold Day-Date President Rolex and quickened his pace along the walkway toward the admin building. When he reached the stone stairway leading into the building, an attractive young woman appeared and walked down the stairs toward him. She smiled as they passed. He returned a pleasant look, thinking, *Another time, sweetie pie.*

The massive doorway was open, and he walked the familiar, long stone hallway to the faculty section. He arrived at the first cluster of private offices in a few minutes. He reached the third door on his left, grabbed the polished brass knob, hesitated, took a deep breath, and glanced at the nameplate: DOCTOR GLORIA GYSIN, PHD. MOLECULAR BIOLOGY: DATA ANALYTICS CHAIR. A jealous twinge tightened his lips. He burst into the spacious room without knocking.

Doctor Gysin, facing her monitor while typing an email, seemed not to notice the sudden intrusion. Her shoulder-length, gold-streaked auburn hair was pulled up onto her head and held by a beautiful, five-inch, dark-blue, gold-plated Japanese hairpin. She was the epitome of class and carried an air of superiority. She was in her early thirties with clear, bright-green eyes and a perfect smile. She was beautiful.

As he waited for her to acknowledge him, he turned to the custom-made mahogany bookshelf and pulled out a book. He opened it and saw she had signed her name on the front page: *Gloria Gysin, New Orleans, Louisiana.*

"I got the notice; you start in three months," he said gruffly as he thumbed through the book.

Gloria smiled without turning to face her brother.

"Why surround yourself with such useless crap?" he asked, glancing around the organized and immaculate room.

The Egyptian floor rug and brass floor lamps looked original and unspoiled. The desk seemed out of place. Its rich, dark-wood and inlaid writing mat belonged in a French minister's office, not on a college campus. On her desk were delicate Waterford crystals, a richly polished, gold-and-blue Bulgari clock, and a silver pencil holder. Placed front and center was a framed copy of her acceptance as a visiting scholar into Bonn University's prestigious Genetic Research Program.

Everything was purposefully placed, pristine, and never out of order. Diplomas from the University of New Orleans and Louisiana State University hung on her walls. Her two most prized accomplishments were the gold-framed copies of her master's in biology and her PhD in molecular biology from Tulane University. Gloria Gysin was the perfect example of an impoverished child's relentless drive to succeed.

Peter tossed the book onto her desk, knocking over a small bottle of hand sanitizer. Gloria quickly picked up the bottle and compulsively wiped the liquid off the desk with a tissue. The slight odor of the spilled disinfectant gave the already obsessively clean room a hospital feel.

"If you weren't lazy and had finished your doctorate, we wouldn't have had to use Lisa," Gloria said with a tinge of anger. She continued cleaning the spot, using a fifth tissue. Finished drying, she opened the top desk drawer and removed a sanitary wipe and meticulously cleaned her hands.

"I didn't hear you bitching about the money, and my grades were better than yours, bitch."

Gloria's face flashed white for a moment. Her right hand twitched slightly and her eyes narrowed as she turned around to face him. "If not for Klaus, you would've been arrested, and we need him, you fool. We can't afford to piss him off." She struggled to control her rage.

For the second time that day, Peter felt a rush of fear and his face betrayed his emotion. "My surgery's set," he said, looking away from his twin sister. "I'll have my new face and identity in a couple of weeks, before the end of October."

"Good. I'll meet Dougdale as soon as you're healed." Her voice had regained its soft tone, and she seemed to relish the thought of what lay ahead for Doctor Dougdale. "If all goes as planned, I'll be assigned and settled at George Washington University by the end of the year. Then I'll coordinate with Klaus about your visa." Gloria glanced at the monitor. "I received an email from Lisa. The pressure at Harvard is affecting her—she's going to snap. Once I'm settled, I'll go see her."

"That's my call," he stated aggressively, leaning toward her slightly.

Gloria's green eyes flashed with primal hate. She leaped up from her chair, her fingers twisting into ugly claws, and lunged at him.

Terrified, Peter fell backward and twisted his face and body toward the door. Before his left hand reached the doorknob, Gloria's first blow struck him on the side of the head.

He dropped to his knees, his face banging into the door. With his face smashed against the wood, Gloria dropped down onto his back, pressing him to the floor. Twisting his hair with her left hand, she reached down and s clawed at his testicles.

Soft cries for forgiveness and muffled rage could be heard in the hallway as sibling heartbreak continued.

Six weeks after Peter Gysin's cosmetic surgery, on a crisp December afternoon, Gloria Gysin, wearing a snow-white cashmere shawl wrapped around her shoulders and a new, fitted, red St. John knit suit, crossed the busy street toward Dougdale's office building. Her auburn hair was pulled up and held in place with the dark-blue Japanese hairpin. She looked radiant and vibrant as she navigated purposefully through the busy street, her persona captivating.

Gloria glanced at the black cage elevator and instead effortlessly climbed the open stairs to the second floor. She walked down the hallway and, on finding Dougdale's office, opened the door and went directly to the front counter. She paused before she rang the push bell with a quick tap of her right palm. She looked through the open reception window into the empty area. After a moment, a man appeared, walking down the hallway. He smiled as he faced Gloria.

"I'm here for my appointment with Doctor Dougdale. I was referred by Mr. Peter Gysin," she said in perfect German.

"Ah, the woman who wouldn't leave her name," the man said, somewhat amused.

"I'm sure you understand." She smiled. "We need our secrets."

"Perfectly."

He closed the glass slider and slid along the counter to the hallway door. Before he opened it, he checked his reflection in a framed poster next to the door, brushed his hair with his fingers, and checked his breath. Satisfied, he smiled at himself, opened the door with a warm expression, and moved into the reception area, closing the door behind him.

"I'm Doctor William Dougdale," he said, offering his hand.

Gloria did not offer her hand. "I have a cold."

Dougdale nodded and moved back a few feet. "Would you like to talk here or in my office?"

"Your office would be perfect."

"This way, please," he said with a gesture as he opened the door and held it for her. "It's at the far end of the hallway. Please follow me."

Old photographs lined the walls, of Dougdale and local politicians, celebrities, and the famous who'd once filled his calendar in much happier times. Nothing recent. His disgrace was simple: greed. He'd engaged in a type of garage surgery, using unqualified assistants and expired drugs and products. To his rich clientele, the suffering of his patients was unforgivable. Now he only worked on the dangerous and outcast.

As they walked down the hallway, they passed three small, empty examination rooms; the fourth room was not empty. The door was cracked open slightly, and sitting on the examination table, covered in a paper gown facing the far wall, was a petite, middle-aged woman staring straight ahead with dark, glassy eyes. There was also a man in the room with her.

Gloria passed the last examination room without hesitation and continued down the hallway behind Dougdale to his private office.

The room was comfortable and warm, exactly what one would expect to see in a successful doctor's private office, the walls covered with vacation pictures, dated awards, diplomas, certificates, and candid photos. Medical folders were neatly stacked on his desk, and a meticulously organized bookshelf covered the back wall.

"Please be seated." He pointed to the small cloth chair facing his desk. Before sitting, he opened a casement window that faced the street below, allowing the morning breeze and sounds to filter into the room. He sat behind his polished pine desk and comfortably leaned back in the leather chair.

Gloria sat.

He looked at her for a moment with a quizzical expression. "Have we met before?" He stared at her face, looking more perplexed. "I'd swear you—"

"I thought I was clear about us meeting alone," Gloria interrupted, her voice cold and threatening.

Dougdale's expression changed, and smugness replaced curiosity. "They're both blind. How can I help you?"

This will still work, she thought. She relaxed, placed her Louis Vuitton handbag on the floor, crossed her legs, and said in an inviting voice, "I had a head injury several years ago. It's very embarrassing." She rubbed her forehead above the hairline. "I'm afraid there's something wrong. Would you please see if there is something that can be done?"

"My pleasure."

Gloria stood and removed the Japanese hairpin with her right hand. Her soft auburn hair dropped to her shoulders. Her relaxed beauty was almost breathtaking. She lowered her right arm to her side.

Dougdale popped a breath mint, put on his glasses, and moved around the desk.

Facing Gloria, he studied her forehead. "I don't see anything. Turn this way; there's more light." He gently placed his hands on her shoulders and turned her to the window. "That's better." He lifted his right hand and softly rubbed her forehead.

Gloria's face was cool, her breathing slow and relaxed.

Dougdale lowered his glasses and probed her forehead with his fingers.

She twisted her fingers around the hairpin, her knuckles turning red, then white. She began to lift the pin, her dilated pupils the only betrayal of her excitement. With sudden ferocity, Gloria clenched her teeth, twisted her lips into a hideous snarl, and plunged the spike deep into Dougdale's brain. The only sound was a gasp of moist, hot air from his gaping mouth as his life escaped.

Gloria released her death grip on the pin and held Dougdale's head between her hands, holding his frozen body in place. Her thin lips quivered; her face twitched with excitement as she watched his eyes die.

At the height of her climactic elation, a horrific explosion, followed by a massive fireball, ripped through the room. The windows exploded outward with incredible force. Pedestrians in the street below screamed as waves of fire and glass rained down on the street.

People rushed from every direction to gawk at the growing blaze. Only one solitary, thin, feminine figure—leaning slightly against a small tree, with face and head covered in clean cotton bandages—showed no reaction to the chaos. A closer examination would have revealed happy green eyes and a perfect smile through the bandage folds, and a clenched left hand, pushed deep into the pocket of the white cashmere coat, a thumb repeatedly pressing the spent detonator button—up and down, up and down, it went.

FOUR

The president's chief of staff, Eric Berg, had called for a meeting in the Oval Office on January 2, 2036. Scheduled to attend were FBI Director Ty Leggett, SecDef Jordan Turner, and HHS Secretary Carol Hallett. Ty held the door as Carol walked past him. As the group mingled before sitting, Ty noticed the front page of the *Washington Times* online edition on Berg's computer screen. The headline read: FEDERAL BUREAU OF INVESTIGATION CRACKS KU KLUX KLAN NETWORK. A yellow highlighted quote from Clarice Kirkland read: "It's about time. All the Klan did was take off sheets and put on ties."

Ty glanced at the story and looked up at Berg.

"A little hard on the boys," Berg said.

"Not hard enough."

Berg glanced around at everyone. "I hope you are all well. Unfortunately, our time will be short. The president canceled his campaign event and scheduled a meeting in forty-five minutes with his Homeland nominee."

No one seemed surprised. Oval Office meetings were always in flux. The chief of staff's small office adjoined the Oval Office and was small. Berg had to schedule his larger meetings when the president was out of the White House.

"The purpose of our meeting is to receive an update on the virus research program and select a team leader." Berg looked at Carol, nodded for her to speak.

She leaned to her right, reached into a briefcase next to her on the floor, and removed four folders. She placed the folders on her lap and, using her index finger, removed the purple rubber band that held the folders together. Finished, she dropped the rubber band into her briefcase.

"I took the liberty of naming our group the Genetic Development Committee, which will obviously be the GDC."

She passed the folders around the table.

Each individual blue-leather folder was sealed with a small red ribbon. Written across the face of each folder in white block lettering was: THE GENETIC DEVELOPMENT COMMITTEE. Below the lettering, stamped in red across the folder, it read: TOP SECRET—FOR YOUR EYES ONLY.

They opened their folders.

"I won't address the administrative detail in this conversation. Those specifics are enclosed with your folder. If you have comments or questions, please reach out to me.

"The proposed research facility is on the outskirts of Reno, Nevada. The history of the building is a question of poor timing. The National Institute of Health requested that HHS build the facility in response to the twenty-thirty Nigerian monkeypox outbreak. NIH, along with WHO, feared the outbreak was the first airborne transmission. The National Institute of Allergy and Infectious Diseases—

NIAID—joined HHS to test monkeypox and other deadly diseases in a remote and secure US facility.

"Their 'Genetic Answer' campus, as it was named, was completed in February of twenty thirty-three. That's where the poor timing comes in, as WHO determined that same month that the monkeypox outbreak was not an aerosol mutation, and funding for NIAID was drastically cut when it was disclosed they were again involved in gain-of-function research outside the US. The project was canceled, and HHS sealed the buildings in March of that year.

"The retrofit is in progress, and local housing has been reserved. The satellite designation has been finalized and activated. We're part of the FBI cybersecurity network. On-site security has been contracted, and auxiliary staffing is complete and scheduled. The executive research team will be formed soon. We are ahead of schedule."

She looked around the table to reassure herself there were no questions. Seeing none, she continued, "The objective for today's meeting is to choose the project director. We have narrowed our choices to two candidates: Doctor Robert A. Royer and Doctor John W. Barber. Both candidates' résumés are enclosed with your folders." She removed each résumé from her folder and held them together. "To conserve time, I'll briefly discuss each candidate. Both men's bona fides are impressive, to say the least." She smiled.

"Doctor Royer, who is probably the reason this committee was formed, is one of America's most distinguished genetic scientists. At seventy years old, his bona fides are too long to list. Doctor Royer is single and was born and raised in New England.

"Doctor Barber, at forty-eight, is twenty-two years younger than Doctor Royer. He was born in Southern California and graduated from Caltech with an undergraduate degree in biochemistry.

"Royer received his undergraduate from Harvard, also in biochemistry. Both men have PhDs in natural sciences and mathematics from Harvard. Interestingly, Barber studied under Royer while pursuing his doctorate. Royer pursued a career in academia and has attained world recognition for his study of genetic chemistry.

"Barber, after receiving his Harvard doctorate in two thousand four, joined a small bio research lab in Virginia. It was there he became interested in cellular mutations and genetic modifications. He led several research teams in his first five years, which patented landmark medications. In two thousand ten, he was named president of Development and Co-Operations. He left the bio company in twenty fourteen and returned to Harvard as a research fellow to study cellular distortions, specifically in children with progeria. In twenty twenty, he joined the FBI as a non-official advisor for medical cybersecurity. He now chairs that committee. Barber is married with two teenage children."

She put down the two pieces of paper and looked at the men seated around the polished table. "Both men are brilliant. The other candidates we looked at fell far short. However, there are some negatives."

"I'd say," Turner said. "For starters, Royer is a pacifist who hates the military, and that's only the beginning of his anti-military credentials. Your second choice is a little too close to the Chinese Communist Party; he's received several grants from the CCP. And he's an unrealistic idealist. This can't be all we have?" Finished, Turner leaned back in his chair, convinced further discussion was pointless.

Ty spoke up. "Doctor Barber and I have worked together

for almost ten years; I have become close to him and his family. He passed our deep background investigation and has attained the highest security clearance possible. Barber is aware of the threats facing America and has helped us fight off several significant Chinese cyberattacks. And something you might find interesting, Secretary Turner: John requested to be admitted into our six-week training course at Quantico. He wanted to understand more than cyber at the FBI. I made the exception and let him do it." Ty smiled. "And, to my joy, he passed. It almost killed him, but he made it through."

Carol smiled. "Lastly," she continued, "Doctor Royer does not work well with people, while Doctor Barber is an effective team leader and surprisingly unassuming, given his accomplishments. His wife, Megan, is a medical doctor."

Silence.

Eric Berg glanced at Barber's résumé while he flicked the edge of the enclosed photograph with his thumb. "Any other additional thoughts on the candidates?" he asked, glancing at the three others. "Hearing none, my vote is for Doctor Barber. Anyone strongly disagree?" He removed his glasses, turned to Hallett. "So now how close are we to being up and running?"

"June or July. Now that we have a director to help with finalizing staff, remodeling, and other managerial details, we should make our deadline."

"Okay, what do we call the project?" Berg asked.

"I say we stick with Genetic Answer—GA," she said.

"What's the first-year goal?"

"To capture all human genetic data from the top five genome laboratories, create an open source link to the European Molecular AlphaFold database, and isolate and categorize every microprotein, peptide, and amino acid for genetic classification. Isolate and categorize all genetic immunities, create an AI database of said immunities, and initiate a gene modification program to match immunities to pathogens."

"Wow." Berg smiled. "That should appease the president." He glanced at this watch. "Our time is almost up. Carol, you and Ty remain co-chairs, and we're the board of directors. The CIA will consult as needed. If you feel DHS help is necessary, I'll consult with them. All security protocols will be followed, and please keep in mind, Genetic Answer has a three-year shelf life beginning this July. Doctor Barber's team must understand they are under the gun. The Chinese are testing vaccines on pigs infected with bird flu and are administering experimental Covid vaccines on Uyghur prisoners. Disgusting."

He took a calming breath. "I know this is a big ask, Carol, and maybe impossible, but Barber's team must find the Holy Grail DNA kill shot, as I call it—a gene that protects us against gain of function. Remember, the Chinese are not our only enemies, and none of them care how many die destroying America."

FIVE

JULY 2036

Five miles outside of Reno, Nevada, secluded by a desolate canyon, a razor-wired, fenced-in compound enclosed a five-hundred-acre industrial complex. The facility housed three buildings: a single-story warehouse of five thousand square feet, a smaller work shed, and a three-story, forty-thousand-square-foot, concrete, tilt-up office building.

The office building housed a subterranean basement of ten thousand square feet, a warehouse of five thousand square feet, a thousand-square-foot medical research lab, a thousand-square-foot animal containment/experimental center, several computer cool rooms, a cryostat room, four clean rooms, three decontamination rooms, three hazmat emergency safe rooms, nine small labs, a video conference center, three research libraries, seven full bathrooms, five executive offices, one principal suite, a kitchen, a cafeteria, and a satellite communication security center.

The second building was a single-story, fifty-thousand-square-foot, concrete, tilt-up warehouse. It stored the hermetically sealed, long-term-emergency bio-safe room, emergency food storage, an emergency helicopter, three military transport trucks, an ambulance, a fire truck, refrigeration vehicles, and other assorted equipment.

The thousand-square-foot shed outbuilding housed hazardous material equipment, retardation chemicals, suppression chemicals, extra isolation gowns, generators, water pumps, air-conditioner compressors, building tools, and a workshop.

The compound was obscured by a five-hundred-thousand-square-foot Amazon distribution warehouse, which faced south toward Interstate 80. With large trucks coming and going throughout the day and night, the concrete road leading to the facility was easily overlooked. A two-lane road led northeast around the distribution center to a small electric gate at the rear of the Amazon property.

Security television cameras surveilled the razor-wire-fence perimeter. Motion and heat detectors protected the balance of the outer compound. Private property and hazardous materials signs were posted on the gate and all along the perimeter to warn curious onlookers.

To gain access to the facility day or night, one had to stop and wait for the gate to slide open. The guards stationed in the compound's main building could hear a whisper and identify every license plate and car exiting the freeway miles from GA. With facial recognition and heat sensors, it was impossible to pass onto the property without approval.

A security guard watched as an electric Ford Bronco traveled along I-80 to the Amazon center off-ramp. She pushed the joystick and zoomed in on the car as it turned off the freeway toward the Amazon center. She twisted the joystick and focused the camera on the driver. She smiled.

Doctor John Barber drove up to the steel gate, stopped, and hit the button to roll down his window. He was wearing a new Caltech baseball cap pulled tightly on his head. She could hear a local Reno sports program coming from the car radio.

"Good morning, Naomi," John said, apparently to no one, as he turned down the radio.

"And a good morning to you, Doctor Barber," came a female voice out of nowhere.

John looked through the windshield down the winding road into the canyon as the gate slid open and thought, *Ugly*.

The outside façade of the three-story building looked dated. The inside did not. The buildings had received a total interior makeover since the Genetic Development Committee took over the site. Everything—including paint, carpet, fiber optics, air-conditioning, air filtration, insulation, windows, electrical, generators, Wi-Fi, mainframe computers, biohazard containment system, satellite receivers, and secure communications—had been upgraded. Everything was new. Only the basement quantum-computing cryostat room was unfinished.

The first floor of the office building contained security offices, the conference center, the kitchen, the cafeteria, mechanical facilities, servers, the supercomputer, server cold rooms, the security reception desk, and the reception foyer.

The second floor contained two laboratories, the computer research library, two full bathrooms, the main lab, two chemical labs, and the executive offices. Barber's suite, the only private room, was at the west end of the building, next to the main lab. The third floor housed the veterinarian research lab, animal containment center, and additional research labs and computational computer rooms.

He drove through the open gate and, a few minutes later, reached the back of the office building and parked. He got out of the car holding his tweed coat and walked along the gravel walkway to the back door.

With his six-foot frame, lean body, and broad shoulders, he had the build of an athlete, although sports had never been part of his life. With jet-black hair, hazel eyes, and olive complexion, he naturally presented a kind demeanor.

Once inside the air-conditioned back hallway, he put on the coat and walked through the narrow passageway toward the foyer and elevators.

The security counter was in the center of the foyer, facing the main door. Scott Wilson, a forty-year-old retired Navy SEAL officer, was sitting at the marble-covered counter, facing a line of security monitors. Scott had volunteered to fight in Ukraine, where he lost an eye. He'd joined the Genetic Answer team to assist Doctor Joyce Dillingham with security.

"Good morning, sir," Scott said as John approached to sign the register.

"How are you this hot July morning?" John asked.

"Had a great day stream-fishing yesterday."

"That sounds very nice."

"Yes, it was," Scott answered.

John held his smile and confidently moved to the elevators and pushed the up button. He watched as the light above one of the elevators showed a car coming up from the basement. After a moment, that elevator's doors opened, and standing inside the metal box was Doctor Robert A. Royer.

The moment Royer saw John, he raised his chin, looked down his nose, and said in his baritone voice, "When will this place run right? The servers we're using are slow. You'd think we could—"

"Good morning, Robert," John interrupted, his expression relaxed. "We've only been in for less than five weeks. Are you getting out?"

"I was, but now that you're here, I'll ride up with you."

As they rode the elevator John patiently listened to Royer's complaints about GA's funding and equipment as the elevator silently lifted to the second floor.

Royer, a thin man in his early seventies with pepper-colored hair and a pale complexion, presented an intimidating first impression at six-five. However, the opposite was true. His doctorial demeanor and intellectual arrogance were a façade to mask a shy and insecure nature.

When the elevator doors opened on the second floor, the conversation had shifted to the Department of Defense and the CIA's involvement with GA, and Royer's hatred for both agencies based on their orchestrating America's wars, beginning with Vietnam.

The two men walked out into the smell of a freshly painted hallway, covered by a cheap, glued-to-the-floor beige carpet, and the conversation continued. The elevator doors closed. Robert waited a moment and pushed the call button to go back down.

"The CIA is responsible for all the violence in the world, and it started with Johnson's Vietnam war, and we're taking those people's money," Royer said with disgust.

John did not agree about the CIA. He blamed Lee Harvey Oswald for Vietnam; President Kennedy would have never escalated that war. As with Abraham Lincoln's assassination,

America's future was destructively altered by a president's death. Both presidents had been murdered by ignorant fools, and America was forever changed.

John understood Royer had lost his father in Vietnam and hated President Johnson. "Johnson did one great thing: He appointed Thurgood Marshall to the Supreme Court," John said.

"Even a blind pig will stumble over an acorn," Royer snapped.

"By the way, why were you coming up from the basement?"

"I was looking at the quantum cryostat room. I love the idea of someday using the fastest machine ever invented matched with our AI database."

The elevator doors opened, and Royer got in. John turned and walked in silence down the hallway past the main lab to his office.

Seated in the small reception area, looking at her computer monitor, was his assistant, Laurie McDuffy. Laurie was a full-figured woman with a warm and outgoing personality. They'd met when she worked at a local Los Angeles restaurant to pay her UCLA graduate school tuition. They became friends when she spilled a chocolate malt on his new tweed coat.

"Good morning, John. A server problem has—"

"I know. I bumped into Robert on the way in, and he mentioned it, along with a lot more." He rubbed his right hand through his hair. "Please set a meeting with IT for this afternoon."

Laurie nodded. "Oh, I almost forgot. Doctor Dillingham left a voicemail; she'd like to see you at lunch."

"I'm busy then. See if she'll meet at two instead?"

John continued into his private office. The walls were lightly decorated with family mementos and pictures of friends. The sitting area looked like a middle-class family room. A cloth couch, several chairs, and a recliner sat to one side of the room. An oak desk, John's pride and joy, faced the door. He'd salvaged it from his grandfather's garage, and every time he sighted the antique, it brought back fond childhood memories of him playing doctor.

There was only one framed photograph on the desk of Megan and their children. Next to the photograph was a small block of wood with a quotation carved into it: NEVER GIVE UP. THERE IS ALWAYS HOPE. Resting on the swivel chair was one of his many Caltech baseball caps.

He took off his jacket and hung it on the chair, then picked up the cap and placed it on the desk along with his cell phone. He sat to read his emails when his cell beeped. He tapped the video button and saw his closest friend, Ty Leggett.

"How's your morning?" Ty asked, a smile on his face.

"Our servers are screwed up. I bumped into Royer in the elevator, and now you call."

"Royer." Ty snickered. "Then this won't help: Megan's leaving you."

"It kills you she married a dork."

"She'll come around."

"Hope not."

"Congratulations, by the way. You've survived almost five weeks in America's banana belt."

"It's hot, and the last thing growing here is bananas."

"Speaking of Royer, how is he working out?"

"Very well. His team has made great progress with the AI database program, and thanks to the AlphaFold open source and the genome database, we're halfway through compiling a workable foundation. Robert believes by year's end his team will have assembled the most complete catalog of amino acids, proteins, and human chemistry in the world. With that process completed, we can start to ask 'what if' questions." John stopped. "What a minute. Why are you asking? You've read my updates."

"Yep, but I like hearing you get excited."

"On that front, I spoke to Carol yesterday. Now that we have some idea of the size and complexity of data we're working with, I asked her to consider finding us a quantum computer."

"That didn't take long. Five weeks and you want more. I'm amazed Carol didn't laugh. Billions for one damn machine."

"Our goal is to have it here by March of next year, and we're after the Clement Syntopicon Q1 system."

"Amazing," Ty said.

"It's the best, a game changer. The AI DeepMind program and supercomputers are fast, but the SQ1 is an unbelievable hundred fifty million times faster. We can answer—"

"Slow down in the harbor, big guy. You're talking to a lawyer."

"Sorry. First, how fast: A quantum did a calculation in less than four minutes. No big deal, right? Except the same calculation would have taken our fastest computers ten thousand years to perform. And that's a fact. It's possible that with the SQ1 quant, we can find Berg's Holy Grail gene before the three-year deadline and other discoveries we haven't even thought of."

"What about the AI revolution we're in the middle of?" Ty asked.

"AI's only as fast as the computer it's using. If you mix it with quantum, you'd have a synthetic god."

"Okay, I get it. By the way, I've learned Turner got a pledge from Carol that Royer will never run GA, and he wants to add his people to GA research."

"Too bad for him; we're fully staffed. Thanks to Carol, we've located our last scientist—a Doctor Gloria Gysin from George Washington University. I'll send her résumé and bona fides in a few minutes. We hope to bring her on by early winter. And tell Turner that Royer is harmless, and it's his genius, along with Joyce Dillingham's programming, that will lead us to stopping gain-of-function viruses."

"I'm glad you've found your last doc. I'll prioritize her background check. As for Turner, he can't help himself—it's politics as usual. Build Royer up in your monthly reports; that'll help. Lastly, I'm forwarding a report from the CIA about the Iranians testing a smallpox variant."

"A new horror. The SQ1 can make everything moot. Its speed will solve our most complex questions, and quite possibly—"

"You don't have to sell me—just the president," Ty interrupted. "But, from your hopeful lips to God's ear."

That afternoon, the Barber children—Lynn, ten years old, and Abby, eight years old—were in their grammar school cafeteria, sitting at a small table talking to friends while the other children were eating and running about the room, when suddenly the room went quiet.

The other children stared at the door and then made giggling sounds. The Barber girls turned and saw their father standing at the door, grinning, holding two In-N-Out Burger bags and a small bag of M&M's.

The girls ran to him and hugged him.

"I told you he'd be here for lunch," Abby said.

"You always keep your promises, Daddy," Lynn said as she grabbed the bag out of his hand and pulled it open.

"M-'n'-M's! Oh, Daddy," Lynn said, hugging him again.

Back at GA after lunch, John was sitting at his desk when the intercom buzzed.

"IT called. They fixed the servers," Laurie said, "and Joyce has arrived for your two o'clock meeting."

Sitting in the reception area was Joyce Dillingham, who had four roles at GA: She oversaw the Cybersecurity, Computer Science, and Human Resources departments, and also assisted Robert Royer in the main lab. She had one of those wonderful dispositions and can-do-anything attitudes that made her a perfect match with Royer. She had a PhD in computer science and data analytics, and a master's in human resources, but her genius was in computer programming. She had a bowl on her desk that was always filled with M&M's. She was light on her feet, quick of mind, and never spoke unkindly of anyone.

John saw Joyce sitting on the reception room couch. "Hi, Joyce, you wanted to see me? Follow me," he said, smiling.

John sat in the cloth recliner, and Joyce sat on the couch in his office.

"Thank you for seeing me. Not to sound alarmist, but I think our little secret is out."

John raised an eyebrow.

"Our satellite system got probed last night. They did not get in or spend much time trying. I used the tracking programs, and the closest I got was Asia."

49

John rubbed his right hand through his hair. "You're sure they left nothing behind?"

"Yes, our firewall is good."

"Okay, then please send an email to Ty Leggett at the FBI, listing the details, and at the end of the message, please add in caps, 'SNEAKY BASTARDS.'"

SIX

It was dusk when John glanced out his office window. He quickly shut down his computer and raced to his car. The winding, thirty-minute drive home gave him time to decompress.

Home, he parked the car in the driveway at the same time as the streetlights popped on. His shirt sleeves were rolled up and his tie loosened. There were plastic buckets, a toy scooter, and assorted Wiffle balls strewn around the lawn, and he spotted a foam baseball next to the walkway. He picked it up and held it for a moment, took several quick steps backward, and threw the ball. *You're out*, he thought as the ball bounced into the neighbor's front yard.

As he reached the front step of his modest, two-story tract home, a smile creased his face. Summer decorations covered the porch. *How does she find the time?*

"Megan," John called out as he pushed the door closed.

"I'm in the kitchen."

John dropped his car keys into the small wicker basket on the bookshelf counter next to the front door. He walked through the family room to the kitchen. Megan stood next to the stove, eating an apple, wearing her medical smock; dinner was almost ready. They had been married eleven years, and John still marveled at her beauty.

Megan was in her early forties; her light-brown hair showed little signs of gray. To her delight, she could still wear the competition swimsuit she had worn in college. At five-six and with a natural glow to her face, Megan provoked pleasant looks from men and admiring eyes from women. Given her gentle personality, her medical patients seldom complained about their visits.

The smell of hamburgers and french fries filled the galley kitchen. Lynn and Abby were sitting at the dinette table doing their homework.

John went to Megan and gave her a kiss and a soft embrace. "How's my bride?"

"Glad you're home."

He reached around her and grabbed a red apple off the granite counter. "I'm starving," he said as he took a big bite.

"Little wonder. You left the house at five this morning, and I understand the girls had a surprise visitor at lunch."

John looked at the children. They quickly looked down at their tablets.

"That's why you leave so early in the morning—so you can sneak off. You're not fooling anyone. The school calls me every time you bring them lunch. Also, I have a brutal week ahead at the hospital and need you to cover for me."

"No problem. You're the one with the crazy schedule. I spoke to Ty Leggett today. He wanted to know why you married me."

"He's a wonderful man." She grinned. "The girls have something to ask."

John looked at the girls.

"We've got a play to show you," Lynn said.

John glanced at Megan, who was smiling.

This is what it's all about, she thought.

"Can we, can we, Daddy, can we?"

"Absolutely," he said.

Dress-up was a big deal in the Barber home. For those impromptu moments, the children dressed in Megan's old skirts and high heels, painted on globs of bright-colored makeup, and fixed their hair with ribbons.

Megan acted as a set designer, draping bedsheets over tables and taping multicolored paper to lampshades. When she was finished, an ordinary family room had been transformed into a playhouse.

John's nightly routine after dinner included reading reports and working in his study. While he sat at his desk, he could hear music playing in the next room as Megan and the girls decorated.

Megan ran out of masking tape after she attached the third sheet of blue paper to the ceiling fan. She left the family room and walked down the short hallway to the study. She opened the French doors and saw John working intently at his desk. She stood for a moment and watched the love of her life pursue his passion: to find a cure for progeria.

Megan knew all about the heartbreaking affliction that drastically accelerated the aging process of children. She had studied the disease in medical school. A child was born with progeria once in eighteen million births, and all died of old age ailments before their tenth birthday.

Megan saw the Caltech baseball cap on John's head.

"John," she said, "you promised to throw that horrible thing away."

"I did. This is a new one."

Megan shook her head and, with a disbelieving look, walked to the desk. Standing next to him, she reached down, opened the second drawer, and removed a roll of tape. With the tape in her left hand, she hesitated, bit her lip, and, in a sudden flash, snatched the cap from his head and turned to run.

John pushed himself backward. As he fell, he grabbed Megan's right leg. He locked his fingers around her ankle and rolled to his stomach. He pulled Megan to the floor, and they wrestled for the cap. Winded, Megan released the cap and laughed. They kissed.

"Someday I'll get that damn thing," she said, trying to catch her breath.

John got to his feet and helped Megan up. Knowing a second attack was not out of the question, he held the cap behind his back. "Not on your life."

"Don't be so sure, Mister Caltech."

Megan glanced at the computer and saw that the machine was on. "You promised not to start something you can't stop."

"It won't take long. The new AI program and database algorithm is installed, and I want to run a quick search."

"John," she said with a serious look, "these moments are more important than work."

"I'll come running as soon as the girls are ready."

"You better, or I'll send Lynn in."

She glanced again at the computer monitor as the screensaver popped on and showed a picture of several children with progeria sitting around a picnic table, eating. The group photo was of a picnic the Barbers had attended in Fairfax, Virginia. Each child looked like a tiny, bald old man.

"When I see that picture, I wonder how any parent could bear the pain of telling their child the facts about progeria." She kissed John on the cheek and whispered, "I know you'll be the one to find a cure and save those children."

As Megan turned to leave, she glanced back as John rubbed his hand through his hair.

"Thinking about your sister Abby?"

"Yes."

"The first child you save will be her memorial."

———————

November 2036: Ty Leggett, DOD Secretary Turner, and HHS Secretary Carol Hallett had been called for a meeting in Chief of Staff Berg's White House office. The meeting was impromptu, which had sent warning bells off in Ty's head.

Ty opened the door to the Oval Office reception room. Mrs. Oland was sitting at her desk.

"Hi, Ty. It's nice to see you two days in a row."

Ty smiled and punned, "Yep, can't have *two* much of me."

She smiled. "Secretary Turner and Secretary Hallett are already here." She picked up the phone and tapped the panel. "Director Leggett is here." She put the phone down and smiled. "You can go in."

As Ty went to the door, he thought, *This can't be good.*

Experience had taught him there were two things he could count on: change and bad deals.

He opened the door to the small, cramped room; he always admired the symbolism on display. The room was adjacent to the Oval Office; no one was closer to the president of the United States. There were photographs of world leaders, athletes, movie stars, and miniature Le Mans race cars on the shelves. An American flag was in a corner hanging from a wooden pole behind the mahogany desk.

Chief of Staff Berg was sitting at his desk, and DOD Secretary Turner was sitting in the leather Queen Ann wingchair. HHS Secretary Carol Hallett was in the chair next to Turner. Ty sat in the other Queen Anne at Carol's right.

"This will be very short," Berg said.

Turner smiled.

Carol glanced at Ty but said nothing. She was not happy.

Ty smiled out of habit and held it while he listened to Berg.

"The president wants to add someone to the GA's team to take some of the pressure off Doctor Dillingham. He wants a Miss Jennifer White to oversee your Human Resources department. And"—Berg turned to look at Carol as he handed out White's résumé—"the president would like her to start as soon as possible." He turned to face Ty. "So please expedite the background check."

Berg stopped speaking.

Silence.

Carol glanced at the résumé, then looked at Secretary Turner. She took a calming breath. Ty watched for Turner's reaction to the news. There was no reaction.

"O-kay," Ty said. "Three and a half weeks." He smiled.

"On a different subject," Carol said, "as you all recall, I mentioned in our first meeting that the only caveat on our budget was the possible purchase of a quantum computer."

Carol looked around the room for understanding, then went on, "The Clement Corporation has perfected the impossible. Their Syntopicon Q1 computing system is the first workable quantum computer, and we need to have one at GA due to the incredible size of the database. For example: The AlphaFold alone covers two hundred million proteins." She looked around the room again. "Those geniuses at GA will perfect it, and—"

Turner interrupted, "We've had our eyes on this for quite some time. The power of that machine is far too important to waste on hunting bugs."

"Saving humanity comes down to bugs," Ty quipped.

"Okay, I get it, we could all use the machine. What's the cost, Carol?" Berg asked.

"Billions. The exact cost depends on how we acquire it."

"That's a lot of bananas for one computer," Berg said.

"Eric, that machine will change everything—it's that fast! The fastest ever!"

"Nothing is secure in the wrong hands," Turner said.

"I like the idea of GA perfecting it." Berg looked at Ty. "You and Carol figure out how we pay for it in the short term. And, Jordan, you negotiate with the Clement Corporation for Defense for the long term. I'll inform the president."

The group left Berg's office.

Carol and Ty walked together to the White House's back parking lot.

"This stinks. Why put a spy at GA?" she whispered.

Ty smiled. "They can't help themselves. It's November; got to raise money. I'll tell Barber, and nice job on the budget-buster."

She laughed.

Early the next morning, John's desk phone rang. He glanced at the screen and saw Ty Leggett's name.

"Hi, Ty."

"Good morning, John. We finished the background on Doctor Gysin. She's okay. Smart lady. Unfortunately, she comes with baggage. The father was a pedophile; he's in a mental facility in Louisiana. Which might explain her twin brother, a real lowlife drug dealer who killed for sport. He disappeared more than a year ago and is presumed dead. Regardless of her family history, she is one sharp lady. I'll send you the full report later today. You can notify Gysin and get her started."

"She'll come in handy. Hopefully, she can be here by early December. We're running a genetic AlphaFold experiment with the AI supercomputer program in the middle of the month."

"I'm excited," Ty said.

"Real funny."

"There's something else. Remember, sometimes they can't help themselves."

"I'm sitting."

"Turner, Hallett, and I had an impromptu meeting with Berg, so this comes from the president, so, a fait accompli. He wants GA to hire a friend's employee. The employer is William Ashby, Ashby Pharmaceuticals. The employee is Ms. Jennifer White. She has all the right credentials. We're running a backgrounder and should have the preliminary results later this week. She should be to you by the eleventh of December."

"This is crazy."

"I know. She'll try to steal something, we'll catch her, and the president's obligation will be fulfilled."

John put the phone down and called Scott.

"This is Scott."

"Would you please add motion cameras to all common areas, libraries, and research labs as soon as possible?"

December 2036: John's GA office phone rang. "Yes."

"Doctor Gysin is here," Laurie said.

"Please send her in."

Gloria Gysin glided elegantly into Barber's private office wearing a light-gray St. John business suit. She looked more like a wealthy business executive than a university professor. Her green eyes sparkled as she walked toward his desk. She was stunning.

"Hello, Doctor Barber, I'm Gloria Gysin." Her voice, soft and pleasant, carried a hint of a Southern accent. She approached John with an air of self-assured confidence.

Her beauty was intimidating. With a quick brush of his hair, he stood. "Welcome to GA, Doctor Gysin."

She extended her hand with a straight arm, and they shook hands.

"Please, call me Gloria. I'm thrilled to be here." A warm smile reinforced an outgoing, self-assured personality.

"Please be seated."

She sat in the chair facing the desk. John sat behind his desk.

"I hope you had an uneventful trip from DC?"

"Long, but not too bad."

"Thank you again for joining our team. I don't want to overload you with information. There will be plenty of time for all of that. What's important to understand is that we are a collaborative team. That is not just a slogan; it's critical to our success. With you, we have a staff of one hundred people and an executive hierarchy of six, you being the sixth. We are very small and must rely on each other. Each member has a specific role. Some have more than one. For example, Joyce Dillingham has four jobs: She manages Cybersecurity, Computer Science, and Human Resources, and also assists Doctor Royer in the lab."

"She's busy," Gysin said sarcastically.

John raised an eyebrow at the tone. "Most of the staff handle data collection and analytics. The balance, like you, are biochemists or geneticists. We're really a very large computer science center. And about to get bigger. It looks like we're installing a Q1 system in March."

"Oh, that's exciting."

"Yes, very. We have no idea how long it'll take to get it up and running, so we're going full-throttle with our supercomputer AI program. As a matter of fact, we have a major test coming up on December sixteenth. Which is why we're so glad you're here. I'm getting too far ahead. Enough of that. How about a tour?"

John stood, Gloria smiled, and he led her out of his office. Their first stop was at the main lab. The room was cold and odorless. Gloria shivered after a few steps into the room.

"I should have warned you. We keep it cool in here. There are sweaters hanging by the door next to the fire extinguisher. Would you like one?"

Gloria didn't respond. Her attention was focused on the lab.

"Impressive, isn't it?"

"Wow," she said.

Computer stations lined the south wall facing the I-80

freeway, and there was a ten-foot-long island in the room. Three sinks and nine flat-screen computer monitors were embedded into the island's Formica countertop. Six flat-screen monitors hung from the ceiling above the island, facing both sides of the island.

A centrifuge was on the west wall, next to Barber's office, along with a seven-foot-wide, double-door refrigerator.

A transmission electron aberration-corrected microscope, called a TEAM, and two twenty-inch monitors were set along the east wall. A smaller electron microscope filled the remaining space.

The north wall was covered by cabinets and a twenty-foot-long Formica counter. Glass and stainless-steel beakers; wide-mouth round bottles; collection canisters; methanol, alcohol, and hydrogen peroxide bottles; surgical gloves; wipes; several different-sized pristine scalpels; scissors; and tongs filled the open-faced cabinets and drawers.

Doctor Royer and lab technician Lisa Ford were standing at the back of the room by the centrifuge machine. Joyce Dillingham and Min Tong were standing at the center of the island, watching numbers flash across the overhead monitors.

As Gloria approached, she glanced at Lisa Ford, and Lisa responded with a not-too-discreet expression of excitement and puzzlement.

Lisa turned and removed a small vial from the centrifuge and withdrew some of its contents with a hypodermic needle. She then injected the clear liquid onto the microscope viewing screen. Finished, she joined Min Tong, Joyce, and Royer at the island.

They watched the monitor.

The clear liquid appeared on the screen. After a few

seconds, the microscopic organisms moved toward the intro-duced material and, with astonishing speed, enveloped it.

"That failed," Royer said. "I can't wait for our quantum. These painfully slow experiments will be obsolete."

Gloria whispered to John, "What is it?"

"They tested a genetic splice to create antibodies against the rhinovirus," he whispered.

"Hardy little bugger," Joyce said, looking at John. "Glad it's in there. I hate colds."

Lisa shot another glance at Gloria, then quickly turned her attention back to Royer.

Royer caught a whiff of Gloria's perfume and, with a smile, turned his attention to her. She seemed to enjoy his double-take.

John asked for attention and introduced her. There were quick handshakes and smiles. After the introductions, the three scientists quickly turned their attention to the computer monitor and resumed working.

Lisa seemed to be the only one interested in meeting Gloria. When they were introduced, Lisa, with a flash of recognition in her eyes, held Gloria's hand a second longer than normal. Gloria did not seem to mind or even to notice.

John did notice. *That's odd.*

"Okay, tomorrow we'll move to step two," Royer announced, holding a clipboard.

"It's time to move on," John whispered to Gloria.

They left the lab, and John showed Gloria the research library, computer center, cafeteria, and remaining laboratories.

The tour was complete in forty-five minutes, and they were back on the second floor, walking to Gloria's new office.

Gloria looked around the small workspace with cold amusement. The metal desk and cubical were sparse of comfort. A computer and telephone were pushed to one side of the desk to make room for a five-inch-high stack of reports and procedural manuals. She walked to the desk, thumbed some papers.

"Light reading?" she asked, looking down at the pile of paper, eyebrows raised.

"Welcome to GA, Doctor Gysin. If you have any questions, please feel free to see me. If they're security-related, see Scott Wilson or Joyce Dillingham."

Gloria picked up the top manual and began to read. With nothing left to say, John turned and started to leave. Catching himself, he said, "Joyce is expecting to see you at five this evening. She'll explain our game plan and expectations."

Gloria nodded. "Thank you for the tour, Doctor Barber. I'm excited about working here."

"Great. There is an executive staff meeting on Monday morning at eight o'clock in the cafeteria. Please join us."

She turned to face the stack of papers.

John smiled as he left, thinking, *What a great addition she will be.*

Late that night, lab technician Lisa Ford walked into Gysin's empty office, leaving the light off, and sat at the desk. Her hands trembled slightly as she brushed her salt-and-pepper-colored hair behind her ears. After a few calming breaths, she picked up the telephone and dialed an outside number. A small bead of perspiration sprouted on her temple.

The phone rang. An answering machine picked up: "This is Doctor Gysin. Please leave your message."

"I've got to see you," she whispered, her hand cupped

around the mouthpiece. "Please, I've got to. I can't take it. I've —I'm so ... so about to explode. The loneliness. This deception is killing me. Where is Peter?"

Her head drooped as she pressed the receiver against her cheek for a second and hung up. Seeing a blue notepad, she wrote a message and hurried out of the room.

SEVEN

Early Monday morning, Gysin arrived at her GA office before her first staff meeting. There was a blue sticky note on her desk. It read: "Where is Peter?"

Her jaw twitched and her fists tightened white. She grabbed the note, tore it up, and left for the 8:00 a.m. staff meeting.

Royer, Dillingham, Min Tong, Scott Wilson, and John Barber were sitting at a long Formica cafeteria table, talking among themselves. Coffee-filled Styrofoam cups and Apple iPads all but covered the table.

Gloria joined the group.

John glanced at his watch. "Good morning. It gives me great pleasure to introduce our newest team member, Doctor Gloria Gysin."

Smiles and words of welcome.

"Quick introductions, even though I know you've met most of the staff already, Doctor Gysin," John said. "To my left is Doctor Robert Royer, our most senior and acclaimed member. Robert chairs the genetics team. To his left is Doctor Joyce Dillingham, who oversees Cybersecurity, Computer Science, and Human Resources, and most importantly is Robert's right hand. Across is Scott Wilson, who oversees our hard security assets and security team. Min Tong is on your other side. She chairs the data collection and analytics teams."

He took a sip of coffee. "Doctor Gysin comes to us by way of Bonn University's Biochemistry Department and she's a George Washington University fellow. She will chair our biochemistry team. Her résumé is on the employee page."

John glanced at his notes. "Doctor Gysin—may we call you Gloria?"

"That's fine," she said with a warm smile.

"Here are some quick facts about GA: We are overseen by Health and Human Services and secured by the FBI. We were created by executive order of the president of the United States and have a three-year sunset. We are tasked to find genetic solutions to all viruses, created or natural. It's a challenging concept given the amount of data we need to analyze. It will take our fastest AI supercomputing systems months to organize the small amount of data we have accumulated—"

Royer interrupted, "Sounds hard—impossible, right? Not if you have an ace in the hole." He grinned. "March of next year, we'll be installing the first Clement Syntopicon Q_1 computing system. Maybe you've heard of it?" He didn't wait for her answer. "It's one hundred fifty-eight million times faster than our supercomputer. That's mind-blowing. We'll be able to do in four minutes what would take ten thousand years to do." He was so excited he was making air pictures with his hands.

Joyce and John smiled; they enjoyed Robert's enthusiasm. John remembered telling Leggett the same thing. *Facts are facts.* John even saw the excitement of Royer's announcement on Min's face.

"Our database," John said, "will contain all five basic human molecules, proteins, enzymes, genetic mutations, and known viruses. I believe with that database and a quantum, we will fulfill our mission and possibly more by our three-year deadline. Regarding our database and AI system, I want to amplify a part of the employee manual: personal research. Some of us have individual projects. Mine is the study of progeria, a genetic cellular disease that ages and kills children. Robert's is the creation of a protective force field."

"I hate war," Robert stated.

"And Min's writing the perfect country western song."

She smiled. "I like cowboys."

John continued, "We are on the honor system and granted fourteen hours a week computer and lab time. You can only use an E2EE secure computer and program from your home office that Joyce has certified. And, of course, all results are the property of the United States government." John stopped and looked at Royer. "Robert, will you give Gloria a quick update on our status?"

"The biochemical database is a work in progress. The SQ1 system, as I mentioned, will be installed in March. Joyce is building programs and algorithms in preparation for that wonderful event. Tuesday night, the sixteenth, we begin testing one of those programs by categorizing a small sample of the AI database algorithm, AlphaFold database, and running genetic comparisons of known diseases. That process will build and repeat until the SQ1 is up and running."

Royer put a smug grin on his face. "So why are we using our supercomputer for tests and cataloging, you ask? It takes an atom bomb to ignite a hydrogen bomb, right? The same thing here: It takes the world's fastest supercomputer to set up the SQ1. When the supercomputers have done their job and the quant is ready, all we'll need is organized data and lots of questions. Now that our team is fully staffed—"

John interrupted, "Excuse me, if I may. The president has added someone from the private sector, a Ms. Jennifer White, to our staff. The FBI is performing a background check now, and if all goes well, she'll join us before January."

"What part of the private sector?" Royer asked aggressively.

"Nonmilitary," John reassured him. "Her bona fides will be addressed after the FBI finishes the background. Please continue, Robert."

After a moment of suspicious contemplation, Royer went on, "The first AI program analysis will focus on Ebola and monkeypox, and that will start in late January." He stopped and looked at Joyce.

"I'm up." She grinned. "The programming team has begun creating algorithms to categorize, define, and connect the AlphaFold to our genetic database. We are compiling viral and medical data from every credible source. The analytic team is inputting, categorizing, and defining that data. I think after four months of collecting and programming, we're ready for our first baby test with the supercomputer. Cross your fingers. One typo will set back all our hard work."

"Sounds scary, right?" John commented. Looking at Gloria, he continued with, "We are assembling and will search through the largest and most complete human chemical and viral database in history. Down to molecules. The data size will be in the quintillions to the hundredth power. This has never been attempted before because it's too damn big. We now believe with the SQ1 the entire database can be analyzed and solutions to life-altering viruses will be discovered. We also believe it's worth the risk of personal ridicule and failure to eliminate disease."

He removed a photograph from his coat pocket and held it out to show the group. "There is something I want to bring to everyone's attention. It's to put a face to why we are working so hard. A little history first: On September eleventh, nineteen seventy-eight, Janet Parker"—he showed her photograph—"was the last person in the world to die of smallpox. A tragic story. Last week, a medical photographer in Tehran was hospitalized with an mpox variant."

Barber's private office telephone flashed. John looked at the video window and saw a picture of Ty Leggett. He answered. "Good afternoon, my friend. What's up?"

"Ms. Jennifer White passed our background check. She is going to stand out, not in a good way. She's a looker, twenty-nine years old, a graduate of Texas Christian University. Did the sorority thing, didn't sleep with too many, and kept away from drugs. She's got a master of communications degree, and an undergraduate in human resources. Her family's loaded." He paused. "Yes, you guessed it: pharmaceuticals. That's how she met Ashby. I don't think Daddy would be too happy about her sleeping with him. Overall, a nice kid with poor taste in men."

"Communications—perfect. We're a research facility."

"Hey, how about a CNN anchor?"

"Real funny."

Ty laughed. "It'll take some pressure off Dillingham. Just

put her in charge of Human Resources like the president wants."

"Send me her sheet and we'll reach out to her. Anything else, Debbie Downer?"

"You're not going to like it: Megan's leaving you."

"Goodbye. Talk to you later." John hung up.

Later that afternoon, Royer and Dillingham knocked on Barber's private office door. They walked in and sat down on the couch. John got up from his desk and joined them, sitting in the reclining chair.

"We want to conduct a sample test run with the AI supercomputer tonight, using the AlphaFold database, and it will run 'til morning. We believe enough data has been inputted to justify the test," Robert said.

"What's the purpose of the test?" John asked.

"To categorize and define our data points," Joyce said.

"You're sure this isn't premature? Why not wait until the sixteenth, when we have more data?"

"We're about forty percent on inputting data. It's time to find the bugs, and it also buys us time to fix things," Joyce said.

John looked at both for a second. "Do we need to firewall the AI system for the test?"

"No, the system partitions will be enough," Joyce said.

"Okay. When do you want to do it?"

"We'll be ready at four-thirty this afternoon," Joyce said.

"That's actually great news. We need to show Washington some research progress before Christmas. I suppose I'm the last to know about this little test." He looked at Joyce.

She nodded and put a shy smile on her face. "Yes."

John snickered. "Okay, do it. Since you two are here, as I mentioned at the staff meeting, the FBI was conducting a background on our last employee. I received a call that she's been cleared."

John stood and went back to his desk to pick up a piece of paper and handed them a notice. It read: "For the Genetic Development Committee by order of the President of the United States: Addition to Genetic Answer team, responsibility Human Resources, Ms. Jennifer White, TCU graduate Human Resources, Master's in Communication, Ashby Pharmaceuticals."

"Did I do something wrong?" Joyce asked, looking unhappy.

"No, Joyce. The president—"

"Are they kidding us?" Robert asked aggressively. "We're a scientific lab. She comes from a pharmaceutical company with an inadequate education in communications. What's this?"

"It's the president of the United States' prerogative. We have no choice."

"This is just the beginning. What's next? The CIA?"

"I'm with Robert on this," Joyce said.

"I'll never let that happen," John replied. "This young lady is harmless, and she'll help you, Joyce, and that's a good thing."

"Not in my lab. I want your solemn oath you will walk out if they try to use this place," Royer demanded.

"Robert, she'll be in Human Resources. And no CIA—ever. And I've never run from a fight; I'll protect us. Ms. White will start around the eleventh. I'll consult both of you with any changes. Good luck with the test. It's very exciting."

After dinner that evening, Megan Barber turned the living room stereo volume up and sang along to the Blake Shelton song "Austin" as she decorated the family room for another family evening of fun.

Finished, she turned down the stereo and called the two girls. She smiled as she heard their plastic high-heeled shoes bang on the hardwood floor. She turned to look at the stairwell and saw Lynn and Abby covered in makeup, wearing purple dresses.

"Where's Daddy?" Lynn asked, disappointed he wasn't in the room.

Megan looked toward the hallway. "John?" she called out. No reply.

"You better go get him. You know how he gets."

"Daddy, Daddy!" Lynn called as she skipped down the hallway to the study.

John heard Lynn's calls and knew the end of his selfish pleasure of working on progeria was fast approaching. He quickly initiated additional voice commands into the GA supercomputer. This search was different: He was comparing the mutation of the LMNA gene, which provided instructions to make certain cell proteins, along with the chemical instructions that would create Werner syndrome. All he had left to do was add three final search parameters and the search would be ready to start.

He hesitated before speaking the final search codes, excited by the prospect. Like winning the lottery, his hope at finding a cure became wishful. With the pangenome imputed, every species on Earth could be compared.

"Daddy?" Lynn shouted as she flew into the study, flinging open the French doors with a loud bang. She ran to his desk. "You need to come *now*. Stop working, Daddy.

Daddy?" she said, reaching toward the touch-screen computer monitor.

Initiate DOWNLOAD.

"No—no!" he yelled.

John turned to catch Lynn as she brushed her hands across the monitor, knocking it onto its side, and he watched in shock as the computer jumped into a search.

"Oh no," he groaned as he held Lynn's tiny hands.

They both watched numbers and genetic codes flash across the monitor.

"Oh, man," he said as he righted the monitor. He rubbed his hand through his hair. With wide-eyed dismay, he took a deep breath and hoped it wasn't locked in a looping search. If it was, his only solution would be to reboot the machine.

Joyce Dillingham had only recently written this software version, and he did not want to crash it with child's play.

He could hear Joyce's voice in his head: "It can compare multiple genetic combinations to programmed variables while it searches for anomalies and paradoxes. Be careful, John. Don't ask too much or leave an open-ended question."

"This is not good," he whispered, looking at the computer screen.

"What's it doing, Daddy?"

"Searching," he said a little roughly.

She started to cry.

"It's okay, my little darling," he said, lifting her onto his lap, adding a kiss on the cheek.

"I'm sorry, Daddy. What's it looking for?"

"I don't really know. I was asking it to find the opposite to aging while looking for the reason people get older."

"Can you make it stop?" she asked, her lower lip quivering.

"No, I can't."

"I'm sorry, Daddy." Lynn's lips curled, and she started to cry.

He kissed her forehead and gave her a gentle hug. "It's okay. Don't cry," he whispered as he kissed her on the cheek again. "It's okay. Nothing's broken." He forced a smile. "It's no big deal."

He rubbed his hand through his hair. "If I'd stopped when you called—It's my fault."

They sat and watched the monitor for a moment. John had no idea what would happen next.

With nothing left to do but wait, John stood with Lynn in his arms, and they left the study, leaving the computer locked in a hunt for God-knew-what. He thought it was probably a waste of a valuable opportunity and hoped it would not crash Joyce's programming.

That evening's play by the children was special, so much so that John forgot all about the computer running in the other room. After the performance was over, he read a bedtime story to the girls and ended the evening sharing a romantic moment with Megan.

The next morning, Megan and John were having their last cup of coffee when the telephone rang. John answered.

"This is your five-fifty-five wake-up call," the mechanical voice said.

John put the phone down. "Do we really need that?" he asked. "Can't we shut that thing off?"

"Sorry, honey. I use it to remind me to go to the gym."

John sighed. "How about I remind you?"

"Sure."

John headed to the front door to leave.

"Aren't you forgetting something?" she asked with a knowing look.

"Wallet," he said.

"And *you're* going to be my wake-up call?"

John went to the study and found his wallet on the desk. He picked it up and in so doing brushed the monitor. The monitor snapped on and instantly reminded him of last night's hiccup with Lynn. Using his voice commands, he logged back into the GA system. To his disappointment, the machine was still searching. He shook his head and pressed the Escape key several times. No reaction. Frustrated, he reached under the desk to reboot the machine. As his hand touched the power button, beeps began coming from the monitor. The search had stopped.

Still leaning over, his finger on the power button, John looked at the monitor and watched the cursor blink on and off. He looked at the cursor for a moment and a message appeared: SEARCH COMPLETED.

What kind of search would take eleven hours? Then he laughed. *It's nothing. Lynn must have screwed things up.*

He again reached down to shut off the computer. Something made him hesitate. He looked at the screen once more, but this time he noticed a genetic equation: 156082573156140081–HGNC 6636–P02545-F1N-V4683761#-GCACAGGGCAG#.

He pulled the chair closer to the desk, sat, and got lost in thought.

"John, you're going to be late," Megan called from the front door.

He saved the numbers under the icon LYNN and quickly

left the study. When he reached the front door, Megan was holding his briefcase. She rolled her eyes when she saw the wallet in his hand.

"You remember that comparison I ran last night? It's finished. It—"

"John, we don't have time for that."

"All right." Laughing at himself, he said, "I can look at it tonight." He left the house.

As he drove to GA, he was excited and filled with hope. *What could those numbers mean?* He tried to visualize the location of the genes and proteins as he drove. He slapped the steering wheel with his right hand. "Ridiculous. It's gibberish."

He turned the radio to his favorite sports station, KPLY Reno, to get his mind off the numbers.

After thirty minutes, he arrived at the GA security gate, stopped, and rolled down his window. The morning air was crisp, with a soft fragrance of fall.

"Good morning, Scott," he said, looking at the camera.

"Hurry in, Doctor Barber. Everyone's excited."

He drove in, followed the bend in the road, and saw GA.

He was surprised for the second time that morning, as people were milling about outside the main building. The GA office complex normally looked deserted; seeing people standing around was unique.

John stopped the car and watched for a moment. Several people moved from one group to another, hugging, clapping, and shaking hands.

What could cause such a commotion? The full database won't be done for months. What happened? He checked his phone. Nothing. *Did last night's test find something major?*

Whatever it is, it looks like good news. He turned the radio to the all-news channel. Nothing; same old noise.

He drove to his parking spot and took the back stairs to reach the second floor faster. He hurried down the hallway to his office, glanced into the main lab, and caught Joyce's eye.

She rushed out. Her cheeks were pink, and her voice shook with excitement: "John! John!" She grabbed his shoulders and hugged him. "We did it! It worked!"

He could feel her emotion. It was infectious.

"The draft program and data sample worked. It worked! Not only did it work, we found the proteins and gene sequences to end smallpox forever, and that's not *all*! Now we need just need size and speed. Our supercomputer worked perfectly."

"What are you talking about?"

"We've got the order of the codes. The supercomputer categorized everything in our sample. We linked everything: AlphaFold, genes, molecules, everything—no bugs. Humanity's genetic history is at our fingertips!" She hugged him. "Now we can find the Adam and Eve gene and follow mankind's genetic immunity. Every inherited immunity from the beginning. It's wonderful! Can you believe it? All we need now is *more*—more data, more computing speed, more everything—and the SQ1 will pull it all together." Her eyes bounced across his face. "To think today, mankind took the first step to unlocking our immunity."

"This can't be. It's too fast." His face was etched in disbelief.

"Our sample size was small, of course. The test finished at five-fifty-nine this morning. Can you imagine what else we'll find?"

"We really did it?"

Joyce bounced on her toes and raced to rejoin Robert, Min, Gloria, Lisa, and several others in the lab. John quickly went to his office and grabbed several bottles of champagne from his small refrigerator. He and Laurie rushed back to the lab. Laurie pulled beakers out of the cabinets. John opened the first bottle with a loud pop and poured generous helpings.

Royer filled a coffee cup with water, as did Joyce.

"A toast to Joyce and our success," Royer proclaimed.

"Let's go to the cafeteria and celebrate with everyone," Joyce said.

It was a party with champagne, hugs, and celebration.

John stood on one of the cafeteria chairs. "Congratulations to all of you. This is wonderful. And worth a day off."

A loud cheer. Only Royer was disappointed; he hated days off. Joyce came out of the kitchen with platters of food and desserts. Scott Wilson turned on country western music and played it through the intercom system. Min grabbed Royer's hand and they danced, and others joined in.

Gloria walked up to Lisa Ford. "I read your note. Don't do it again." Her eyes were cold. Scary.

EIGHT

A slender man walked nonchalantly down a drab apartment hallway. A gold Japanese hairpin held his long hair tightly together on top of his head. He was dressed in running shoes, gray sweatpants, and a dark-blue hoodie.

He stopped halfway down the hallway and looked at the number on an apartment door: 269. He knocked and listened as a childlike pitter-patter of quick steps raced to the door.

The door opened with a rush of air. Lisa Ford held onto the doorknob for a moment, then her eyes sparkled with joy as she looked at her lover. Lisa's makeup was perfect. She was dressed in a new cotton blouse and tight Levi's. Her eyes bounced with life. Her breathing was fast and excited.

"Your hair? And you're so thin," Lisa said as she reached to touch him.

"Stop," he snarled and pushed her arm away.

"Don't be mad. Please don't."

His jaw was tight, his left hand in a fist by his side as he aggressively pushed by her. Lisa quickly followed and raced to face him. With her standing before him, he reached back with his foot and kicked the door closed. It slammed shut.

Lisa moved closer. They kissed.

"I can't stand the loneliness," she whispered, her eyes excited and breath moist. "This deception, it's—"

"Our time will come. You must wait."

"Yes yes, I understand. You're right, it's—but I've got to know if you love me."

They embraced and kissed with lust-inspired excitement. Their bodies pulsated and moved as they felt each other's passion.

"Nothing can interfere, nothing. Do you understand me?" he said in a menacing voice.

"Yes ... yes. I'm sorry, but I can't control the pain. I need you. I'm so alone." She watched his eyes turn as cold as death. Panic gripped her. "Don't get angry. I can't take it. Please don't torture me."

"Stop," he said. He gently pulled their bodies together.

They kissed and moved as one. With each breath, Lisa's pelvis pressed harder against his. After several moments, he removed the hairpin and shook his head, his hair dropping to his shoulders. Holding the hairpin in his left hand, he wrapped his right arm around her waist and they kissed. She took a breath and closed her eyes.

Her heart was pounding; she could taste the passion. Lisa's excitement was overpowering, an obsession. Their bodies were now hot and their breathing short, panting. A sexual hunger raced through their clothes.

It had been a long time since *he'd* felt this rush of lust.

Sex held them and the hunger would not let go.

Like lust, the passion ended all too quickly as the hairpin

plunged deep into Lisa's temple. The ecstasy was complete. He stared at her frozen, shocked expression.

There were no high-pitched sounds, no fighting or flailing hands or bulging eyes—just a slow last exhale of life. He let go of the pin and placed a hand on her jaw, watching her eyes fog over to death.

With the moment passed, he reluctantly dropped her body to the cold tile floor. He stood over the corpse, studying the lifeless shell. He felt no regret. Well, he would miss the sex.

He bent down, placed one knee on the floor, and leaned over her warm body. He touched the hairpin with his index finger, took hold of it, and played. In and out, in and out, delighting in the sexual pleasure.

After several moments, he removed the hairpin and held it up to the light. He twisted it to see all around the slime-covered spike. Finished, he wiped a lifetime of memories on the crisp white collar of her blouse and calmly returned the pin to his hair.

He stood and looked around the apartment. After a moment, he stepped over Lisa's body and walked into the kitchen. He opened the cabinet under the sink and removed bleach, dish soap, and several rolls of paper towels. He cleaned himself. As he scrubbed, he softly sang an old Crosby, Stills, Nash, and Young song:

"Find the cost of freedom buried in the ground. Mother Earth will swallow you...."

NINE

The next morning, John walked through the empty second-floor GA hallway. As he passed the main lab, he glanced in and saw Robert and Joyce standing by the center island, talking. He didn't stop. He had a hammer pounding in his head and did not have the energy to talk. He was glad Joyce had driven him home the night before instead of going to the local biker bar with Min Tong and other GA employees.

"Good morning, John. Feeling tiptop, I'm sure," Laurie said, smiling.

"Good morning to you, and as a matter of fact, I feel fine. Not like some." He pointed to the bottle of Motrin on her desk.

He saw a young, attractive, well-built, light-haired woman in his reception room, sitting on the cloth chair against the back wall. She was dressed in blue jeans, a white silk blouse, and tan, ankle-high boots. She looked professional, yet casual. Her gold Rolex watch and twenty-four-karat gold cross necklace bespoke wealth.

John smiled at the young lady, then went straight into his office. He sat at his desk and opened the lower left drawer and grabbed a small bottle of Bayer aspirin, removed four tablets, and swallowed them dry. He took a deep breath, opened his computer.

After five minutes, he tapped his intercom. "Laurie, would you tell Ms. White I'll be right out, and would you contact Joyce? She's in the main lab. See if she'll meet with Ms. White after our meeting."

John stood up from his desk and moved to the reception room. Before he could say anything, Jennifer jumped up.

"Hello, Doctor Barber! I'm Jennifer White. I'm so excited to meet you." She reached out, took his hand, and shook it enthusiastically.

"Good morning, Ms. White."

"Please, call me Jennifer." She smiled.

"Okay. Please." He gestured with his right hand for her to go into his office.

"Laurie, please join us," he said.

Jennifer sat on the couch.

Laurie followed and asked, "May I get you either of you anything to drink? Coffee, water?"

"No, thank you, I'm quite fine," she said with a hint of a New England accent.

"I'll take a Diet Coke. Just the bottle. I don't need a glass."

Laurie smiled. Her head also hurt; she'd had three cups of black coffee already. She left the room.

"Welcome to GA, Jennifer. It's a pleasure to have you on our team." John sat facing the couch.

Laurie returned, handed John his Coke, and moved the wood chair facing his desk to the side, facing Jennifer and John, then she sat and smiled.

John said, "I won't overload you with information. Doctor Joyce Dillingham will do that. What's important to understand is we are a team. That is not a slogan; it's critical to our success. We have a staff of one hundred—now a hundred and one—with an executive staff of six. We are very small and must rely on each other. Each member has a specific role to play. Some have more than one job. For example, Joyce, whom you will meet after we're done, has four jobs. For the time being, you will work with her and eventually take over her responsibilities in Human Resources. Laurie will give you a brief tour of GA and introduce you to Doctor Dillingham." He stood. "If you have any questions or need anything, please reach out to Laurie or Joyce or, if it's critical, me."

Jennifer stood. "I'm super-excited."

They shook hands, and Jennifer and Laurie left the room.

John returned to his desk and called Scott Wilson. "Scott, I want to double-check which rooms are covered by cameras."

"All but yours, the main lab, and the executive offices. All the hallways and everything else is covered."

"Add some cameras to the main lab, my office, and the executive offices, except Doctor Royer's." He brushed his hair with his hand. "Actually, don't put cameras inside the executive offices except for mine—just outside. We want to make sure we can see who comes and goes." He glanced at the ceiling. "Are the computer rooms, including the quant cold room, covered?"

"All are covered, except the basement cold room."

"I know it's premature, but please cover that one and set an alarm on the door."

"Yes, sir. Anything else?"

"How long do we keep the camera footage?"

"Indefinitely, sir. It's digitalized and stored in the security safe."

The following week, as John was walking to his GA office and passed the main lab, Joyce saw him, waved, and met him in the hallway. She looked concerned.

"Lisa Ford hasn't reported to work for a week. I've called her apartment several times, and no one's answered. This is not like her. I'm worried."

"When was the last time you saw her?"

"She was here the day we had the big celebration last Tuesday."

"Okay, so if we don't hear anything today, I'll send someone to her apartment. It's almost Christmas. Maybe something came up."

The following morning at GA, John checked with Human Resources and learned that Lisa had still not reported for work. He clicked on his videophone and called Ty.

"What's up?" Ty asked, looking happy.

"Everything's great. Our test run of the new research program last week was promising. I had a hangover to prove it."

Ty laughed. "I'm sure with your teetotaling body, it didn't take much."

"Some of the staff ended up at a biker bar and didn't make work the next day."

"Ouch."

"The reason I called, there's something curious. One of our employees—our lab tech, Lisa Ford—hasn't come to work for over a week. She's not the kind of person to not show up or call. I stopped by her apartment last night. It was dark, and I got the feeling it was deserted. Could you send someone by before Christmas?"

"Absolutely. Before you hang up, how's our little spy doing?"

"Fine. Joyce is happy and Royer isn't complaining."

"Great. I'll send a couple agents over to Ford's apartment and get back to you."

John hung up, leaned back in his chair, and looked at the photograph of Megan standing between Ty and himself, in front of their favorite Georgetown Italian restaurant. They looked happy. *That was a great night—no kids.* He smiled.

An FBI agent from the Reno FBI office was dispatched to Lisa Ford's apartment after the missing report came to them. The agent knocked on the door several times. Getting no response and hearing nothing, she went to the manager's apartment. She returned several minutes later with the manager and a key. They unlocked the apartment and walked in.

After a cursory walk-through, the agent asked, "Did you clean this place?"

"No. The lease is paid for another six months."

The agent reached into a coat pocket for her cell phone and called her supervisor. "I'm at the Lisa Ford apartment. Nothing to report. It's empty. Really empty, like no one ever lived here, and it's scary clean with a strong smell of bleach."

A missing person report was filed with the Reno police, and several hours later, two FBI agents showed up at Lisa's modest, one-bedroom apartment: Agent Angie Ripple, a petite, middle-aged chief investigator, along with a rookie agent, Charlie Benjamin. They were tasked with conducting a forensic search.

After a quick glance around the living room, they put the two suitcases they were carrying next to the main door to hold it open. The air was stale and hot and smelled of bleach. They walked around the apartment to familiarize themselves with the layout and look for anything unusual.

Agent Ripple turned on the air conditioner. "That's better," she said.

They went back to the door, picked up the two black suitcases, and closed the door. They placed the cases on the tile floor, opened them, and removed the cloth suits from the sealed bag and put them on over their clothes. Finished, they put on cloth shoe covers.

"Man, from the looks of this place, this Ford babe was clean. No rush job here," Benjamin said.

Ripple nodded. She picked up the larger of the two suitcases and placed it on the small coffee table in the center of the room. She opened it. The contents included fingerprint dust, brushes, a small hand vacuum, rubber gloves, infrared goggles, double-sided tape, an infrared flashlight, scissors, toothpicks, tweezers, several small dental picks, and cutting knives.

"Ready here, so let's get started," she said, snapping on one of her surgical gloves.

Several hours later, the apartment was a mess. Powdery white dust was everywhere. Most of the room had been torn apart and smaller furniture tossed into a pile. They had finished the bedroom.

They looked at each other, hot and frustrated.

Benjamin held the vacuum cleaner and stood by an over-turned chair. Ripple stood next to the bed, her suit wet with perspiration. She held double-sided sticky tape.

"Nothing. Not even a single dirty hair. Whoever cleaned this place is a freak," she said as she crushed the tape in her hand. She pulled off her gloves and tossed everything to the floor.

"Look here. I'll bet even the inside of the telephone is clean," Benjamin said as he reached down, picked up the telephone, unscrewed the mouthpiece, and looked inside. He held the telephone up to his partner. "Can you believe this? She washed the freaking phone. We're done. We're not going to find shit."

"Keep looking. Let's finish with the ultraviolet."

Benjamin picked up the smaller suitcase, put it on the side table, opened it, and pulled out an orange, handgun-sized ultraviolet lamp. He plugged it into the wall and handed it to her. She put on goggles and gestured "Okay." He closed the window shades and switched the lights off.

Ripple moved over to the bed with the ultraviolet lamp. She scanned the bed. Finished, they pulled the bedding off, dumping the sheets and comforter in a pile on the floor. She scanned the bare mattress, floor walls, ceiling. Ripple took a deep, frustrated breath.

"Nothing. No fluids. Not a damn thing. Not shit. Not a drop of blood, semen, drool, nothing. We're through," Ripple barked as she tossed the lamp onto the mattress.

Benjamin turned to the wall and flicked the overhead light on.

Suddenly, there was a loud bang. He quickly turned to watch Ripple kick the bed frame a second time. She kicked it several more times. On the last kick, the wood headboard holding the mattress frame dropped against the wall with a loud thud. She looked down at the fallen headboard, shook her head, and walked away.

"Damn it," she said as she went into the bathroom.

Benjamin walked to the bed and picked up the ultraviolet lamp. He started to coil the cord; it was stuck. He followed the cord and realized the bed frame had fallen on it.

"Figures," he said with a sigh.

He bent down, lifted the frame, and removed the plug from the wall. As he did so, he noticed something white sticking out from the wood headboard where the bed frame connected. He lifted the mattress away, then bent down again to get a better look. There was something under the wood. He picked a sliver off with his fingernail. There was paper wedged in a cavity. He pulled a small penknife out of his pocket, opened the blade with his thumb, and cut away some wood from the bed frame, exposing a piece of white paper.

He again reached into his pocket and pulled out a fresh pair of rubber gloves, putting them on. Using the tip of the knife, he gently removed more wood, further exposing the paper. Using the tip of the knife again, he lifted the paper up so he could grip it with his tweezers. He gently pried the paper out of the cavity.

With the rolled, cigarette-sized paper in his hand, he held it up to the overhead light. He twisted it and moved it back and forth.

His eyes brightened with excitement when he saw writing under the folds. He carefully unrolled the paper, exposing several sets of seemingly random nonsensical numbers and letters. Some numbers were crossed out, but one set was clear.

With raised eyebrows and an ever-so-slight smile, he straightened up, looked toward Ripple standing at the bathroom door drying her hands, and read, "Twenty-three sixty-nine at unibonn dot de."

Ripple's face beamed: 2369@uni-bonn.de.

TEN

John was at his desk working when Laurie hailed him on the intercom. "It's Doctor Wipsing. He'd like to speak to you."

"Hello, George."

"Hi, John, thanks for taking my call."

"Sure, what's up?"

"Are you still studying progeria?"

"Yes."

"I'm giving a speech this Friday evening on cybernetics at the Reno Hilton before I head to China. Two friends of mine who are also studying progeria would like to meet you. Can you join us Friday around five?"

John glanced at his calendar. "Yes, I'm open."

"Great. Meet us at the Hilton, room seven fifty-two."

John arrived at the Hilton at 4:45, found room 752. He

knocked on the door and was greeted by his old friend, George Wipsing.

"Thank you for joining us. It's great to see you," Wipsing said as they shook hands.

"It's been a long time. Five years, right?" John asked.

John liked and trusted Wipsing. They had spent many hours studying together or playing poker at Harvard.

Wipsing was a short man, in his late forties, and looked every bit the genius: thick glasses, bad teeth, and hair that had never met a comb.

John saw two other people standing in the room as he walked farther in. John didn't recognize either of them. One was in his late fifties, with white hair and bad skin. The other was in her late sixties, thin and worn-looking. Of the two, the woman was the most intriguing. Her eyes were intense, yet they had a veil of concern to them.

"This is Doctor Josephine Khoury and Doctor William Ping," Wipsing said as he gestured toward them.

John smiled and shook Khoury's hand first, and to his pleasant surprise, she had a strong and reassuring grip. He then shook Ping's hand and was welcomed by a cold, damp, slippery grip. John almost cringed as he held the man's hand. He forced a smile and sat on the couch.

"Thank you again for coming," Wipsing said, continuing to stand.

The other two sat in the chairs that faced the couch.

"By way of introductions, they both study progeria, as I told you. William is a geneticist from Taiwan. His focus is aging. Josephine is from Israel, and her focus is cybernetics."

"I'm always interested in hearing anything new regarding progeria," John said.

"We've some disturbing news, not one hundred percent

related to progeria," Ping said with a heavy Asian accent. "The Chinese have modified the LMNA gene to accelerate aging in pigs. It worked."

John glanced at Wipsing with surprise.

"This should also concern you," Doctor Khoury said nervously as she crossed her arms. "Several weeks ago, a French research team implanted a revolutionary crystal CPU chip into an adolescent chimpanzee. Yesterday, they accessed the chip and began downloading simple commands. The animal responded—it spoke. This morning, they found the animal dead. It killed itself."

"Doctor Barber," Ping said, "the Chinese are trying to accelerate meat production. The French are trying to create an education chip for the disabled. Worthy ideals until nature responds."

"We understand the American government is on the verge of having a working quantum computer and it has in fact bought a Clement Syntopicon Q1. If that's true, God help us." Khoury focused on John's face. "Mankind is not ready to know all the answers."

John rubbed his hand through his hair and leaned back. "Why are you telling me this?"

"We understand you and Robert Royer are working together," Khoury said.

"This is inappropriate." John stood abruptly and left the room and hotel.

On the drive home, John sent a text message to Laurie: *Please notify the executive staff there will be a meeting at eight o'clock Monday morning in the cafeteria.*

Earlier that same Friday afternoon, Scott Wilson visited Joyce's office.

"Hey, Scott. How can I help you?"

"Doctor Barber asked me to make some improvements to the internal security cameras. He also asked about our digital storage. I thought I'd better double-check what I told him. So I scanned the files, and to my surprise, I found something odd."

"One of the cameras not working?"

"No. The cameras are all working perfectly, twenty-four/seven, as they should."

"Then what was odd?"

"To save on storage, our cameras are motion-activated. It also makes it easier to search. Out of curiosity, I scanned through the footage when the motion detectors activated a camera at night and found this."

He placed his iPad on her desk. The screen had a still image of a dark room.

"That's Doctor Gysin's office," Scott said. "Unfortunately, with the camera being out in the hall, the angle is from behind —plus the room is very dark."

"What's the date of this video?" she asked.

"Friday, December fifth." He tapped the screen.

Joyce leaned forward to watch. Someone walked into the room and sat at Gysin's desk, not moving for several moments. It appeared the person was staring at the blank computer screen. Then, with their back to the camera, he or she picked up the telephone and dialed.

"That's odd," Joyce said. She leaned closer to the iPad screen.

The person sat motionless for a few seconds, then cupped a hand around the mouthpiece before speaking.

"Why are they doing that? No one else is around," Scott said.

The person put the phone back into its cradle, slumped forward, head in both hands, then seemed to be writing something before standing up abruptly and hurrying out of the office.

"Pause it, Scott." Joyce went into the iPad settings and enhanced the lighting. "Okay, let's start it in slow motion where the person is leaving the room."

Scott reversed the video, adjusted to slow motion, and tapped *Play*.

They watched as, for just a fleeting moment, the person faced the camera almost straight on while leaving the room, illuminated by the hallway's soft overhead lighting.

"Freeze it there," Joyce said.

It took several tries to capture the person's face. Joyce put her fingers on the screen and expanded the picture. They both leaned forward and looked at the slightly fuzzy image.

Joyce gasped. "It's Lisa Ford."

John walked into the GA cafeteria to meet with his senior staff on Monday morning. He took a breath and smelled coffee, bacon, and freshly sprayed Lysol. The room was virtually empty. Two members of the kitchen staff were cleaning up the remaining breakfast dishes. Royer, Joyce, Min, and Gloria were already sitting at the table.

With the sound of clinking dishes in the background, John approached the waiting group and sat at the cleaned Formica table.

"Good Monday morning. As you know, the holiday break

starts Wednesday. I can't believe twenty thirty-six went so fast. This is our last meeting for the year, and we've had a great six months." John smiled. "Something odd has happened, though. Lisa Ford has not been at work for almost two weeks. Does anyone know anything?" He looked around the table.

"I don't," Royer said.

"The last time I spoke to her was the day of our celebration. I asked her to join us at Pete's. She told me she had plans," Min said.

"Same here. That's the last time I saw her," Gloria said.

"Me too," Joyce added.

John nodded. "A police report has been filed, and the FBI is investigating. With that said, there is nothing more to talk about, but should anyone hear something about Lisa, please tell Joyce, Jennifer, or me." He looked down at his notes. "As I already said, Wednesday is the beginning of the holiday break, so GA will be closed for two weeks starting then. Only security and maintenance personnel will be on campus." He smiled. "Word has gotten out about us, so please do not come to GA. Go someplace and have a well-deserved break. I'm actually off tomorrow, so I'll see you all in 'thirty-seven. Happy New Year."

The next morning, John walked into his kitchen dressed in blue jeans and a hoodie, relaxed and at ease. Megan was standing by the counter holding a cup of coffee. The children were sitting at the small dinette table eating pancakes, dressed for their last day of school before their own holiday break. Megan was wearing her white lab coat. John grabbed himself a cup of coffee and a piece of toast and then sat at the table with the children.

"Dressed for success?" Megan asked, eyeing his outfit.

"Day off."

"On a Tuesday?" Megan asked as she took a sip of coffee. "Good, then you get to take the kids to school and pick them up at five. And don't send them in the car on autonomous drive. I want you to drive them, not the car alone take them."

"You know I hate using that system. I love to control the car."

"You mean speed," she said.

Megan, having experienced the bus' pecking order, smells, obnoxious boys, and painful ride, would drive the girls to and from school even though the car could deliver them without a driver. Unlike Megan, John had walked to school and wanted them to ride the bus. He seldom drove them now; he left too early and stayed too late at GA.

John's favorite part of taking the children to school that morning was the sing-along. It developed with starts and stops, until the perfect song came on the radio. And ended with swinging doors, music blasting into the schoolyard, and the girls running to class. Pure joy.

Back at home, John was alone. Megan was at the hospital seeing patients. The children would not need picked up until five o'clock. He could do as he pleased. It had been two weeks since the celebration day at GA and since he'd ventured into the study. Except for a thin layer of dust clinging to the computer screen, the room was as he had left it since the morning after Lynn had sent the machine into a crazy search.

Before he turned on the computer, he sat, picked up his Caltech cap, and took a moment to think about all the possibilities the Clement Syntopicon Q1 could bring once it was installed. There was no telling what they could find, including —and most important, with a little luck—a cure for progeria.

He looked at his little sister's photograph, a beautiful smile on a thin, wrinkled face. Then John wiped the dust from the monitor screen with a piece of tissue, turned on the computer, and hoped for an adventure. He moved the cursor to the *Progeria* icon, but his attention was drawn to another one on the left side of the screen, titled *LYNN*.

He flashed back to innocent fingers flashing across the touch-screen and starting an endless computer search.

He clicked the *LYNN* icon and opened the file. Suddenly, there it was: 12/8/26, 5:59PM: 156082573156140081–HGNC 6636–P02545-F1N-V4683761#-GCACAGGGCAG#.

John asked the same question he'd considered a couple weeks ago: *Why did the computer pick that equation?*

When Lynn brushed the screen, he'd been about to compare mayfly cells, which lived twenty-four hours, a 4,850-year-old California bristlecone pine, and children with faulty cell repair due to a defective LMNA gene.

His question had been simple: "How do we rejuvenate cells and repair the lining?"

"What have I got to lose?" he asked the ether. "It'll only take a second to get ready for a new search."

He logged in to the GA supercomputer and curiosity stole all time. Hours disappeared, each moment filled with wonder and excitement. John felt as he did the moment before his first kiss. Everything was moving too fast; each step led to another positive result. This exact combination of acids and proteins was not present in the fly or children with progeria. More astonishingly, older cells had reduced amounts of these compounds, and stem cells had the most.

"Oh God," John whispered, "what've I found?"

The room went dark for a moment. He jumped to his feet and jumped back from the desk, almost falling to the floor. He glanced at the monitor clock: 2:00 p.m.

Standing there, he thought, *Finding these genes, acids, and proteins in this combination is impossible. It's luck. Not in a thousand years ... never could I find this exact sequence of chemicals. Like any lottery, only the exact combination wins. In this lottery, the winner lives forever.*

It can't be this easy to violate God's Tree of Life. Death.

He returned to his desk, determined to prove this wrong.

ELEVEN

At GA late that afternoon, Jennifer White walked into John's outer office and found Laurie sitting at her desk, working on the computer.

"Is he in?" Jennifer asked.

"No. He took the day off, and it's about time."

"I've got the information he asked for."

"He's home," Laurie said.

Jennifer smiled and left the office.

At home, John was still consumed with the genetic comparison. He'd lost track of time. Each test: six-year-olds, same; three-year-olds, same; newborns, same. He could not find one adverse result: in every case, the older the cells, the smaller the quantity of these acids and proteins.

He stood up and walked away from the computer. He rubbed his hand through his hair and moved around the small room, talking to himself. "It can't be! There must be an error." He walked to the computer monitor, stared at the screen, and thought, *God is not simple.*

He sat back at the computer and started from the beginning, and again everything moved at lightning speed. Each result the same: yes, yes, and yes.

John's mind flashed to the unthinkable: *I've found the Tree of Eternal Life, God's most guarded treasure.*

Adam and Eve were punished for eating from the Tree of Knowledge, and God sent cherubim to guard the Tree of Life. *What am I going to do?*

He leaned back in his chair, sweating with excitement. There was nothing more he could do at home; only quantum computing or testing these acids and proteins on living creatures remained. The thought was unbelievable. He glanced at the clock: 4:45.

"Shit! The girls."

He quickly stood, ran out of the house, and jumped into the car.

"I can still make it." He started the car, backed out of the driveway, and raced along the two-lane road toward the school.

Suddenly, he came to a familiar 25-mph curve—and face to face with reality. Adrenaline instantly shot through his body, his fear not caused by the impending curve itself, though it soon would, but by the right-angle arrow affixed to the signpost before the curve. Seeing the sign, John glanced down at the speedometer, and to his shock, the needle was waving atop 80 mph.

The pending crash began with skidding tires and a slide off the right side of the road. When all four tires reached the loose gravel shoulder, the car spun around.

The car passed over the shoulder with screaming tires and slid onto the grass field that bordered the road. On reaching the grass, the car started to spin a second time. John's world suddenly changed in that instant. Time seemed to slow, and silence enveloped a slow-motion and surreal world. He felt himself a helpless bystander to his own recklessness.

Although the car was spinning out of control, he felt no fear; a sense of peace encompassed him. His fingers and hands relaxed from the steering wheel and dropped onto his lap. He watched in the third person as the car spun in circles.

It's hard to describe a second when one instantly comprehends he is about to die. That moment arrived when John saw the trees. At first, the trees seemed far away, unreachable—suddenly, they looked to be one terrifying mass that he would hit.

Uncontrollable fear shot through his body. *I'm about to die!*

He lifted his hands from his lap, grabbed the steering wheel, and turned to the left as hard as he could. At first, there was nothing, no reaction, only a continuation of the slow-motion slide to death. He closed his eyes.

Without warning, a violent jerk swung the car back toward the road. John opened his eyes. The car spun one last time before it came to a stop in the middle of the road.

Shocked, John sat for a moment and watched the dust settle around him. He opened the door and got out. He walked a few feet away from the car and looked back down the road. He followed the black, muddy grass trench that marked its journey through the field. He was dumbfounded by what he saw: It turned just before the trees.

Why am I alive?

He walked across the street to follow his path to death.

His surreal, tranquil world abruptly ended. Seeing the field's long skid mark and deep gash cut into the grass, John realized that, while his mind was at peace, he'd had the brake pedal floored from start to finish.

He looked disbelieving at the sudden left turn in the grass. *What made the car turn?* There was no visible reason.

Astonished by this miracle, he walked to the spot where the car made its inexplicable turn. There was nothing there except a deep cut in the grass.

I should have hit those trees. Unbelievable.

He walked back to his Bronco, looking over his shoulder every so often. When he reached the vehicle, he looked for damage. Except for mud, there was none. He knew he'd hit something, but there was not a scratch, only the three-hundred-foot skid mark.

He leaned against the gently vibrating hood of the car for a moment. *How stupid. How stupid.* Now his heart began to race, and a weakness he had never known gripped his body. The pressure inside his chest grew stronger with each breath. He pulled his shirt open, hoping to catch his breath; it did not help. The pressure kept building; it was so great he wanted to slice his chest open and free the fear.

Panic, the most unforgiving of all horrors, had wrapped its oppressive arms around him and was tightening its death grip.

"Breathe," he whispered. "Relax. Think."

He took a deep breath and forced himself to relax.

Suddenly, a truck passed with its horn blaring. The blast of wind and sound brought him back to reality. He lifted himself up from the hood, brushed the dust from his pants, and drove to the girls' school.

Returning home after picking up Lynn and Abby, John parked in the driveway with the car radio off and the girls sitting quietly in the back seat. He switched the engine off and sat in the car and watched the girls run into the house.

He relaxed back into his seat for a moment, then opened the car door and walked toward the house. Lying on the walkway a few steps from the front door was a purple pickle-ball. He picked it up, took a couple quick steps, and tossed it across the lawn and smiled.

"You're out," he said.

He called for Megan as he tossed his keys onto the entryway table. Not hearing a reply, he walked into the kitchen.

"Hi, darling," Megan said, still dressed in her medical smock, looking happy. "Late getting the girls?"

"Interesting day. How is the love of my life?"

"Lynn said the ride home was very quiet and the car is covered in mud."

"I think I've done it."

"Great, honey, but we've got company."

John turned and looked to the dining room.

"I hope you don't mind me dropping in like this," Jennifer said.

In the dim background light, she looked radiant. Her expression was welcoming and comfortable. She was dressed in faded jeans, extra-worn cowboy boots, and a white silk blouse. Her hair was pulled up under a Dodgers baseball cap.

"I finished the personnel file on Lisa Ford, and Laurie said you were home, so here I am." She handed John the flash drive.

"This is totally unnecessary," John said with an uncomfortable smile.

"I know I could have emailed it. But I needed an excuse to leave GA early. I hope you don't mind."

"Well, you're here. How about a glass of wine?"

Jennifer and John moved to the living room.

"Your Christmas tree is beautiful," she said.

"Thank you. It's all Megan."

John opened a small wine refrigerator and removed a bottle of chardonnay and poured three glasses. He handed one to Jennifer and sat on the couch.

Jennifer was looking at the tree.

After a few moments, Megan walked in carrying a small tray of hors d'oeuvres.

"I poured you a glass of wine," John said.

"Your tree reminds me of home," Jennifer said, looking at Megan. She moved to the cloth chair facing the couch and sat. "That tray of food looks wonderful, though you didn't need to go to any trouble on my account. I can't stay long; I'm flying home tonight on the red-eye, and I must finish packing."

Megan smiled. "We've taken that flight. It's a long one." She placed the tray on the glass coffee table and sat next to John on the couch. "I interrupted you in the kitchen, sweetheart. You said you've 'done it.' What've you done?"

"Nothing, really. I solved a silly problem that was bugging me." He took a sip of wine.

"I hear children," Jennifer said.

"Yes, we have two girls. They're upstairs washing up for dinner," Megan said.

After several minutes of light conversation, Megan and John excused themselves to go into the kitchen. The children came down the stairs and rushed to the food tray and started eating.

"Hello," Jennifer said.

"Hello to you," Lynn said.

"Are you excited about Christmas?" Jennifer asked.

"Yes, and I hope Daddy doesn't work."

"Your daddy works a lot at home?"

"He's late to everything. He's always in the study."

Still in the kitchen and speaking in a whisper, Megan asked, "What's going on, John? You're acting strange. What's wrong?"

"This is weird."

"That she's here? Give her a break. She used you as an excuse to leave work early. So what's wrong?"

John did not reply.

"What is it?" Megan asked, this time touching his right hand.

"I had a little mishap on the way to pick up the girls."

"And?"

"I was driving too fast and thinking too much."

"That's not smart, and why do cars have auto-drive? So smart people don't drive out of control."

"I know."

Megan looked at him for a moment before releasing his hand and shaking her head. "Go ask Jennifer if she'd like to join us for dinner."

To his surprise, the living room was empty. He walked into the hallway. "Jennifer?"

"You caught me," she said, grinning, standing in the hallway looking into the room. "The girls are showing me your office."

John passed by her and looked into the room.

Lynn was sitting in his chair, and Abby was standing next to her. The computer screen was still on, and his last search results were on display. The automatic logout had not reached its time limit and closed the system. The cursor was blinking by the last word of the statement It read: LMNA ADJUSTED ENZYMES FOUND IN PINUS LONGAEVA.

Jennifer smiled as she looked at the desk.

John walked to the desk, logged off the computer, and started to pick up the small piles of papers on the floor.

Standing at the doorway, she said, "That's a new system, isn't it?"

"Yes."

"I love new computers."

"Daddy, can we play on the computer before dinner?" Lynn asked.

"Not tonight."

Disappointed, the girls left and ran into the living room.

"Is that a picture of your sister?" Jennifer asked, pointing at the desk.

"Yes, she was ten years old when it was taken."

"It's a terrible disease. So I want to thank you for making me feel so welcome at GA, Doctor Barber."

"We're trying to build a team. We're happy you're with us." Finished picking up, John said, "Let's go back into the living room."

Megan was sitting on the couch, finishing her wine while thumbing through a magazine. The girls were reading.

Jennifer glanced at her watch. "I had no idea of the time. I've got to go."

"Won't you stay for dinner?" Megan asked.

"Thank you, but I can't. This has been very nice."

With that said, John and Megan walked Jennifer out of the house. They stood on the porch and watched her drive away.

Megan, with her arm around John, said, "What a nice young woman."

He did not respond.

When Megan and the children were asleep, John returned to the study. He walked to the desk, sat down, and pulled up the genetic formula. 156082573156140081–HGNC 6636-P02545-F1N-V4683761#-GCACAGGGCAG# appeared on the monitor.

He sipped his glass of wine and thought, *How arrogant to think I've discovered God's gift of life.*

With the wine finished, he closed the program, stood, and went to the door. He put his hand on the door frame to steady himself. "No one can know."

TWELVE

"Welcome to twenty thirty-seven," John said at the new year's first GA staff meeting. "I hope you all had a wonderful holiday celebration." He put a warm smile on his face. "For the next six weeks, we will continue to move forward with our department goals, and I don't foresee see any operational changes." He put a youthful grin on his face. "Now for some exciting news: While we were away, the Syntopicon Q1 cold room was completed, and the system is now scheduled to be installed earlier than expected—Presidents' Day weekend next month. From what we've been told, it will take four days to complete the installation: Friday, the thirteenth, through Monday, the sixteenth. I will be requesting all staff start that weekend holiday on Friday and not return until Tuesday."

"I don't think that's going to happen," Min said. "I for one will be here."

John looked around the table. Everyone was nodding.

"Well, it looks like you'll be on-site for the installation," he said with a laugh in his voice.

"I'm excited and looking forward to it," Joyce said.

"We'll be the first," John said, "thanks to Secretary Hallett pulling a lot of strings, the first and only government program to have sole use of an SQ1. We're the guinea pigs. The exact time of installation is being held until the last minute, for obvious reasons. All we can do is follow our daily goals, ready our database, and wait for the semi to arrive. To that point, security will become much tighter. There are some who are very concerned about quantum computing. Others will try to hack us to get what we learn. The FBI will conduct random checks on personnel and—"

"What kind of checks?" Royer interrupted.

"Cyber, nothing more," John said immediately, studying each face as he looked around the group. "Please instruct your staff."

"What does 'random' mean?" Royer cut in again, his voice a little harsher.

"It means no one would dare bother you," Joyce said with a laugh.

"They better not." Royer nodded.

"When the SQ1 installation is completed, personal projects will only be conducted off-site and after work hours. We must dedicate our attention to the SQ1 formatting and algorithms. The first challenge will be to keep the SQ1 room at minus two hundred seventy-three degrees Celsius. From there, it's a breeze." John smiled and looked at his notes again. "Until that time, daily tasks will not change. It's all about collecting data, programming, and preparing for our second AI supercomputer test."

John looked at Min, who stood. She liked to stand when she talked. The petite, four-foot-tall mathematician was holding a multicolored plastic chart. The red-black-and-blue chart listed the sequenced genome of the Drosophila fly.

"Our little friend has been studied for a very long time. Lots of data. We are going to ask four simple questions—of course, using our little supercomputer."

Joyce smiled at the joke.

"What molecules are not in our database? And why not? Third, what molecules and proteins are in our little fly and not humans? Lastly, compare it all. Easy-peasy." Min abruptly sat down.

"Something interesting," John said. "A French research team implanted their revolutionary crystal CPU chip into an adolescent chimpanzee and downloaded simple commands. According to reports, the animal responded to the commands, but unfortunately, it died the next day."

Min gasped and covered her mouth with her fingertips. "I hate animal testing. I look forward to the day when all that stops and it can be done with an SQ1."

"Their hope is to create an education chip," John said.

"Impressive," Royer whispered.

"Just because a billionaire wants it doesn't make it right," Min said.

Heads nodded.

"I agree," John said. "Well, that's all I have. We can begin our individual reports. Who would like to start?"

"I will," Min said, jumping to her feet again.

On Monday morning, February second, at FBI headquarters, Ty Leggett picked up the telephone and called HHS Secretary Carol Hallett.

"Hi, Ty. What's up?"

"Just a quick question regarding Doctor Gloria Gysin. How did you hear about her?"

"An old friend, former German Ambassador Gerhard Klaus, called and asked if I could help her. Why do you ask?"

"I'm trying to put a scorecard together for the players."

Workers began the task of installing the Syntopicon $Q1$ computer mid-morning on Friday, February thirteenth, heading into the Presidents' Day weekend.

Excited about watching the magnificent machine being installed, John tapped his fingers on the steering wheel as the GA gate bounced opened. He then drove to the back of the three-story office building.

The industrial-sized liftgate was open. An eCascadia semi-truck and two Mercedes vans were parked inside the building. Joyce's car was parked outside, facing the open lift-gate, alongside Min's candy-apple-red Mini Cooper. Gloria's car was parked inside the building next to Royer's gray Honda Accord, facing the vans.

John had dressed in a new, polyester-blended, winter-cotton, gray-and-blue sweatsuit with a hoodie. He parked next to Joyce's car, opened his door, and walked into the giant ground-floor warehouse of five thousand square feet. There were several men dressed in workman uniforms standing at the rear of the semi-truck. Royer, Min, and Gloria stood next to the truck, watching the $SQ1$ being removed. Another group of people, dressed in casual business attire, were standing alongside Joyce, facing the truck, talking.

As John approached, a counterbalance Reach electric

forklift was removing the SQ1 from the semi-truck and placing it onto a ten-square-foot motorized rolling cart.

John joined Joyce. "Good morning, all," he said.

"I'm so excited," Joyce said, her face beaming. "These wonderful people"—she pointed with a wave of her right hand —"are the geniuses who are going to assemble our once-in-a-lifetime gift."

John introduced himself to the people standing next to her. Gloria and the others joined them as the SQ1 was wheeled to the elevator and its home in the basement's cold room.

"You're right: It's quite a gift," John said. He turned and looked at Min. "And you were right too: Not a chance that any of us would miss a billion-dollar show like this." He glanced at Royer. "Well, what do you think, Robert?"

"All I can do is grin. Two thousand qubits, entanglement forging, near-perfect error mitigation, an all-in-one supercon-ducting package. I wonder what our first real question is going to be."

Min was almost giggling and dancing. "I can't wait to flip the switch and hear it think."

Late afternoon that same Friday in Germany, the assistant federal minister of finance, Gerhard Klaus, was in his home sitting room, reading national banking reports, when his aide knocked on the door.

"A Mr. Otto Heinz has arrived, sir. Should I show him in?"

The aide left the room after a gruff nod from Klaus, who

got to his feet, buttoned his cashmere reading jacket, and walked to his executive desk.

Otto Heinz, a self-made billionaire, feared no one and showed even less respect. He was one of Germany's most successful businessmen and had built the largest international drug company in Europe—and he wanted more.

He was tall, with a full head of silver hair and especially fit for seventy years of age. He loved the conquest of rivals and women. He was driven by the memory of forced labor on the docks at Kiel as a child. His pockmarked face and low-class slang bespoke a man who could and would kill to get what he wanted.

"He's been over there more than a year, and we got nothin'," Otto spit out as he burst into the room.

"I would suggest you remember who you're addressing," Klaus said in a low, menacing tone.

"I know how you got here," Otto said, his eyes filled with contempt. "The whore is not moving fast enough."

"Don't worry."

"I have five million reasons to worry, you worthless cow."

Klaus suddenly stood, grabbed Heinz by the shirt collar. "*Enough.*"

The two men stared at each other without fear, the threat of pending violence filling the air.

"Okay," Otto said, glaring at Klaus.

Klaus released his grip on Otto's shirt, turned, went back to his desk, and sat. "He needs more time," Klaus said in a relaxed tone.

"I want to see him, now. I want his lazy ass working. And living in fear of me."

"It's too early for that."

"Then I want my money."

"That's a mistake. I'm warning you: Don't go after the money."

"I don't make mistakes. And that whore better be here soon," Otto snarled. He turned and strutted toward the doorway. As he was about to leave, he turned to face Klaus, pointing his fat, gnarled index finger while almost spitting the words, "It's my fucking money."

Gloria returned to her apartment building at 7:00 p.m. that night after watching the SQ1 being installed. She parked in the underground garage in her assigned slot and took the elevator to the second floor. Before she opened the apartment, she checked the door frame to see that the hair she'd placed was still in place. Seeing it, she unlocked the door and went into the cold, undecorated one-bedroom apartment.

Gloria felt her patience was about to pay off; soon she would work with Royer. She went into the master bathroom and took her hour-long bath. Finished, she returned to the living room, switched on her laptop computer, and scrolled through her emails.

Adrenaline flashed to her head when she saw a message from Bank Bern Freya in Switzerland. She opened it, thinking, *My money!*

The message read: "We regret to inform you that your account has been frozen effective 9:00 PM GMT, February 12. Issuer has demanded repayment of deposit. Account holder shall contact Bern Freya, as per account restrictions, by February 26, or the disputed funds shall be returned to issuer. Mr. Thomas Elander, President, Bank Bern Freya."

She slammed her left hand on the table, knocking the

lamp to the floor. She had a numbered account, and only a personal visit would fulfill her security arrangements. She also knew her benefactor *could* get his money back.

That Friday at midnight, John was in the GA third-floor lab. He had written his last notation. He felt good, thinking everything was ready for the next experiment. He sat at the work-table facing a row of specimen jars filled with fruit flies. As he always did before leaving, he flipped to the first page of his research diary to review the progress. He had done this since his first year in college. His grandmother had taught him to go over his project notes from beginning to end each day.

She'd say, "Do this and everyone will think you're a genius." Every time he did it, he thought of her. It worked.

The first page read:

Notes to Diary — 12:00 AM 12/27/2036

What if this works?

Preparing experiment #1 for Drosophila Fly #1:

Study cell gene expression using derived genetic code on Drosophila melanogaster Fly #1 to determine effect on aging process. Removed genetic altered/spliced DNA, inserted new sequence into Fly #1.

Fly #1 has a remaining life expectancy of 2 days. I've been able to duplicate the exact molecules, amino acids, and proteins sequenced in formula. Will reexamine tomorrow evening. Hope this experiment fails. Fear consequences.

. . .

He turned the page:

Notes to Diary — 12:00 AM 12/28/2036

Results Experiment #1: Success. Drosophila melanogaster Fly #1 is alive and shows no adverse effects. Visual observations suggest reverse of aging process. Fly #1 appears to have been rejuvenated. No further actions planned.

He flipped through the next several days:

Notes to Diary — 11:30 PM 12/29/2036

Results Experiment #1: Fly #1 alive.

Notes to Diary — 11:30 PM 12/30/2036

Results Experiment: Fly #1 alive.

Notes to Diary — 12:30 AM 1/1/2037

Results Experiment: Fly 1 still alive.

Notes to Diary — 11:30 PM 1/2/2037

Results Experiment: Fly #1 alive. Day 7. Fly #1 shows no signs of deterioration. All placebo contemporaries dead. Will conduct rejuvenation on mice tonight.

He turned to the last page:

Notes to Diary — 12:30 AM 2/14/2037

All modified test mice have lived. Scary. Rejuvenation remarkable. SQ1 installation began today. There is nothing left for me to do but test this on a human. Unthinkable. Will ask Royer to run experiment on SQ1.

John called the GA executive staff to his office on Tuesday morning, February 17, 2037. Royer, Min, Gloria, and Joyce arrived, and he opened the meeting with a question.

"Now that the SQ1 has been installed, what do we do with it? What are our next steps?"

"May I?" Joyce asked.

"Of course."

"We know we must keep the room temperature at zero Kelvin. We're close; we're at minus two hundred sixty-five point five Celsius. The last seven point six five will prove challenging. Robert and I believe we will reach and can maintain that temperature by next week. Once we reach those magic numbers, we'll be able to turn the machine on and initiate several tests to calibrate the computing accuracy. Those tests will continue until we reach ninety-nine point nine-nine percent accuracy.

"That could take some time, maybe several months. Our standards are very high. The manufacturer says we will reach acceptable accuracy within a month of operation. Our guess is it will take longer. At worst, our goal is to be fully operational and start asking important questions by May first." She smiled and looked at John.

"Okay, team, May first is our deadline. Can your team meet that goal, Robert?" John asked.

"We'll be ready."

"Min?" John asked.

"Easy-peasy."

John looked around the table. "Okay, I'll leave the logistics and coordination to you and your teams. I'm excited. Let's get to it."

John stood and glanced at his cell phone. There was a text from Ty Leggett: *Please call tomorrow. Not urgent. When you have time.*

"John, may I have a moment?" Gloria asked.

He looked away from his phone. "Sure."

"I have some personal business. I'm catching a flight tonight and I'll return in a week."

"Not the best timing, but okay. Check with Jennifer so she can coordinate the Human Resources reports."

"Also, if I may, when I return, I believe it's time my team joins with Royer's to create and facilitate a biochemical regimen."

"That call is up to Royer."

THIRTEEN

Later that day after lunch in the GA cafeteria, John returned to his office. He pressed the speed dial at about 2:00 p.m. to call Leggett's Washington DC FBI office.

A smile warmed his face before the video screen popped on.

"How y'all doing?" Ty asked enthusiastically.

"Fine. What's going on? You asked me to call?"

"I wanted to give you a heads-up." Ty's tone went serious. "We've been monitoring Gysin's communications."

"Why?"

"We found an email address hidden in Ford's apartment. We traced it to a Bonn University computer. We're not sure Gysin ever used that computer; however, it was in the same department."

John leaned slightly closer to the video screen.

"And she's been sending and receiving encrypted emails from her apartment."

John rubbed his hand through his hair.

"We managed to trace one of the emails to the home of Gerhard Klaus, a German finance minister who's also the person who recommended Gysin to Carol." Ty put a grin on his face. "To tie it together, Klaus is an investor in one of Europe's largest drug companies, Heinz Pharmaceutical."

"Well, that, my friend, is interesting. Doctor Gysin asked this morning to work with Royer, and to my surprise, she also asked for a week off for personal reasons."

"When is she taking off?" Ty asked.

"Tonight."

"Where's she going?"

"No idea, and this doesn't make sense. Gloria is doing a good job. Her team members only complain about her obsessive cleanliness. And that's a good thing. She certainly does not come across as a patsy or a thief."

"I agree. I reread her file. She's got quite a comeback story: Mother's dead, father's in an institution, and her brother's one bad hombre who hasn't been seen in over a year. She's never married, two master's, two doctorates. Impressive. I also reread the CIA interview conducted at Bonn University. She knocked their socks off. To quote the file: 'She's brilliant.'"

"That doesn't sound like a thief," John said.

"You never know."

"What do you want to do?"

"I'll keep an eye on her," Ty said. "She hasn't done anything illegal. Our only mystery is still: Where's Lisa Ford?"

FOURTEEN

Leggett hung up, checked his watch—5:10 p.m.—and pressed the intercom button on his desk phone.

"Yes, sir?" a pleasant female voice asked.

"Contact our GA team and have them meet in the conference room in ten minutes."

Ty Leggett's Washington DC office was full of personalities. There were pictures of him with celebrities and political figures, and a full-sized skunk skin was tacked to the wall with various Western artifacts. The only picture on his deck was of him, Megan, and John holding Lynn at her baptism. Written across the bottom, in gold ink, was "Godfather."

After checking his GA notes, he picked up Gloria Gysin's blue personnel file folder, left his office, and walked down a short private hallway to the main conference room. The hallway was lined with photographs of athletes, politicians, Old West gunfighters, and signed photographs of the Tuskegee Airmen and also Justice Marshall.

Twenty minutes after requesting a meeting with his DC

GA-assigned staff, Ty walked into a small, nondescript conference room filled with a ten-chair conference table. The room
went quiet.

"Lady and gentlemen," he said as he took his seat at the
head of a coffee-cup-ring-stained mahogany table. "Doctor
Gloria Gysin is taking some time off. We have no idea where
she's going or planning. All we know is that she's flying out
tonight. Finding her location and itinerary is your number one
priority."

Sitting at the table were his best agents: Peter Smith,
Mitch Meehan, Jamie O'Grady, Josh Jacob, and Daniel
Whitehead. All were dressed in khaki pants, black shoes, and
white, long-sleeved, buttoned-collar dress shirts, except Jamie
O'Grady, who was wearing a light-purple silk blouse with
jeans. She was Ty's favorite agent.

"Where is she going and who is she seeing?" Ty said to the
group.

The room was silent.

"Now that I've got your attention, no one goes home until
those questions are answered."

Ty tossed a blue folder on the center of the table that
contained photographs and every fact the FBI had found on
Doctor Gloria Gysin.

"From all available information," Ty continued, "it
appears, and I stress *appears*, that Gysin is working with a
foreign interest. We're going to watch her every move wher-
ever she goes until she returns to GA." He leaned forward,
jabbed his index finger on the table, his eyes wide with intent.
"So that there's no misunderstanding: If a busboy, street
vendor, or any other living human being comes closer than
five feet of Gysin, they're investigated back to birth."

He looked at each person sitting at the table.

There was a knock on the conference room door. It opened and a young-looking male agent handed Ty a note.

It read: Doctor Gloria Gysin booked American Airways Flight 362 to Heathrow Airport, departing San Francisco at 9:00 PM Pacific time tonight. Expected to land at 4:15 PM London time tomorrow, 2/18.

Ty smiled. "Our first question has been answered. Gysin is going to London. We have eighteen hours or so before she lands. I want those of you who are assigned to fly to London tomorrow"—he checked his watch—"to get an eight a.m. departure and coordinate our surveillance of Doctor Gysin.

"So, assignments: Peter, first thing, call San Francisco and get an agent on her plane. After that, you coordinate European operations, contact our London office, and have a team at Heathrow to follow Gysin. Mitch, you'll continue to follow the money. I want to know where she spends every penny and where every penny comes from. Jamie," his voice softened slightly, "you'll coordinate the female surveillance team.

"And, everyone, please note"—he leaned forward for emphasis—"in addition to the email address, we've found another possible connection between Lisa Ford and Gysin: Ms. Ford disappeared within days of Gysin arriving at GA."

He looked at Whitehead. "You trace her electronic messages. Hopefully, we'll find her European money." Ty rubbed his chin, looked down, thinking, and looked back at Whitehead. "Doctor Gysin is very smart. I'm sure she has an exotic encryption code hiding something we want to know. I want that code found and broken. I want to know why that Bonn email address was hidden in Ford's bed frame, for God's sake. Gysin worked at Bonn University; there has to be a connection. Ford was also a smart person; why was she so afraid of losing that email address, and who was she hiding it from?"

"Yes, sir," Whitehead said.

"When you answer those questions, I want each link sourced and followed back to Creation."

"Yes, sir, understood."

"I especially want the names, addresses, and cell numbers of those bastards in Bonn."

Ty picked up the blue folder, flipped through the pages for a moment. "Per our understanding with the CIA, copy them on all reports sent to me. I want them to know what we know. Don't worry about Homeland; this does not affect them." Ty turned to face Josh Jacob, his senior agent. "I want a twenty-four-hour detail at Gysin's apartment, and I want it searched.

"Any questions?" Ty finished, taking one last glance around the table.

"What do you want to do about Jennifer White?" Jamie asked.

"Nothing. Let her play for now. We know the actors. Any other questions?" He looked around the room. "Okay, let's catch those bastards in Bonn and hopefully find Lisa Ford."

Gloria listened to the announcements as the flight attendant in first class handed out champagne and a moist cloth.

"Welcome aboard American Airlines Flight 362. Please fasten your seat belts and bring your seats and tray tables to their full upright and locked position. Our flight time is eleven hours and fifteen minutes to Heathrow. Our anticipated arrival time is Wednesday, four-fifteen p.m. London time."

FIFTEEN

Gloria noticed something out of the ordinary when leaving Heathrow customs on late Wednesday afternoon. She was accustomed to having men stare at her, but not women. Women generally glanced, moving their eyes up and down to check her outfit. She turned to face the airport exit glass doors and glanced at the crowd of people moving about behind her. Five were looking in her direction.

I'm being followed. This didn't surprise her since the FBI was watching GA. *But so many? Do they suspect something?* Gloria walked out onto the crowded sidewalk to meet her private car service. A man, dressed in black pants, a white dress shirt, and black leather jacket, was standing at the curb holding a small sign with her name on it. Gloria got into the black taxi as the man loaded her luggage into the trunk.

"The Haymarket Hotel," she said without looking at the driver.

Halfway into the hour drive, she noticed the driver was gawking at her through the rearview mirror. She glanced at the right sun visor, which was turned down to display the driver's name.

"Is there something I can help you with or do you always stare at your fares?"

"No, lady," he said with a thick east Indian accent. "You planning on staying at Haymarket?"

"What business is it to you, Mr. Rajinder Singh?" Her tone dripped with disgust.

"You very beautiful, and being American, I thought you not know the Haymarket is a gay hotel."

"What I'm aware of is none of your business. Just get me there."

Without saying another word or further glances via his mirror, Singh drove a little faster to the hotel.

The taxi stopped at the hotel, Singh got out, walked around the back of the taxi, removed her luggage, and opened her door. She got out and took a moment to survey the area.

Gloria had studied the Haymarket's location by AI street map, but she needed a moment to get her bearings. After looking around, she whispered, "Perfect." Without saying another word or tipping the driver, she turned to face the hotel.

She was greeted by a tall, slender man in his mid-twenties, dressed in a pristine, perfectly tailored, traditional, blue-and-gold bell captain's uniform, complete with an oversized whistle.

"Oh, dahling, you're dazzling," the captain shrieked with joyous enthusiasm.

With overacted dramatics of formality, he raised his whistle to his lips and blew until his pale cheeks popped out and a piercing blast called his junior captains outside.

He turned with military precision to the now assembled

group of four similarly dressed men lined up facing the taxi, barking out, "Attend this goddess."

The assembled group rushed toward Gloria and the taxi with great fanfare.

"Madam," the captain said, his chin lifted with military formality, "allow me to escort you to the front desk of the *glorious* Haymarket Hotel." He clicked his heels and raised his bent left elbow.

With a smile, she took his arm, and he guided her through the ornate glass doorway of the hotel, followed by several bell-hops carrying her luggage.

With a bounce in his step and swinging his straight right arm, the bell captain led Gloria into the plush and tasteful lobby to the vacant front desk. When they reached the flower-draped marble counter, the bell captain gently released Gloria's arm and with ceremonial panache lifted his right arm and with his flat hand flicked his wrist twice and rang the gold push bell.

After a moment, a door behind the reception counter opened, and a short, thin, well-manicured man dressed in a white silk shirt, dark-blue cashmere jacket, and tailored gray slacks appeared.

"May I help you, madam?" he asked with a thick English accent.

With that said, the bell captain clicked his heels and marched out of the lobby.

"Yes. I am Doctor Gloria Gysin."

"Yes, madam, we've been expecting you. It's a pleasure to serve the only non-athlete this glorious weekend." He nodded to the people moving around the lobby. "This week is the qualifying round to attend the Bonn Games. And you, madam, are our only non-sporting guest."

"That is why I chose the Haymarket Hotel."

He smiled. "My name is Jerrold Pincushion. I am the assistant manager."

Gloria smiled when she heard his name.

"We've selected our most exclusive suite for your stay. It's exceptional, madam. Which is quite necessary with these sporting enthusiasts running about." He again gestured to the lobby. "Your suite," he said with a lifted left eyebrow and a smile, handing Gloria a silver key, "is on the top floor, suite double oh seven." He giggled, covering his mouth with his fingers. "A bit of English humor, madam. I hope you don't mind."

"Not at all, and I'm sure it won't disappoint."

The assistant manager, still smiling, signaled with a wave of his left hand to a lone junior bellhop standing by the elevator to come forward.

Gloria turned and followed the bellhop. After a few steps, she stopped and turned with a look of uncertainty at Pincushion.

"Is there something I can help with?" he asked in a whispered voice.

Gloria glanced at the bellhop and then back to Pincushion. Sensing what Gloria wanted, he dismissed the bellhop with a toss of his head.

"I'm traveling alone, and my lover is very possessive and unaware of my true desires," Gloria said. "Driven by distrust, I believe he's hired people to follow me."

"Madam, you need not say another word." He lifted his chin. "We at the Haymarket Hotel are protective of our guests' privacy. Each member of our staff has been with us for years. I assure you not even the ever-present Mossad could infiltrate this establishment. If madam wishes, I'll discreetly advise each member of our family to ensure your anonymity."

Gloria smiled softly, turned, and walked to the bellhop standing by the elevator to take her up to her suite. *Done*, she thought.

They walked along a plush carpeted hallway in silence. The bellhop stopped halfway, then opened the door to number 007. He walked into the suite; Gloria followed. She took a moment to look around the spacious one-bedroom suite.

"You may bring in my luggage." She reached into her purse and removed five £100 notes and tipped the bellhop without saying another word.

With him gone, she locked and bolted the door and quickly pulled off her clothes, except her panties, tossed the clothes into a corner of the room, opened her suitcase, and removed disinfectant and other cleaning materials.

After several hours of cleaning the suite, she showered and scrubbed her body pink.

Dressed for bed, she picked up the telephone and called the front desk. "Hotel manager, please."

"This is the manager speaking. How may I assist you, Doctor Gysin?"

"My plans have changed. I'm taking a trip Friday morning."

"Do you wish to cancel your reservation?"

"No, I'll only be away a short time. Please arrange to have a bicycle ready for me Friday morning. I want to start my tour by bicycle."

"Of course, madam. I'll personally arrange the details and select our most comfortable bicycle."

"Thank you. I'll only use the bike to a specific point, so

please arrange to have it returned. Also, I'd like to attend tomorrow's finals for the Bonn Games. Can I get a ticket?"

"Of course, madam. Shall I add the ticket charge along with the bicycle rental to your room?"

"Yes, also add a forty-five percent gratuity."

"Thank you, madam; you're very generous. I'll leave the ticket at the front desk. The bicycle will be waiting for you at the bell captain's desk Friday morning. Is there anything else madam wishes?"

He patiently waited for her response.

"Yes, come to think of it. Since tomorrow is the final day of the qualifier, is there a celebration or party at the conclusion?"

"Yes, madam. There'll be a ceremony at Horne Hill Stadium. Medals will be awarded and a fireworks display. Later that evening, there'll be a party at London's most popular club, the Mahiki Mayfair."

"Will it be difficult to attend?"

"Yes, madam. I'm sorry to say, it'll be impossible."

"Oh, you must help me get into that party. It sounds so perfect." Her voice went high-pitched and overly dramatic.

"Since you are our special guest, I'll contact the club manager. He's a very close friend, and I'll tell him you'll be attending as my guest."

"That's glorious, and since I'm to be your date, I must know your full name."

"It's Robert, madam—Robert Hurlbutt. I'm the executive manager."

"Wonderful, Robert. What time and where should we meet?"

"At eleven p.m. in the lobby, madam."

"Thank you, Robert. I look forward to an entertaining day and special evening." A warm smile lifted her cheeks, and she added, "Oh," sounding as though she had remembered something, "one last thing. Have there been any inquiries about my stay?"

"Sadly, madam, yes. But we've rebuked all efforts."

"Thanks, Robert. My lover is quite the jealous type and will employ any deceit. Once," Gloria said with a soft laugh in her voice, "he even hired actors." She laughed. "Thanks again, Robert, for being a lifesaver."

Gloria put down the telephone and smiled. *It's falling into place.*

SIXTEEN

Early Thursday afternoon, Gloria arrived at Horne Hill Stadium. There were thousands of spectators, and it looked more like a carnival than a track and field competition. Concession stands were everywhere and filled with loud barkers hawking every imaginable item—hats, cotton candy, hot dogs, T-shirts, adult toys, pom-poms, electric concept cars, and exotic adventures. The excitement was infective.

The grandstands were filled with brightly dressed, enthusiastic people waving team flags, cheering, and singing songs of local flavor. Whenever a well-known competitor performed, cheers of support would ring out.

Gloria proceeded directly to her seat even though she received many invitations to stop and talk. She looked cold and aloof. Once seated, she did not leave. She was not watching the competition, though; she was studying the competitors.

Finally, Gloria spotted what she was looking for: a woman with features and coloring similar to her own. The woman had run a race, and from the way she waved her hands and celebrated, it appeared she had qualified for Bonn.

Gloria quickly left the stands and walked to the competitors' changing area. She reached the roped-off space at the same time as the athlete she had been watching. She moved into the walkway and, as if by accident, bumped into the distracted athlete and stumbled to the ground.

The young woman quickly turned and reached for Gloria. "Oh, I'm terribly sorry," the athlete said as she helped Gloria up.

Not looking at the woman, Gloria brushed the grass and dirt from her tight, straight-leg jeans. Finished, she looked at the concerned athlete with tender eyes. The two of them looked at each other for a moment. Gloria gave a warm and seductive smile.

"Are you okay?" the woman asked.

"It was my fault," Gloria said.

"That's sweet, darling, but—"

"Please don't apologize."

"Are you sure?"

"Yes, I'm fine. I got carried away seeing such beautiful creatures and forgot to watch where I was going," Gloria said, sounding excited. She fixed her hair with a flip of her hand.

"I hope I'm one of those beautiful creatures," the woman said with a Cockney accent—and a cocky little smile.

"To be quite honest, yes, you are," Gloria said seductively. "I was watching you perform and you're terrific." She reached out her hand. "My name is Gloria."

"Nice to meet you. I'm Chris Withering."

"I'm sure you have more important things to do than talk to starstruck fans," Gloria said as she released Chris' hand.

"Unfortunately, yes. They're about to award the medals

and I must change. I hope we'll meet again and I'm sorry about knocking you down."

"To show there's no hard feelings, I'll buy you a drink if you're going to the Mahiki Mayfair this evening."

"I'll make a point of looking for you," Withering said with a building smile.

"Perfect. I'll be in the emerald dress."

With that said, Gloria spun around and headed back to the Haymarket Hotel. There was no point staying any longer. Her goal was completed—*And quite satisfactorily*, she thought.

Thursday, February 19, 2037

Report to: Director Tyler Leggett

FBI Headquarters, Washington DC

From: Special Agent Peter Smith, FBI European Operations, London

Suspect arrived London yesterday at Haymarket Hotel

1: Agent on plane to London with Gysin, nothing suspicious, subject had no interactions.

2: Hotel is host for Gay Games qualifiers.

3: Subject had no outside contact upon arrival.

4: Subject left hotel Thursday 12:30 pm local time for Horne Hill Stadium to attend games.

5: Large crowds presented problems for surveillance. Games ended today.

6: Special Agent Jamie O'Grady is attempting to coordinate hotel assets; no success to date.

7: Special Agent O'Grady interviewing supportive members of gay community for advice and counsel. Challenge: Overcome protective nature of the community. Hope to convince them we are solely interested in subject for national security reasons. London gay community is tight-knit and protective of newcomers. Advantage: They are friendly to American law enforcement.

8: Due to the nature of this investigation, we are precluded from contacting local authorities to secure additional assets. With limited agents at our disposal, complete surveillance is questionable.

END

Ty tossed the memo onto his desk, leaned forward, and hit the intercom button. "Are they ready?" he asked.

"Yes, sir."

Ty stood up, unrolled his white, long shirt sleeves, and left his office. He walked down the short hallway into the small conference room. He glanced at the agents sitting at the table, went to a side table, and poured himself a cup of coffee.

Four people sat around the table, collars loose and their sleeves rolled up. Agent Josh Jacob was laughing as Ty poured the coffee.

"What did they find in Doctor Gysin's apartment?" Ty asked as he turned to face the group.

"It was clean," Jacob said with a slight snicker.

The other people in the room exchanged looks and smiles.

"Okay, I'll bite," Ty said as he sat down. "What's the joke?"

"Boss, her apartment was clean, like NASA clean. Her underwear was packed in sandwich bags, and each panty was lined with gauze."

"Gauze?" Ty said incredulously.

"She's a real clean freak. Sir, she even cleans the tracks inside her dresser."

"Wow, that's odd. What about her computer?"

"Wasn't there," Jacob said. "Except for some very expensive clothing, the place looked like it had never been lived in. The agents who performed the search said it reminded them of Lisa Ford's apartment, except cleaner."

"Well, what do you know," Ty said.

Gloria exited the elevator at exactly 11:00 p.m. and walked across the lobby of the Haymarket Hotel, greeted by gasps, covered mouths, and high-pitched shrieks of approval from the hotel staff and several guests. The bell captain strutted to Gloria with exaggerated military pomp, his cap pulled tightly down and held by the black strap under his chin. His eyes were wide and beaming with excitement as he high-stepped to Gloria.

"May I have the privilege of escorting you to your waiting carriage, Doctor Gysin?" he asked, looking thrilled to be in her company.

"Why of course." Gloria smiled and lifted her arm for him to take.

Gloria and the bell captain floated gracefully out of the hotel to a waiting horse-drawn carriage. Hotel manager Robert Hurlbutt was standing next to the carriage door as Gloria left the hotel. He took an admiring breath of awe.

"You bring tears to this old queen's eyes, madam. Tonight, the world will be yours."

Gloria gave him a radiant smile.

New York City's long-gone Studio 54 or any party club in

the world could not compare to the Mahiki Mayfair: velvet ropes, red carpet, spotlights, flashbulbs, limousines, hundreds of screaming fans. Famous and not-so-famous people were trying to gain access to the most exclusive party in London.

Some were offering the velvet-lined rope attendants thousands of dollars to allow them admittance. All in vain. If your name was not on the guest list, access was denied, regardless of station or wealth. Lady Phyll and a companion were being escorted inside the Mahiki as Gloria's carriage reached the unloading zone.

Robert got out of the carriage and turned to assist Gloria. When her legs reached for the street, her dress, which was slit up both sides, opened, exposing most of her perfect thighs. There were gasps and waves of white flashes, and questions buzzed through the paparazzi:

"Who is she?" ... "She's beautiful. What's her name?" ... "Is she an actress? What's your name, lady?"

Other solicitations were hurled at Gloria and Robert as they walked up the red carpet to the purple-velvet rope. Automatic cameras and cell phones flashed across the walkway with each step. They approached the handsome and massively built security guard standing at the end of the red carpet, who raised his hand to stop them.

A distinguished-looking, tall, thin man, dressed in a perfect-fitting red-and-black tuxedo, greeted Robert when they reached the velvet-lined opening. The two men exchanged cheek kisses, whereupon Robert introduced Gloria.

"It's a pleasure to have someone of your stunning beauty grace my humble club. Tonight, my lady, you're my personal guest," he said as he handed Gloria a plastic badge, labeled "Personal Guest" in bright-red letters.

"You bitch," Robert said. "I never got one of those badges."
He glared at the owner. Both men laughed.

Robert and Gloria passed through the ropes and walked
into the club. Everything and everyone looked perfect. Not
one costume or eyelash was left to chance.

The building was alive like Times Square at midnight or
the Champs-Élysées after a World Cup victory. The glittering
lights and throbbing music united the crowd into a vibration
of sexual glamour.

Gloria could not make out individuals while standing at
the top of the stairs that led to the main ballroom. She could
only see a throbbing mass of bodies.

"This is magnificent. Look who's here!" Robert shouted
over the music to Gloria.

Gloria could not believe what she was seeing. She had
never allowed herself to go to such a place. Work always came
first. *This is it*, she thought. She had always wanted this life,
and as soon as she had GA's secrets, this would become her
world. Never again would she be someone's tool. *Soon. Very
soon.* But first she had to find Chris Withering.

Robert and Gloria walked down the stairs and moved
through the throng of sweating bodies to the back of the room.
He spotted a friend sitting at an almost empty booth, and they
joined him.

After several drinks and laughter, Gloria started watching
a group of beautiful hard-bodies dancing. One dancer caught
Gloria watching. The woman stopped for a moment and
looked at Gloria, then she left the dance floor and moved
to her.

When the woman was within a few feet of the table, the
sinuous creature, while staring into Gloria's eyes, began to
rhythmically glide her hips from side to side. Dressed in a full-

length, sheer silk gown, she began to lift her dress with each graceful swing of her hips, exposing a magnificent bare body. Gloria watched with little interest.

Finished with her dance, the woman lowered her dress, bent down, and kissed Gloria on the cheek to Robert and his friend's cheers, then turned and rejoined the throng of dancers.

As the departing suitor turned to leave, Gloria spotted Chris Withering. Chris had also been watching the table dance. Gloria could see that Chris was interested in the performance.

Now. Gloria quickly got up from the table, walked to Chris, gently took her left hand, and pulled herself directly in front of Chris. They kissed. Gloria then reached down and held Chris' other hand, lifted them both up, and held them between their chests. They kissed even more deeply.

For a moment, they stared at each other, their stomachs gently touching with each breath. Their bodies began to sway with the music. Gloria knew she could take Chris back to the hotel. But no, that was not to be. They could not go there or anywhere else. This was where it had to end. No one could see them leave together.

After what seemed like an eternity of desire, Gloria whispered into Chris' ear, "Follow me." Gloria released Chris and walked to the women's bathroom. Chris followed in mindless pursuit.

Gloria walked into the large, elegant bathroom. She moved down the row of stalls, opened a door, and walked in. Chris followed. Gloria kissed Chris and gently turned and pressed her against the now-closed stall door. Gloria again gently held both of Chris' hands and lifted them to her chest. They kissed. Chris' breath was short, panting. Lust pressed their bodies against the door as they kissed.

Sounds of passion reverberated throughout the room.

"Let me touch you," Chris whispered.

The seduction was complete.

"No. Tonight is not our time. We cannot be together," Gloria whispered.

They kissed.

"Yes, yes, we must, we must. You can't leave me like this—it's not fair. This isn't enough," Chris pleaded breathlessly, staring into Gloria's eyes.

"Not here, not tonight," Gloria whispered.

They kissed.

"Why? We can leave, find a place; we must."

"No." A hint of aggression tinged Gloria's voice, and she gently pushed Chris away. "I want you," Gloria continued in a soft voice, "but we can't. I'll meet you in Bonn Saturday, and only exhaustion will stop us."

They kissed.

"How can you be so strong?" Chris asked. "Please, now."

"No." Gloria placed her hands on Chris' face and asked, "Which hotel are you staying at in Bonn?"

Realizing it was over, Chris said with a weak, disappointed voice, "Hotel Belmont Classic."

Gloria leaned back and looked at the wreck of a woman. "I'll meet you Saturday," she whispered.

Gloria opened the stall door and rejoined Robert and his friends at the table. After several minutes, Gloria turned discreetly to Robert and asked if he would take her back to the hotel. Robert excused himself from the table without complaint and they left.

The ride back to the hotel was quiet and uneventful; only

the FBI was awake on the streets of London. Back in her suite, Gloria cleaned herself pink and covered her hands and face in antiseptic cream.

After four hours of sleep, the alarm buzzed; it was 8:00 a.m. Gloria showered again, and then dressed in beige shorts, a white tennis blouse, white tennis shoes, and a small white waist pack. She left the room.

"Good morning, madam. Are you ready for your scenic tour?" the bell captain asked as Gloria walked to the reception counter.

"Yes, quite ready."

"We at the Haymarket will miss you and look forward to your return."

With that said, Gloria walked to the side counter and saw a woman's ten-speed bicycle there. She walked the bike out of the hotel to begin her ride through the streets of London.

The FBI, having been tipped by an angry employee that Gloria was planning to ride along with a mass bicycle ride, planned on following her. What they were not prepared for was the spontaneous chaos and calamity to follow Gloria as she joined the fast-moving throng of a thousand-plus bike riders in London's noontime Critical Mass Bicycle Ride.

The London bobbies tried to control the event by setting up barricades and closing most of downtown to automobile and lorry traffic. However, like every previous mass bike ride, the police failed and chaos won the day.

With a quick turn and a sudden burst of speed, Gloria joined the bike parade near Victoria and flowed along, past the Palace, past Trafalgar Square, around Parliament, and through Hyde Park to Piccadilly.

The bobbies had set up a roadblock at Westminster Bridge to prevent the chaotic throng from pedaling across the Thames River. Chaos again prevailed, and the mass detoured from their scripted route, destroying the FBI's planned surveillance on Gloria.

As the first riders met the roadblock at Westminster Bridge, they turned left and proceeded as planned. Gloria's group, however, suddenly veered right, sliding through the offset barricades onto the bridge. The three bobbies standing at the bridge were shocked. Two of them were knocked down and the third jumped out of the way, all to the cheers of the spectators lining the bridge as the riders sped past.

By the time the FBI reassembled, Gloria was sitting comfortably belowdecks in a chartered cabin cruiser sipping chilled French spring water. The small craft gently powered her to Waterloo Bridge and away from prying eyes.

Gloria left the boat at Waterloo and walked to a waiting taxi. After being driven to London Executive Aviation, she boarded a Beechcraft King Air 200. The plane began its taxi the moment she buckled her seat belt and took off to Bonn/Hangelar.

Upon landing, the plane quickly refueled and took off again for its destination: Lugano Airport, Switzerland. The plane landed in time for Gloria to change and take a two-hour limo ride for her ten o'clock dinner in Zurich with Bank Bern Freya's president, Mr. Thomas Elander.

That morning, as Ty was leaving for a congressional hearing, he made one last check of his emails. He activated the security protocols and logged on to his email account. There was only one message—the one he was hoping for.

3:00 PM GMT, Friday, February 20, 2037
    Report to: Director Tyler Leggett
    FBI Headquarters, Washington DC
    From: Special Agent Smith and Special Agent Jamie O'Grady— European Operations, London
    1: We lost Doctor Gysin while riding in a mass bicycle race. Agent Smith was injured trying to navigate through a police barricade. Agent Mitchell was arrested for assaulting a constable while assisting Agent Smith. Agent Roberts is in a London hospital with a skull fracture, caused when he fell off a bridge and hit the water. We have returned to the Haymarket Hotel.
    2: We have limited support from hotel staff in our effort to discover Doctor Gysin's current whereabouts. We will attempt to survey her room tonight. Doctor Gysin has not checked out and will return to the Haymarket. Unable to determine if bicycle evasion was deliberate.
    3: We have interviewed several guests who attended Thursday night's celebration at the Mahiki Mayfair. According to most reports, Doctor Gysin did not meet or leave with anyone. There is, however, one report she might have had a brief sexual encounter with a female guest in a bathroom. This cannot be confirmed, and we cannot ascertain the identity of the bathroom woman.
    4: Other than that possible brief encounter at Horne Hill Stadium with one athlete, and her appearance with the hotel

manager at the Mahiki Mayfair, Doctor Gysin has not met or contacted anyone. We have reviewed all incoming, outgoing calls, emails, instant messages, etc., from the hotel and have learned nothing helpful.

5: We will inform you of any further developments.

END

What a cluster, Ty thought.

Frustrated, he downloaded the report into Doctor Gysin's file, stood, and walked out of his office.

"How could they screw up so badly?" he whispered.

SEVENTEEN

Gloria arrived by limousine precisely at 10:00 p.m. on the twentieth as agreed, dressed in a tailored, silk St. John business suit, draped in a white mink shawl. Her hair was jet-black and pulled up underneath a white silk scarf. Her wide and beautiful light-green eyes were now a rich almond-brown.

She got out of the limousine and walked up ten wide, carved marble steps leading to the mansion of Switzerland's most prominent banker.

Having reached the heavy, ornate doors, she pressed the bell and was quickly greeted by an impeccably manicured and formally dressed butler.

"Yes, madam, may I help you?" he asked in German.

"I'm here to meet Mr. Elander," Gloria said in perfect German.

"Yes, madam, he's expecting you. Please, allow me to guide you," he replied in German.

Gloria passed into the ornate home and followed the

butler through the heirloom-rich foyer, past a grand two-level staircase, down a magnificently wide and opulent hallway, and into a dignified, bauble-decorated private library.

Dark, freshly oiled cherrywood bookshelves covered the walls, filled with first-edition classics. The ceiling was high and crisscrossed with raw, hand-honed wooden beams. The rest of the ceiling was covered with a thick cork tile, which filled the room with a delicately perfumed fragrance of blended pipe tobacco. A fire gently burned in a large, stone-faced fireplace and provided most of the light in the room, adding a hint of smoky pine to the air.

When Gloria and the butler came into the room, a tall, slender man, dressed in a dark-blue dinner jacket and gray slacks, stood up from a rich, soft-looking, dark-leather chair facing the fireplace. He was holding a small, leather-bound book. He placed the book on the shimmering, dark-wood side table and turned to face Gloria.

"Mr. Elander, sir, I present your ten p.m. engagement," the butler said in German, his chin held high. On the introduction, the butler moved aside, turned, and left the room.

With the servant gone, Gloria moved to her reticent host and reached out her right hand to the banker.

Before Gloria could speak, Elander said, "Good evening, *mademoiselle*. May I please see your account identity card," he asked in German.

"Yes. And I prefer English," Gloria said.

She reached into her coat and removed a small, gold-engraved Bank Bern Freya AG card and handed it to him.

Without looking at Gloria or the card, he left the room, then returned several minutes later. "May I offer you a glass of champagne?" he asked in perfect English.

"Yes."

"It is a pleasure to meet you." With that said, Elander turned and moved back to the side table and pressed a small white button underneath the table.

The butler returned. "Sir."

"Two vintage bottles of Louis Roederer Cristal champagne, please."

Elander gestured for Gloria to move toward the fireplace. "Please," he said, "it's quite pleasant."

A moment later, the butler returned to the room, carrying an ornately decorated silver tray, two crystal flute glasses, an ice-filled sterling silver bucket, and two unopened bottles of champagne. He placed the tray on the richly polished, antique Victorian coffee table.

He turned to face Gloria. "May I take your shawl, madam?" At her nod, he gently removed her white mink shawl, left the room, and as quickly returned.

After a moment of hesitation, Elander selected one bottle of champagne and showed it to Gloria. She approved, and he handed the chosen bottle to the butler. He opened the bottle and placed it in the bucket and left the room.

Elander poured the wine into a glass and handed the drink to Gloria, then poured himself one. She took a sip.

The butler returned, holding a plate-sized silver tray sprinkled with an assortment of fine, hand-cut European cheeses, meats, and candy delicacies. He waited patiently as she took another sip of her wine, then passed the tray to Gloria, who took one of the hors d'oeuvres. He handed her a silk napkin, turned, and presented the tray to Elander. Finished, he placed the tray on the coffee table and left the room.

After a moment, Gloria asked about the financial management of her account. Satisfied with Elander's explanations, she reached into her Chanel flap bag and removed a folded piece of paper on which she'd listed investments she wanted to fund for the following twelve months, along with instructions should she fail to return in a year. She unceremoniously presented the paper to him.

"Mr. Elander," Gloria asked after taking a sip of her champagne, "have there been any inquiries made concerning my account?"

"Yes, madam, there's been one such inquiry. We cooperate with international law enforcement to ascertain if any of our funds are derived from drug trafficking or other forms of elicit business."

"I'm aware of your policy, Mr. Elander. That's the reason my account is with your institution. Are you saying that a law enforcement agency approached you regarding my account?"

"Yes, madam."

"Who made this inquiry?"

"I'm sorry, madam, but we at Bank Bern Freya have had a strict policy since seventeen fifty-five of not answering questions about the bank's associations. We do not suspect your account, and their questions went unanswered."

"Thank you, Mr. Elander. Now to your request for return of funds."

"Yes, madam, we were quite specific."

For a moment, she flushed with anger but just as quickly regained control of herself and nodded for him to continue.

"We received a request for the return of the most recent deposit from Mr. Otto Heinz. He has also requested that we refund all previous deposits, which we're not obligated to do." He politely hesitated.

Gloria nodded for him to go on.

"Regardless, it is our policy to contact the account holder of any such demands. Due to the unique nature of your account, we had to request you make a personal visit."

"I find being forced to meet with you on such short notice unacceptable. I am not a school child." Her eyes were wide with anger.

"Our policy, and the nature of your account, serve Bank Bern Freya and our clients well. Unlike most institutions, we believe urgency is preferred in exceptional circumstances. Our customers demand anonymity and want to keep their assets esoteric. That is why I summoned you."

Gloria bristled at "summoned."

"When we received the request for fund retrieval, we reviewed the deposit documents and discovered a clause stating the issuer had one year to retrieve said funds."

He turned and picked up several pieces of paper off the fireplace mantel. He handed Gloria the document, with the clause highlighted in yellow.

Gloria took the paper and read it. "How much time do I have?"

"With proper legal guidance, these matters generally—"

"I want you to close my account tomorrow morning."

"That will not help matters. We've frozen the requested monies, and those funds cannot be transferred."

"It's my money," Gloria snarled, her fingernails digging into her palm.

"That is true, madam. Unfortunately, Bank Bern Freya cannot release those funds to you. You may close your account and withdraw the balance of your unencumbered funds if you desire. We would then immediately comply with Mr. Heinz's request—"

"That would be a grave error," she said, almost growling.

"Be that as it may, madam, that's what we'll do. I suggest you seek legal counsel or have Mr. Heinz withdraw his demand."

Gloria stared at him, her mind racing for a solution. "Thank you for your advice. I believe you will hear from Minister Gerhard Klaus regarding this matter very soon."

"As you wish," he said.

Gloria put her half-filled glass on the side table. "I believe that concludes our business."

They left the library and walked outside to the waiting limousine.

Gloria got into the car, and the driver closed the door. After sitting comfortably, she rolled the window down and motioned for Elander to come closer. "If Heinz does not withdraw his demand in the next five days, you may return the funds."

She rolled the window up, and the limo drove away. She reached into her evening purse and called Gerhard Klaus' private number.

"This is Klaus."

She whispered into the phone with a clenched jaw. "If Otto does not remove his demand on my money by tomorrow afternoon, he will suffer a great tragedy."

She ended the call abruptly and instructed the driver to proceed to Lugano Airport, where she was to meet the private airplane for Bonn.

Gloria sat in silence as the car drove through the dark streets, thinking of Heinz trying to steal her money. "That bastard," she whispered. Her hands began to shake. Her left hand was fisted so tightly her knuckles were white and her fingernails dug deep into her palm. She was biting the right side of her lip, coloring her white teeth pink with blood.

She glanced up to see the driver staring at her in the rearview mirror with wide-eyed amazement. She forced herself to relax and looked out the window at the passing darkness and thought, *That leech will pay.*

EIGHTEEN

Ty had returned to his office from an early-evening meeting with the president when he received a third status report from Europe.

11:00 PM GMT, Friday, February 20, 2037
    Report to: Director Tyler Leggett
    FBI Headquarters, Washington DC
    From: Special Agents Peter Smith and Jamie O'Grady—European Operations, London
    1: We have inspected Doctor Gysin's suite at the Haymarket Hotel. Nothing too much out of the ordinary, except dresser drawers filled with undergarments in plastic bags and a strong scent of disinfectant.
    Lying on top of one piece of carry-on luggage was an itinerary for a bicycle trip abroad. According to said itinerary, she is in Paris and scheduled to leave for England at 8:30 a.m. on

Sunday, the 22nd. No specific locations were listed for Paris bicycle tour.

2: We sent a team to Paris to reacquire Doctor Gysin. We will monitor the Channel Tunnel, airports, and Paris bicycle shops. The evidence in her room suggests her disappearance was unintentional.

END

Ty put the memo down and thought, *This is too neat—I don't buy it. She wanted us to find that itinerary.*

He looked at the memo for a moment, interrupted by a knock at his door, and CIA Director Robert Pensky poked his head in, a curious look on his face.

"Got a moment?" he asked.

"Yes, it's the end of a long day, and if you'll join me for a short one?"

Pensky smiled and sat in the worn cloth chair facing Ty's desk. Ty reached into his lower desk drawer, pulled out a half-filled bottle of Jack Daniel's and two short tumbler glasses, poured one full shot each, and handed Pensky his glass. Ty took a sip and leaned back in his chair with a warm smile on his face.

Pensky took a sip and let out a deep sigh. "Tough day. Thanks."

"How can I help you?" Ty asked after another sip.

"Thanks for the heads-up on Klaus. He's a greedy, well-connected, powerful man. While researching him, we also learned something interesting about your missing person, Lisa Ford, and the Gysin family." Pensky loosened his tie.

Ty put a "How so?" look on his face, leaned a little farther back into his chair.

"In the late nineteen nineties, Lisa Ford's father was hired as a professor to teach organic chemistry at LSU in Baton Rouge. While there, he pulled the standard anti-Iraq war crap. Nothing outrageous—holding signs, blocking traffic, petty shit." Pensky took another sip. "But he did get arrested, and guess who bailed him out of jail?"

Ty shrugged.

"Professor Jonathan Gysin, who happened to be visiting from New Orleans." Pensky smiled.

"Whaddaya know," Ty said as he raised his eyebrows and smiled.

"Professor Gysin taught at the University of New Orleans and the two families were close, until Professor Gysin was arrested for molesting Gloria and Peter. He's still in a Louisiana mental institution. You'll never guess what his hobby is: knitting. He'd rape the kids and then make them a sweater."

Ty took a breath. "F-ing pig," he whispered.

Pensky took another sip. "Which might explain why Peter Gysin turned to crime rather than science like his sister."

Recalling Peter's criminal record, Ty nodded.

"The only reason we ran across Peter Gysin's name was in our background search on Klaus," Pensky went on. "We don't know anything about the relationship, but my bet is more drugs. Regardless, as you know, Peter Gysin has vanished."

Another nod from Ty, then, "I wonder why Jonathan Gysin's arrest didn't come up on Gloria's background report like Peter's stuff did?" he asked, seeming to talk to himself as he put his empty glass on the desk.

"No idea," Pensky said with a shrug. "Gloria and Peter were only in Bonn for a couple of years." Pensky finished his drink and placed it on the desk too. "And, as you also know,

Peter is presumed dead. It's believed he was killed in a terrorist attack on a Bonn office building. A firebomb destroyed the building and killed dozens. Gloria left Bonn soon after the bombing and moved to George Washington University." Pensky leaned forward and put a little grin on his face. "Here's the kicker." He lifted his eyebrows for effect. "Peter Gysin dated Lisa Ford while they were in high school."

Gloria landed at Bonn/Hangelar Airport before sunrise on Saturday. She went directly to the empty customs center and casually walked through the roped maze to the inspection cage. She slipped her passport through the steel slot and looked up at the agent.

The only thing on the gray-haired customs agent's mind, as he glanced at her passport, was going back to his nap. He slid the passport back to Gloria and, with his normal cold glare, nodded for her to pass through.

Finished with customs, Gloria went into the women's lounge. She entered one of the two toilet stalls, closed the door, took off the black wig, and changed out of the silk blouse and skirt. She then put on an authentic Great Britain Gay Games team sweatsuit outfit.

Leaving the toilet stall, she went to the sink and removed her makeup and dark contact lenses, washed her face, and wet her auburn hair. Finished, Gloria looked into the mirror and smiled. Now she looked like every other female athlete visiting Bonn that day.

Gloria left the bathroom, tossed her clothing into the trash bin, and walked nonchalantly to the front of the airport and hailed a taxi.

"Hotel Belmont Classic," she said as she climbed into the back seat of the Mercedes taxi.

After a twenty-minute drive, Gloria said, "Stop here." The taxi pulled over several blocks from the hotel. She got out and jogged the remaining distance to it.

She stopped running before reaching the hotel doorway, put the Japanese hairpin into her hair, and, breathing heavily, walked inside. Gloria looked like every other athlete in the lobby, insignificant.

She went to the house phone. "Chris Withering's room, please."

"This is Chris."

"I'm here. What's your room number?"

"Who's this?" she asked.

"Your surprise from London."

"Who...? Ah, okay. Fifth floor, number ten."

Gloria put the phone down and moved quickly through the lobby to the back stairs. She did not look directly at anyone. She walked up the stairs to the fifth floor and opened the stairwell door to check that the hallway was empty. Seeing no one, she left the stairwell and nonchalantly walked to room 10.

She took several deep breaths before knocking. The door opened, and Chris Withering stood by the door dressed in a sheer robe. Before Chris could say anything, Gloria pushed the door open and pressed herself into the room by softly kissing Chris and dancing her around.

Chris pulled back to see who was kissing her, and as she did so, Gloria gently pushed the door closed with her right foot.

Chris did not recognize Gloria at first, then she smiled. "You *are* the chick from the Mahiki," she said in her Cockney accent. "I thought you were another pussy teaser when you said you'd meet me in Bonn." She put a wry smile on her face. "Our timing's not good this time either, luv. I must be at the welcoming brunch in forty-five minutes and don't have time or the energy to entertain. Sorry, you'll have to give me a rain check."

"Is there any way I can go with you?" Gloria asked, facing Chris with her hands gently resting on Chris' hips.

Chris turned away from Gloria and walked to a night table to pick up her security badge. "Not unless you've got one of *these* little babies." She held the blue-and-gold ID badge between her thin fingers.

Gloria walked up to Chris and looked at the plastic security pass.

"Thanks to the local homophobes, security is so tight that these badges were handed out and every competitor had to be in her room to get it. So, unless you've got one of these blue devils, you're screwed," Chris said with a grin.

Gloria smiled and fingered the badge as it hung from Chris' hand. "Why is this event so special?" she asked as she sat on the edge of the bed, looking coy.

"It's a big deal. The welcome reception is at Beethoven-Haus. Lots of government types are gonna be there. The organizers don't want any trouble, so they put us through this 'top secret' crap. I guess having fancy Nazi-land bastards attend proves we're gaining acceptance."

"Well," Gloria said with a seductive smile, "if we can't be together now, how about a little love to tide me over until later?" Gloria again placed her hands on Chris' hips and smiled, her eyes and face warmed by the pending joy. She removed her hairpin.

Chris smiled as Gloria leaned forward and gently pulled

them together. As they kissed, Gloria put her right hand around Chris' shoulder and gently fondled her ear, while her left hand, holding the hairpin, softly slid to the small of Chris' back and firmly pressed their bodies together.

Gloria could feel Chris' body temperature rise, and her heart pound harder. The kiss grew into passion. Gloria leaned her head back to catch her breath, smiled, and focused on Chris' dilated eyes. Her breathing was deep and slow; their bodies were pressed together and had begun to pulsate.

Gloria's sexual stare suddenly turned into a snarl. Her fingers twisted around the hairpin; her knuckles turned white. Her hand flashed up with violent savagery, and she plunged the spike deep into Withering's brain. The only sound was a gasp of moist, hot air from Chris' mouth as her life escaped.

Releasing her death grip on the spike, Gloria held Withering's head between her hands, holding the body in place. Gloria's lips quivered as she watched the pupils turn hollow.

"You're wrong, my little pie. I do have one of those little babies," Gloria whispered with a sick smile.

Gloria dropped the lifeless shell and dragged the body onto the bed and removed Chris' outer clothing. Finished, she pulled the bed covers over the semi-naked body and went into the bathroom to clean herself.

Thirty minutes later, Gloria finished washing, dried off, walked back into the bedroom, picked up her sweatsuit and backpack, removed a plastic bag containing her undergarments, returned to the bathroom, and used Chris' makeup to match the security badge photo. Satisfied with the likeness, Gloria changed into Chris' clothes, called for a taxi, and stepped out of the room.

Gloria smiled as she placed the Do Not Disturb sign on the hallway doorknob. She walked to the stairwell, looking like every athlete dressed in formal attire, the blue-and-gold security badge placed neatly in her backpack. As she walked down the stairs, she sang softly, "Find the cost of freedom buried in the ground. Mother Earth will swallow you ... buried in the ground."

NINETEEN

Gloria was not afraid of being recognized; she knew no one would recognize Chris Withering dressed in formal wear. Gloria looked directly ahead as she left the hotel. Her eyes did not wander; she focused all her attention on the taxi station and the waiting car.

She got into the taxi.

"Beethoven-Haus," she said in a soft, shy voice, looking down at the car floor. After a short ride and a turn onto the destination street, she said, "Stop here."

Gloria exited the taxi a block from Beethoven-Haus and walked along the ivy-laced wall to the main gate. Standing at the gate were two heavyset security guards dressed in dark-blue uniforms, with silver badges, gun belts, and stiff, black-billed caps.

She continued along the narrow pathway without a glance at the military soldiers stationed at the second checkpoint. With her security badge bouncing against her unusually flat chest, she nonchalantly continued through the beautiful, flower-draped courtyard toward the check-in table.

She smiled. A large crowd pressed against the long table, and the elderly volunteers were too busy checking names to guard the mansion doorway.

"They'll never know," she snickered softly.

She passed the check-in table without stopping and walked directly to the name tag table. Three hundred name tags, in alphabetical order, filled the cluttered tabletop. Blank name tags were piled on an adjacent table with several black marker pins. She quickly found Chris Withering's name, then picked it up along with a blank name tag and marker pin. She wrote "Chris" on the blank name tag, crumpled Withering's tag, and tossed it into the small trash can next to the table.

With her new, fake name tag properly placed above her right breast, Gloria moved into the mansion. Inside, she was directed by a volunteer to join the receiving line. She studied the great room while standing in the slow-moving line. She slipped her identity badge inside her blouse. At first glance, she saw no security, and to her joy, the dignitaries had not arrived.

She left the receiving line and mingled among the other guests for several minutes, then moved to the bar and got a glass of ice water. She turned away from the bar and the line of people, looking for the doorway to the main dining room. Seeing two floor-to-ceiling oak sliding doors, she walked up to them and peeked through the crack to see how many people were in the room.

Several members of the catering staff were finishing up.

Holding the glass of water, Gloria turned away from the doors and looked for the bathroom. Seeing the sign across the room from the bar, she went into the small, single-toilet bathroom, locked the door, and placed the glass of water on the sink.

She reached inside her silk blouse with her left hand and removed the right breast cup. The small, gel-filled pasty contained a second packet of clear jelly. She opened the packet and poured the contents into the glass of water. She tossed the empty packet into the toilet and flushed it several times. She picked up the glass of water and rejoined the growing crowd in the reception room.

After a quick glance around the room looking for security, Gloria walked directly to the dining room doors, pulled them apart, and slid into the room. She found several small groups of people, along with catering staff, in the room. Several individuals were meandering among the tables looking at nameplates and gossiping.

Gloria smiled at one small group when she approached a table, and, like them, she continued walking around the room reading the table tents and nameplates. To her amusement, she came across Chris Withering's nameplate and smiled, wondering if she should remove it or not. She turned and continued walking around the room, all the while getting closer to the head table.

Once there, she drifted from seat to seat, reading each nameplate, not wanting to appear purposeful. She paused a moment and smiled at reading the nameplate for the center-right seat: "Mr. Otto Heinz, Chairman, Heinz Pharmaceutical."

With a quick glance over her shoulder, a wicked grin crossed her lips as she exchanged water glasses.

Finished, Gloria gracefully turned and left the head table, casually moving through the dining room and out into the main reception room.

Soon, she thought, *the perfect death scene. He will grab his chest, stand, vomit, and die—and my money will be safe.*

Gloria left Beethoven-Haus and walked several blocks to the first of what would be numerous taxi rides leading to an untraceable trip back to Paris.

Sunday morning, an FBI agent was sitting in a Paris train terminal reading the newspaper when he glanced up to see Doctor Gysin walk past.

He checked his watch: 8:30 a.m. "Wow, right on schedule," he said to himself. He whispered into his coat sleeve microphone, "Contact Captain Smith and tell him Doctor Gysin's boarding the Eurostar at the Gare du Nord station." He looked at the television monitor hanging from the ceiling to double-check the train schedule.

"Ready eyes to follow target. She will arrive on the ten a.m. St. Pancras International. See attached photo of subject." Finished, he followed Gloria and boarded the train. He sat several rows behind her.

As the train lurched forward to leave the station, a homeless woman dressed in a tattered, dirty burka with a stained face veil sat across the aisle from Gloria. The agent paid little attention to the homeless-looking woman, feeling she had no relation to Gloria.

A second woman walked up the aisle, this one dressed in a fresh cotton burka with a pristine silk veil over her face. She stopped at Gloria's row and asked with a heavy Middle Eastern accent, "May I sit next to the window?"

"No," Gloria said in a strong voice.

The woman hesitated a moment, then continued up the aisle toward the front of the car.

The train reached London, and Gloria got off, with the FBI agent close behind. Walking through the terminal, Gloria glanced at one of the televisions, and underneath the talking CNN heads, the scroll read: GERMAN INDUSTRIALIST OTTO HEINZ DEAD OF APPARENT HEART ATTACK.

When Gloria strolled into the lobby of the Haymarket Hotel that afternoon, Robert Hurlbutt was working at the front desk. He smiled and walked around the counter to greet her.

"Welcome back to the Haymarket, Doctor Gysin. I trust you had a pleasant tour abroad."

"Perfect," Gloria replied.

"Unfortunately, madam," Robert said, looking serious and lowering his voice, "one of my girls has betrayed us and given information about your stay to outsiders. I apologize, and I've—"

"I'm very disappointed," Gloria interrupted, her face cold, then as suddenly, she smiled, creating a wondrous warm expression. "I told you my lover was resourceful. I'm sure he learned nothing new. I'll be leaving tonight. Please make all the necessary arrangements?"

"Yes, madam, and again, please accept my apology."

Without acknowledging Robert's words, Gloria turned and walked to the elevator and thought, *Too perfect, too perfect.*

TWENTY

It was a beautiful Sunday afternoon, a week after they'd installed the SQ1, and one of those special Sacramento days when the wind is gentle, warm, and dry. People were sitting around picnic tables at William Land Park, watching small children playing and running about. There were birthday balloons and colorful tablecloths draped over tables. A large banner had been staked into the ground that read, "Welcome Friends of the Progeria Research Foundation."

The Barber family arrived in Megan's used silver Tesla Model Y SUV. The rear passenger doors popped open. "Love Shack" was playing on the stereo and blasting throughout the parking lot. John and Megan sat and listened to the end of the song as the girls ran across the grass to join the party. With the song finished, they walked around the picnic area, making a point of touching every child and hugging every parent. Megan stopped at one of the picnic tables and made a place for them to sit. Then she joined a game of tag with several children.

After games of tag, leapfrog, and Pin the Tail on the Donkey, John and Megan went to their table for glasses of lemonade. They sat and watched the children play. John turned and glanced to see the parking lot and watched Jennifer White's red Mercedes C-Class pull into the driveway.

Jennifer parked her car and walked to the picnic area. She was wearing white shorts and a light-blue silk blouse knotted at the waist, and her hair was held up by a Sacramento River Cats baseball cap. She walked directly to Megan and John.

"I'm glad you decided to come and support this fundraiser," Megan said with a warm smile.

"I wouldn't have missed it. I've been thinking about these special children ever since Doctor Barber mentioned progeria at a staff meeting."

They watched two children run after a balloon and play tag on the grass. Smiling, Jennifer stood, left the table, and joined several children chasing after a balloon.

After a half hour, a woman called for lunch and everyone sat at the concrete public picnic tables. They said grace, served hot dogs, potato salad, potato chips, and water. Megan and John sat across from a woman in her late twenties, the mother of a child with progeria.

"Hello, my name is Audrey. That's my son at the other table."

"Nice to meet you. I'm Megan, and this is my husband, John."

After lunch, the Barbers and Audrey watched the children continue to play.

"They deserve more days like this," Audrey said, with her eyes tearing up. "My son doesn't have much time left, but look how happy he is."

John looked past her to a group of little boys playing musical chairs with Jennifer. Bringing his attention back to Audrey, he said, "We'll beat this disease," sounding overly confident.

"Maybe for my son; he's got five or six years left. Unfortunately, time has all but run out for a boy named Billy Pinehorse."

"Who?" John asked.

"Billy Pinehorse. Today's his eleventh birthday," she said as she pointed at the birthday balloons. "He's too weak to be here. He could go anytime."

"Where is he?"

"UC Davis Children's Hospital."

With an expression of recognition, John said, "I know that hospital very well. They have a state-of-the-art biochemistry lab and the best gerontology specialists in California. Billy is in the best hands."

Audrey smiled politely, not convinced Billy had much of a chance.

John left the table and joined Jennifer and several other children in a game of tag. Megan and Audrey watched and laughed as several boys and girls pulled John to the ground.

"He really loves them, doesn't he?" Audrey asked.

"You have no idea," Megan said with a laugh in her voice.

"How long have you and your husband supported the foundation?"

"John lost his sister Abby to progeria thirty years ago. He hasn't given up hope of finding a cure or stopped contributing ever since. It really hurt him to lose her. We follow the fundraising events on the Progeria Research website and try to attend when we can," Megan said, watching John and the children roll on the grass, playing and laughing.

Many hours later, John sat in the GA third-floor lab, recording the results of his most recent test. It was after midnight.

Notes to Diary — 12:10 AM, 2/23/2037

Results: Fly #1 still alive!

With continued resubmission of genetic formula, fly appears to have achieved extended life!

Other GF test subjects alive and following Fly #1 eternal progression.

Conclusion: With GF administered, Drosophila melanogaster flies do not die of age. Total regeneration occurs six hours after introduction. Continuation of normal two-week lifespan follows each administration of GF.

Mice: Same results as Drosophila fly; regeneration/restorative process follows amount of formula administered; full dose resets subject to age of birth.

Full regeneration in mammals occurs 12 hours after introduction.

Regardless of the amount of formula administered, body subsequently follows normal aging and development process. Mice do not seem to lose cognitive memory. Mice appear to have significant challenges adjusting to slow pace of physical development.

Assumption: Genetic formula is recipe for eternal life and must be reintroduced or aging/natural death will occur.

Conclusion: It works!

· · ·

John put the pen down, thought for a moment, though he knew exactly what he would do next. He packed up his papers quickly, cleaned the lab, locked his journal into his private office safe, and hurried out of GA.

After a two-hour-thirty-minute drive to the University of California Davis Children's Hospital, he parked the car behind the fourteen-story building and walked to the back stairwell door. He walked up two flights of stairs looking for an unlocked door. Luckily, the third-floor door was unlocked. He gently pulled the door open and walked down a cold, freshly painted, hundred-foot-long white hallway. Bright-colored crayon drawings and posters displaying every type of animal covered the walls. Photographs of smiling, happy children were pasted on every door he passed.

The hallway was quiet. John glanced at his watch—2:45 a.m.—and he knew the floor nurse had finished last rounds. He walked down the sterile hallway looking for the nurses' station. When he found it, he input Billy Pinehorse's name and found the child's room number, 222, on the second floor.

He quickly left the station and went back down the hallway to the staff lounge. After a quick search, he located the hanging locker, opened the closet door, and removed one of the green dressing gowns and put it on. He opened several wall-cabinet doors, looking for N95 medical masks. He found an open box and put a mask on, pulling it halfway up, covering his chin.

He went to the elevator and took it down to the second floor. He ventured out, looking natural and relaxed. Not seeing anyone or hearing footsteps or talking, he continued down the hallway, following the room numbers. Room 222 was halfway down the hallway on his right. He listened at the open doorway for a moment. Not hearing anything, he pulled the mask up, covering his mouth and nose before pushing the door open.

The room was dark and cold; the only movement was coming from the colored ribbons waving from the air-conditioning vent. There were two beds in the room; the bed closest to the door was empty, with only a stiff white bedsheet pulled tightly across it. The other bed was hidden behind a flimsy, pale-green privacy curtain.

He pulled back the edge of the curtain next to the wall and moved closer to the bed, letting the curtain close behind him. He stood for a moment next to the bed, studying a bald, thin, sickly looking little person lying there asleep. John watched Billy for a moment before he removed the IV tube attached to the cannula from the child's arm.

He took a syringe from his coat pocket, pulled off the needle's protective cover, and placed the needle into the cannula and filled a small glass vial with Billy's blood. Finished, he reattached the IV plastic tube, silently slipped out of the room, and returned to Reno.

John returned to UC Davis Children's Hospital at 3:00 a.m. twenty-four hours later. He parked his car as he had the previous night. He put on the same medical gown and N95. As before, he wore the mask under his chin. He went to the same stairwell door and walked up the stairs. The second-floor door was locked. He continued up; the third-floor door was again unlocked. He turned the knob and opened the stairwell door enough to listen.

Everything was quiet. He walked casually to the elevators and pressed the down button. He cringed when the bell rang, announcing the elevator. He quickly jumped in and pushed the second-floor button. The door opened, and he carefully stepped out, listening for the slightest sound. The hallway was again quiet and empty. He walked confidently to Billy's room.

He listened at Billy's door for a moment, and not hearing anything, he pushed the door open. Like before, the first bed was empty and the privacy curtain was pulled around the second bed.

John tiptoed around the first bed while he lifted his mask to cover his nose and mouth. He pulled the curtain open, walked around the bed, and stood next to the IV bottle tree. He reached into his pocket and removed a one-milliliter glass injection vial and an empty syringe with a needle attached. He filled the syringe with the contents of the vial. He held up the filled syringe and eliminated several air bubbles. He removed the plastic tube from the cannula, inserted the needle into Billy's arm, and injected the liquid.

Suddenly, Billy's eyes opened, and he looked up at John. "Hello," he said in a high-pitched, weak whisper.

"Hi," John said softly, his eyes kind, face smiling under the mask.

"Who are you?"

"An angel. God wants you to meet your grandchildren." John placed his left hand on Billy's forehead and whispered, "Close your eyes and dream of tomorrow."

Billy closed his eyes and fell asleep.

John reinserted the plastic tube, glanced around the bed to ensure everything was in its place. He again gently touched Billy's forehead, turned, and left the hospital.

That morning at UC Davis Children's Hospital, a nurse was walking down the second-floor hallway, pushing a medical cart containing charts and room supplies. He stopped before the next room on his route, thumbing through several charts, looking for the one with room 222 on it. He removed the chart and said a quick prayer before going into Billy Pinehorse's room.

"Please be alive," he whispered.

He walked past the empty bed and softly pulled the privacy curtain back. Before the curtain was all the way open, he took a deep breath, closed his eyes, and again whispered, "Please be alive." He finished opening the curtain.

It took a moment for him to comprehend what he was seeing, then he gasped and dropped the chart to the floor. "Where's Billy?"

Sitting up in bed, grinning, looking back at him, was a very thin but otherwise perfect-looking eleven-year-old child.

TWENTY-ONE

John had just left the first-floor computer center after a late Tuesday morning meeting when he saw Gloria walk into the building from the main parking lot.

"Welcome back," he said when they reached the elevator. "I trust you had a good vacation."

"Yes, it met all of my expectations," she said with a smile.

"It has been hectic since you left—you were missed. I spoke to Royer about your offer to merge your teams, and I'm sure he'll welcome your help."

"That's great. I'm on my way to meet him now for coffee."

John continued up the elevator and went to his office. He sat at his desk and logged in to his computer. The private phone light flashed; he saw Ty Leggett's face on the screen.

"Hey, Ty, how are you?"

"Fine. How 'bout you?"

"Now that Doctor Gysin has returned, everything should get back on track."

"Doctor Gysin is the reason I called. I finished reading the report on her trip to Europe. To sum it up, she lives an active lifestyle. Other than that, nothing much to report."

"So she's okay?"

"Keep your eye on her."

"So you called to tell me she's active and to keep my eye on her?"

"Yep."

"That's definitive."

"That's me: Mister Precise. By the way, I am planning a trip to Northern California, and if I can swing into Reno, I'll call."

"Sounds great. I'll tell Megan."

"I've got to go. Remember to keep an eye on Gysin."

Leggett got up from his desk at the Washington DC FBI headquarters and went into the sixth-floor conference room; his team was assembled.

"Okay," Ty said as he sat at the head of the table. "Let me see if I got this right: We lose Doctor Gysin for three days, and agents go swimming, to the hospital, and get arrested. Right," he said with a pained smile. He looked around the table. "And now, you all have concluded that Gysin went to London to attend a sponsored track competition, to meet an athlete, attend a party, and kill the athlete two days later in a Bonn hotel." He paused with a doubtful expression, shaking his head side to side. "That same day, again in Bonn, a well-known German businessman"—he looked down at his notes— "a Mr. Otto Heinz, is murdered by state-of-the-art poison, coincidentally at an event for said athletes from the London games. All this from a cluster-F surveillance."

The assembled team looked down and avoided eye contact with Leggett.

"Okay. I'll play along: You all believe Doctor Gysin traveled over ten thousand miles in five days to kill two unrelated people? Then returned to GA like nothing happened?"

"Yes, sir, that's what we think," O'Grady said. "The target was not the athlete; the killer needed the dead girl's ID to attend the reception. The target was the business exec."

"What's the link to Gysin and the dead guy?" Ty asked.

"German Minister Gerhard Klaus is a major investor in the dead businessman's pharmaceutical company."

"So? Why kill him?"

"We don't know that," O'Grady answered.

"Oh, come on. Klaus introduces Gysin to Secretary Hallett and we've got nothing? How did the athlete"—Ty looked down at his notes—"Chris Withering, die?"

"The mortician who performed the autopsy said she was killed by a spike or long needle stabbed through her temple."

"Was there any foreign DNA found on the body or in her room?" Ty asked.

"No, sir, the girl's body had been scrubbed after death and the room was clean," O'Grady said.

"How clean?"

"Scary clean, like Gysin's apartment and Lisa Ford's place, sir."

"Again, so what? Unless you find direct links to Gysin and Heinz, or better yet, a motive, all we got is nothing," Ty said.

Royer was sitting at one of the Formica tables in the cafeteria, sipping a cup of black coffee and reading the latest report on the human trials for cyber implants, waiting for Gloria to arrive for their meeting.

She came in and said, "Thank you for meeting with me."

Royer looked up with a smile and waved at the report. "This could be scary," he said, tossing it onto the table.

Gloria glanced at the papers and showed no interest.

"Welcome back. It's good to see you."

"Thank you." She smiled. "Bad timing, I know. We're all working so hard; I didn't want to miss a minute. Which is why I mentioned to John about us combining our teams and doubling our efforts."

"Yes, he spoke to me, but I feel it's premature to merge. We're not quite done with the data-collection process and still months away from a working quantum. Joyce is writing the AI algorithms, and those tests could last several months. Maybe then we can talk about merging."

She smiled, thinking, *Damn it.* "That's frustrating. I was hoping that working together we could move faster—"

"Gloria, these things normally take careers, and sometimes that's not long even enough. Our advantage is the SQ1 quantum, and when it's up and running. our discoveries could become geometric. We're administrators, and patience is our true gift."

Gloria smiled and nodded, thinking, *Sanctimonious bastard.* She stood up. "Thank you for your wisdom. It's greatly appreciated. I look forward to that time when we discover something great—"

"We could be closer than we know," Royer interrupted with an insightful grin. "You notice the insect jars in the third-floor lab?"

Gloria sat back down, leaned forward, hoping to hear a secret. "They've been there for months."

"Guess how old some of those flies are?" he teased after a sip of coffee.

"The Drosophila fly lives two weeks," she said, giving a "So what?" shrug.

"Unless someone is playing a joke, some of those bugs are months old."

"That's impossible. It must be a joke," she said, her eyes betraying her excitement.

"If true, the scientist will announce his or her findings at the appropriate time."

Gloria smiled. *It's a joke—or a trap.* "That would be exciting. Something to look forward to."

Royer smiled and glanced at his watch. "I've got to run." He collected his papers, stood, said, "I'm glad you're back," and rushed out of the cafeteria.

Gloria's mind raced as she watched him leave. *Whose project is it? Could flies live forever?*

Her cell phone vibrated; she had an instant message in her secure file. It was from Bank Bern Freya. She opened the message, which read, "Your account has been restored; all funds are unencumbered. Issuer of stop-payment has rescinded all demands. Thomas Elander, President, Bank Bern Freya."

Wednesday night, feeling wonderful, John was working late in the third-floor GA lab when the door opened.

"John, I can't believe you're here. It's almost one o'clock in the morning."

The instant he heard that voice a chill shot through him.

Gloria was standing at the lab doorway. She walked to

him. John kept his back to her and finished writing in his journal. Finished, he closed the book.

Gloria stopped several feet from the center counter.

"I'm not having any fun," he said as he turned to face her.

"Can I help?"

Her eyes were flashing across the table. They stopped and focused on his phone. The screen was partially covered by John's journal, but she caught a bit of a headline: "Miracle in—"

"It's late for you, too," he said.

"I often work late. I like the quiet. But you, this is extraordinary."

"It's the only time I can be alone."

After an uncomfortable pause, she sighed. "Okay, you don't have to hit me over the head." She turned and left the lab.

John cleaned up and returned to his office, locked the journal in his safe, and left for his car. As was his habit, before he got in, he turned and took a last look at GA. A light suddenly snapped on in the main lab. *Gloria*, he thought.

TWENTY-TWO

Gloria walked through the lab, checking the trash bins and tables. Not finding anything of interest, she left and returned to her office. She sat at her computer and searched for the article she'd seen under John's journal.

She found:

Miracle in Davis, California

By Katherine O'Keefe | Sacramento Bee | Online 2.24.37

Eleven-year-old Billy Pinehorse has joined the ranks of millennium miracles: Billy has seen an angel!

Until early in the morning on Tuesday, February 24, 2037, little Billy Pinehorse had been living a nightmare, when, according to Billy, "An angel appeared and said God wanted me to be a grandfather."

Before that hallowed visit, Billy had been afflicted with progeria, a genetic disorder that kills most of its victims before they reach their twelfth birthday. Children with this heartless disease age seven times faster than normal, forcing old age and death on our most innocent.

Billy is now quite the star in California and around the world. He shows no signs of the deadly disease. According to Doctor Johanna Harris, chief of staff at the University of California Davis Children's Hospital, "Billy is the first child on record to have progeria and recover. It's truly a miracle."

Scientists and religious figures from around the world are calling Children's Hospital to meet little Billy.

Gloria clicked off the Sacramento newspaper site, leaned back in her chair, and wondered, *Why was he here so late?*

Gloria arrived at GA earlier than normal on Thursday morning. She went straight to her office and called UC Davis Children's Hospital. She had tried several times to contact the hospital on her way to GA, and to her frustration, each time a recorded message answered.

"Children's Hospital, how may I direct your call?" a strong, deep voice finally answered.

"This is Doctor Gysin, and I would like to speak to Billy Pinehorse's supervising physician to schedule an appointment to visit the child."

"Good luck with that," she said, snickering. "Right now, the pope couldn't get an audience. We're swamped with requests from street nuts to celebrities. Other than midday nap time—uh, please hold."

Gloria squeezed her left hand so hard her fingers turned white around the phone.

"Thank you for holding. Your best bet is to wait for the press conference."

"What time is his nap?"

"One-thirty to two-thirty. But—"

Gloria hung up, left her office, and hurried to the GA main lab. She grabbed a green surgical smock from the closet, a new N95 mask with attached respirator tub, surgical gloves, hair nets, and caps. She held everything together in her arms and went back to her office and neatly placed the lab contents into her empty wastebasket trash bag.

She checked the time: 8:00 a.m.—*I'll leave at ten.*

Before 10:00 a.m., she picked up the desk phone and called John's voicemail. "John, this is Gloria. I'll be away for most of today for a doctor's appointment in Sacramento."

She put the phone down, left her office carrying the filled trash bag, and went to her car.

Two and half hours later, Gloria arrived at the main parking lot of the Davis Children's Hospital. She parked and impatiently watched the dashboard clock: 12:45 p.m., 1:00, 1:05, 1:09, 1:15, 1:25, 1:30.

Finally. She watched the last small groups of people file out of the hospital.

The parking lot, once filled with staff and visitors walking about, was now empty. She got out of the car, put on a surgical smock, N95 mask with attached air hose, hairnet, and cap. Finished, she walked into the hospital with a purposeful, hurried air of determination.

The security guard did not, for a moment, think about stopping Gloria as she passed by the security podium on her way to the elevators. Her eyes never wavered and were glaring straight ahead.

She pushed the elevator button. The empty car opened, and she got in and pressed the fifth-floor button. Once the doors closed, she removed the mask, tube, net, and cap and placed them into a bag she carried under her gown. She removed her blue GA security badge from her pocket and pinned it to the front of the gown.

The elevator doors opened. Gloria walked down the cold, sterile hallway, looking for an empty room, found one, went to the telephone, and called the operator.

"This is Doctor Simmons speaking. Have they moved Billy Pinehorse yet?"

"No, Doctor. He's still in room two twenty-two."

"Thank you." She hung up and took the elevator down to the second floor. The hallway and nurses' station were quiet and empty. She confidently walked down the hallway to room 222, then walked around the privacy curtain and saw Billy sitting up in bed reading J. K. Rowling's novel *The Christmas Pig*. A card rested on the bed signed by Rowling. It read: "To America's newest wizard. I look forward to meeting you one day."

"Hello, Billy, my name's Doctor Gysin. How are you?" she asked in her softest, happiest voice.

"Okay."

"You're quite the star," Gloria said with a smile as she sat on the edge of the bed. She looked around the room for a moment. "Is it okay for me to ask you a few questions?"

"Sure." He shrugged.

"Tell me about the angel," she said with an engaging expression.

"He was nice," Billy said with a big grin.

"Was he tall?"

"Taller than my daddy."

"Did the angel give you anything to eat or drink?"

"No."

"What was the angel wearing?"

"Doctor stuff."

Gloria picked up a soft toy baseball lying on the bed and rolled it in her left hand several times. "What makes you think the angel was a man?"

"He smelled like my daddy."

Gloria thought for a moment, then reached into her jacket pocket, took out her cell phone, and showed Billy a photograph of John Barber.

"Ever see this man before?" she asked, handing the phone to Billy.

Billy shook his head and handed the phone back.

Frustrated, Gloria stood and with a forced smile said, "The angel was right; you'll make a fine grandfather."

"I never gave up hope," Billy said.

"Never do, Billy. Surviving is what keeps us going. Well, I've got to go. Thank you for answering my questions."

She left Billy's room, headed to the nurses' station, and asked if Billy's parents were in the hospital. The nurse told her that Billy's father worked in the hospital as a nurse.

The nurse glanced at her watch. "He could be in the nurses' lounge. Down the hallway on the left."

"Thank you," Gloria said.

She went to the nurses' lounge and found a young, tall, lean man sitting with his feet up on the table, looking at his phone.

"Are you Billy's father?"

"Yes."

"My name is Doctor Gloria Gysin. May I ask you a few questions?"

"Sure." He lifted his feet off the table and stood.

"Has Billy described to you what the angel looked like or if he was touched or given anything?"

"No. All he said was the angel was nice."

"Are you sure? He said nothing else?"

"Well, he did say the angel was tall and smelled like me. Other than that, nothing."

Again frustrated, Gloria turned and started to leave the room. When she reached the door, she stopped and turned to face Billy's father. "What's that cologne you're wearing?" she asked with a disarming smile, acting embarrassed.

"Surgical soap," he said with a laugh. "I get so many compliments, I don't need to wear cologne."

"You're kidding," she said.

She abruptly turned and left the room and went to the elevator, muttering under her breath, "Nothing, nothing, not shit."

Once back at GA late that afternoon, Gloria went directly to Doctor Barber's office.

"How can I help you, Doctor Gysin?" Laurie asked.

"Is John in?"

"Yes, but he's in a meeting with Doctor Royer."

"When will he be available?"

"I really can't say. They went in, and from the memo Doctor Royer was carrying, it could be a long meeting. You know how Doctor Royer can be. If you want, I'll have Doctor Barber call as soon as they're done." Laurie glanced at her watch. "That might be after five."

"That won't be necessary. I'll try to catch him tomorrow." She turned and started out of the reception area. Pretending

185

to catch a thought, she stopped at the door. "Oh, before I forget, do you know if anyone at GA shares John's interest in progeria? I'd like to join them."

"I'm not aware of any—Well, maybe Jennifer?"

"Thank you."

"Do you want me to find out? He'd love the help in finding a cure."

"No, that's not necessary."

Gloria left, and as she walked back to her office, she reached into her coat pocket and tapped her cell phone several times. Billy Pinehorse's picture was on the screen. She could not suppress the emerging smile. "I think he already has," she whispered.

TWENTY-THREE

"Robert," John said, frustrated, "I spend twenty hours a week in budget meetings, another twenty hours dealing with logistics and securing future funding. There isn't—"

"Is the government funding another lab to match our mission?" Robert interrupted.

"No."

Royer studied John's face. "Okay. Are the security cameras operating around the clock?"

"Robert, can we discuss this at the staff meeting?"

"No."

"Yes, the cameras are on."

"Please turn them off; it feels like a prison. My staff is beginning to act paranoid."

"There're sound reasons for—"

"John, please, at least during the day. People aren't under suspicion or guilty of anything. We're a research lab, not a military facility, aren't we?" Royer interrupted.

John thought for a moment. "Okay, the inside cameras will be turned off during working hours."

"Will you announce this at the staff meeting?"

"Of course."

"Thank you. The last item: Sunday night, we kept the SQ1 computer at absolute zero for fifteen minutes and reduced the noise to acceptable levels. If we successfully repeat that tonight, we'll start coding sample test questions, and then we'll ask one question on Friday the sixth."

"This is exciting! Fifteen minutes is an eternity for the SQ1, and to be at this point so quickly is marvelous. Don't you want to announce this at tomorrow's upcoming staff meeting?"

"No, you're the only one who doesn't know." Royer laughed.

"Perfect." John smiled. "Why would I need to know?"

Royer stood to leave, holding his papers. "You know, to think about it, one major benefit of the SQ1 is we'll no longer need to test drugs or viruses on animals. Never again will a virus escape a lab—or a fly, for that matter," Royer said with a wily, knowing smirk as he left the room.

———

That Thursday night, Gloria studied progeria on her apartment computer. The computer monitor provided the only light in the room. There was a beeping sound, and scrambled letters popped up on the screen.

She initiated the decoding program and the letters disappeared and reappeared, reading: "Spy at GA. Min test algorithm given to American pharmaceutical company. Find them."

She slammed her left hand on the table.

Late Tuesday morning the following week, Ty Leggett was sitting at his desk reading a memo when there was a soft knock at the door, followed by Agent Whitehead poking his head into the room.

"Got a moment?"

Ty nodded and waved his right hand for Whitehead to come in. Propping his feet up onto his desk, Ty leaned back in his high-backed chair.

"What's up?"

Whitehead sat in the cloth chair facing the desk. "Today we finally got something tangible on Gysin."

He reached across the desk and handed a piece of paper to Ty; written in black ink across the top of the paper was: March 3, 2037. It read: *hat alle Forderungen zuruckgezogen. Elander.*

After a quick glance, Ty tossed it onto the desk and looked at Whitehead with a blank look.

"We ran a new algorithm search this morning, looking for top-level encrypted messages sent to Reno. An hour ago, we found two such messages. Both were sent to Doctor Gysin's computer. We think it's the break we've been looking for.

"The encryption Gysin's using is an amazing viral program that mutates into different logarithms every nanosecond. We couldn't decode the first message; for all we know, it was received before Gysin left for Europe. Our computers were, however, able to make an educated guess on part of the second message—what you've got there now—and Gysin received it a week ago on Tuesday, February twenty-four. The translation falls inside our ninety percent accuracy requirement. Translated from German to English the message reads: 'has rescinded all demands. Elander.'" He glanced at a second paper he was holding. "The message originated from Bank Bern Freya in Switzerland and was sent by the bank's president, Thomas Elander."

Ty smiled, his eyes searching Whitehead's face. "And?"

Whitehead continued, "We believe the first message is why she went to Europe. The second message is completion. We got her coming and going, sir."

"We got our link. Good job." Ty leaned back, smiling. "Now, what law has she broken?"

Whitehead took a deep breath, shook his head, stood, and left, dejected. Ty glanced at his watch, five o'clock in Bonn. He buzzed his assistant. "Would you please locate the name of the chief investigator for the Bonn police department and ask him or her to call me?"

Ten minutes later, Ty's intercom buzzed. He pushed the button and his assistant said, "Bonn Chief Investigator Edward von Grub is returning your call."

Ty picked up the phone. "This is Tyler Leggett, director of the FBI. Thank you for returning my call. Does your department have any information on a Doctor Gloria Gysin? She taught at Bonn University not long ago."

"Please hold. I'll check our database," he said with a deep, raspy voice and heavy German accent. He came back after a couple minutes. "Yes, we have a small file on her."

"Why the file?"

"Bad family connections."

"We know about the brother, Peter Gysin. Do you know where he is?" Ty asked.

"We're not sure. He hasn't been seen since December, twenty thirty-five."

"You think he's dead?"

"We hope so, but we're not sure. We believe he was in a building destroyed by a firebomb."

"What makes you think he was in the building?"

"We had information he was meeting with someone there at the time of the explosion."

"Why were you interested in him?"

"Drugs and murder."

"Was Doctor Gysin involved?"

"There were rumors, but I'd say not."

"Why?"

"They hated each other. Doctor Gysin once almost beat him to death with a baseball bat."

"Do you have a photo of the brother?"

"Yes, I'll email it now."

Ty clicked on his computer and downloaded the photograph. "Peter Gysin" was typed on the bottom of the mug shot.

"Wow, he sure looks like his sister."

"They were fraternal twins. The only noticeable difference was that he was left-handed and she right."

"Twins. Humph. Thanks, Chief Investigator. I'll let you know if we come across Mr. Gysin."

Ty put the telephone down, glanced at his calendar, then clicked on the intercom. "Please arrange a flight to Reno for me on Friday, March twentieth."

That Tuesday afternoon at GA, Barber's desk phone buzzed. "John, there're two men here from Homeland Security Science and Tech to see you."

"Okay, I'll be right out."

John opened his door to the reception room. The two men were standing in the reception area. They were professionally dressed in pinstriped suits, yet they displayed all the telltale signs of government employees: over-polished black shoes, sunglasses lifted on top of their heads, and palpable arrogance.

"Doctor Barber," the older of the two men said, "I'm Brad Smith and this is Bob Rosa. We're from the DHS Science and Technology Directorate." He handed his card to John. "We're here to—"

"Gentlemen, we're very busy. I'll schedule a briefing next time I'm in DC, so—"

"Doctor Barber, this won't take long," Smith interrupted.

"Mr. Smith, I'm very busy."

"Doctor, it's important we speak today," Smith said as he took a small step forward.

For a moment, John and Smith stared at each other.

"Like I said, make an appointment." Without another word, John turned and returned to his office, leaving the two men staring at each other.

Back in his office, John sent a text to Leggett. It read: *Two people from DHS ST arrived at my office, want to meet. I don't.*

Leggett replied: *Do meet them, and I'll be in Reno on March* 20.

That evening, Megan came into the home office carrying a FedEx mail package. "This was delivered a few minutes ago."

She handed the envelope to him and left the room. The front of the envelope read: "Registered mail. IMPORTANT." The return address was Xi'an, China. *Well, that's odd.*

John looked closer at the envelope and saw it had been forwarded by Doctor Josephine Khoury.

He felt the envelope before opening it, held it up to the ceiling light. Seeing no paper enclosed, he ripped the edge and removed a flash drive. Handwritten in black ink on the drive was Doctor George Wipsing's name.

John thought about his last meeting with Wipsing—and his doctor friends, Khoury and Ping—at the Reno Hilton and recalled leaving abruptly when the conversation turned inappropriate with questions about GA. He also remembered Wipsing saying he was going to China. John opened his bottom desk drawer and removed a seldom-used laptop.

If there's a virus in the flash drive, no harm done.

He plugged the computer into the surge protector, waited for it to boot up. Ready, he inserted the drive.

The screen snapped on, and he saw four people with flashlights moving around a dark medical lab. The room looked larger than GA's main lab. He could hear whispers but could not make out the words. As the group walked around, it was clear the lab was as sophisticated as he had ever seen. He recognized the type of computers and the transmission electron aberration-corrected microscopes, and everything looked brand-new.

The way they were moving, it seemed they were searching for something specific.

Suddenly and clearly, John heard a woman's voice: "Here! Here it is, over here."

He heard more whispers, but again he could not make out the words.

The person holding the camera suddenly stopped, focused the camera on a workbench, and zoomed in on a two-gallon glass container. It was filled with liquid and contained what looked like a deformed spider monkey with two heads and six arms.

The camera and people continued their search. They worked their way around the room. When they reached the back of the lab, the camera again focused, this time on three two-high stacks of empty cages. One crate was covered by a thick blanket.

John heard, "That's it."

The flashlights focused on the covered box. In doing so, a beam struck one intruder's face: Wipsing.

A person reached over and pulled the blanket away from the box, revealing a four-by-four-square-foot, reinforced metal cage. The lights focused on the cage; no one moved. Suddenly, something at the back of the cage jumped, hitting the top of the cage with a significant thud.

Doctor Wipsing tapped the cage several times. The person holding the camera moved closer and shined a flashlight at the thing in the cage.

"Jesus, it *is* a hybrid," Wipsing cried out.

The camera focused on the animal. It had a bald human head, face, and hands—and a spider monkey's body, arms, and legs.

It screamed "No!" with a baby's voice.

Suddenly, there was a loud bang behind the group. The monitor went black.

John, thinking the drama was over, leaned back in his chair, rubbing his hand through his hair.

Suddenly, the monitor snapped back on, showing a dimly lit street. A loud car horn honked, and John jerked in his chair. The horn was followed by police sirens blaring.

John stared at the monitor as the camera panned to a Chinese soldier standing in front of a taped-off area in the street. Crowds of people were lined up along the bright-yellow tape. They were all looking at something inside the taped-off area.

The camera bounced around for a few seconds, then one person along the tape moved aside, and the camera focused and zoomed in on something on the ground: George Wipsing's bloody face—he was dead.

Horrified, John rubbed his hand through his hair again and fell back into his chair. "Christ."

That same night, Gloria went into the main lab and quickly moved to the insect-filled jars. Finding the right jar, she picked it up and watched the flies move about. She removed a small suction tube from her pocket, then carefully opened the jar and removed a fly. She restrained the fly under a tiny wire mesh, held the fly still, removed a small eyedropper filled with radioactive iodine, and marked the fly. She returned the fly to the jar and left the lab.

On Wednesday morning, March 4, the same two DHS Science and Technology agents were waiting in Barber's reception room.

John recognized the men on his way in. "Come with me."

Agent Smith was in his mid-forties, with graying hair and thirty pounds overweight. Agent Rosa was in his late twenties and very fit-looking.

They went into Barber's private office. John walked to his oak desk and sat, opened the top drawer, got a small bottle of aspirin, and took three pills with a sip of Diet Coke. Smith sat on the couch while Rosa roamed the room, his dark eyes darting from corner to corner.

"We understand your team is about to bring the quant into operation. Is that right?" Smith leaned back and crossed his legs.

"No, that is not correct. We are still conducting tests."

Smith was about to speak when Rosa abruptly sat on the couch, pushed his aviator sunglasses farther back on his forehead, and asked, "How long before you break the virus code?"

"Young man," John said after another sip of his Coke, "it could take many years before we know how each virus functions, if ever." He stood. "If that's the extent of your questions, you're wasting our time and—"

"I don't think you understand who's paying the bills," Rosa interrupted. "We control this facility, not you or your clutch of dreamers."

After a disapproving glance, Smith touched Rosa on the elbow and said to John, "Please excuse Bob's lack of manners." Smith shot another glance at Rosa. "The secretary asked us to extend his appreciation for your accomplishments. He also instructed us to have a candid conversation on enhancing your mission."

John sat back in his chair.

Smith smiled and leaned forward, resting his arms on his legs. The look on his face suggested he was choosing his next words carefully. "We've learned that the Chinese tested Ebola on a vaccinated pig and the pig lived. They are developing a therapy to create a plague that'll make Ebola look like a cold. Or worse, the nineteen-eighteen flu. In the secretary's opinion, it will be very difficult to protect Americans from billions of Chinese androids when most Americans are sick or dying."

John's face said it all: skeptical, if not contemptuous.

Smith continued, "To assist your efforts, I've been instructed to inform you that S-and-T is doubling your funding and the secretary has instructed several top-level analysts to join GA—"

"First," John interrupted, "the plague you mentioned was a pandemic flu carried on troopships returning soldiers home after World War One, and the Ebola outbreak was mainly in Liberia, Guinea, and Sierra Leone in twenty fourteen. The United States has faced several cases of Ebola and all of them were contained."

"The flu started in China. It was the beginning," Rosa blurted out.

What a fool, John thought. "It was Europe, and we don't need additional staffing. Lastly, the White House wouldn't have authorized this without notifying me."

"Doctor—"

John put his right hand up to stop Smith from speaking. "As long as I lead GA, my staff will formulate our research direction and I'll determine our staffing needs, and we will not use the SQ1 for gain-of-function research."

"I didn't say anything about gain of function, Doctor Barber," Smith said as his eyes shifted down and he pinched the crease on his polyester slacks.

"You didn't have to."

"All the secretary asks is a little consideration. It's important that all options are discreetly researched," Smith said.

"I understand fully what S-and-T intends. Please inform the secretary the answer's no." John stood.

Smith looked down at the floor; Rosa jumped to his feet and left the room. After a moment, Smith reluctantly walked to the door. John walked around his desk toward the door.

"The secretary," Smith said with his hand on the doorknob, "is interested in reaching an accommodation." He took a breath, seeming to measure his next words. "There's something more. What I'm about to say is top secret." Surprisingly, his face looked sincere. "We have a report that the Chinese have successfully implanted a microchip and created a hybrid-android monkey at the Tangdu Air Force Medical Hospital. Doctor, they're winning the soulless race to weaponize animals."

John rubbed his hand through his hair as Smith pulled the door open and left the room.

Joyce Dillingham was in the reception room when Smith and Rosa left John's office. She hurried to him. "I've got to see you," she said in a somber voice.

"Sure." John turned his attention back to Smith. "Have the secretary call me; however, my answer will still be a no."

Smith left.

Joyce and John went into his private office. John sat behind his desk, his headache pounding—too much wine after watching that stolen video. Joyce pulled a chair up to his desk, so close she almost hit her knees on it. She placed a red manila folder she'd been carrying on the desk. She leaned forward and rested her arms on the desktop.

John took a sip of a Diet Coke.

"John, are you authorizing emails or calls to Ashby Pharmaceutical?" she asked in a whisper.

"No," John said incredulously.

"On Monday afternoon, two days ago," she said after a deep breath, "I was emailing a report to HHS when my computer was kicked offline. Frustrated, I used my transmittal report to catalog the times I've been disconnected, along with other members of the staff, and I noticed an email address I've never seen before. So I sent an old cafeteria menu and asked for an acknowledgment. I got a reply."

Joyce handed him a copy of her transmittal sheet with the email address circled in red. She then handed him a copy of their reply. "Ashby Pharmaceuticals" was printed on the top of the paper.

John rubbed his hand through his hair. *That's a bad habit. I'd better stop doing that; my hair will fall out.* "Unbelievable," he whispered. He took four more pills followed by a gulp of warm Coke.

"After receiving that reply, I ran a search to find the dates and times that address had been emailed. I also asked the computer to locate the terminal used."

Joyce handed John another sheet of paper. She pointed at the bottom of the paper. "I could only retrieve records for the last six months. So I can't say when these messages started, but from this search, five emails have been sent to that address."

"Whose computer was used?"

"The one in the research library, which is not under anyone's authority."

"Only one computer was used to send these emails?"

"Yes."

"Is there a pattern? Day? Time?"

"No. The day or week doesn't seem to matter. The only trend is the emails were sent after working hours." She leaned forward and pointed at a second piece of paper in her folder.

"I also checked the phone logs. Look here, see this?" She pointed to it. "It's the only daytime activity—a call to this phone number. At first, I couldn't figure out why the change in routine, then I saw it." She again pointed at the piece of paper. "It's after our Monday, February second, staff meeting where Min detailed her algorithm. Whoever it was apparently couldn't wait to tell Ashby, so they called."

"What?"

"You betcha. I searched for the phone number online and didn't find anything, but I did see it's an Omaha area code." She handed John another piece of paper.

After looking for a moment, John again rubbed his hand through his hair. "Wow," he whispered, then asked, "So you called the number?"

"Yes. It was Ashby's private line."

He leaned back and looked at the ceiling. "Okay, meet with Scott this afternoon. Have him run a diagnostic on the phone system and cameras; see if we can learn more about our spy." He leaned forward and lowered his voice. "We don't dare let this get out among staff."

"I understand," Joyce said, her brown eyes fixed on his every move.

"Thank you for the fine work. When you and Scott are finished, please send everything to Ty Leggett at the FBI."

Joyce stood. When she reached the door, John called out, "Thanks again for the great work, Joyce."

They looked at each other for a moment.

With Joyce gone, he took another long swallow of warm Diet Coke. He leaned back in his chair and thought: *Jennifer*.

He activated his computer and initiated his videophone.

"Hey, John," Leggett answered.

"Man, a tough day," John said.

"You don't look too good."

"Thanks, Ty."

"I'm about to go into a meeting. How can I help?"

"Dillingham found several emails and one call to Ashby Pharmaceuticals. There's no reason for anyone from here to call a pharmaceutical company."

"Sounds like Jennifer. I'll look into it and get back to you. Anything else?"

"I just finished a BS meeting with those two Homeland S-and-T boys. I'm worried."

"It's nothing. Homeland wants to show off. It'll all be fine. The White House wants to throw more money at you, and Homeland wants credit."

"The two agents were talking about us hiring more staff and researching crazy stuff, force us to do something stupid and dangerous."

"Don't worry. I'll talk to Berg." Ty looked away from the phone camera. "I've got to go."

"Okay, Megan and I are looking forward to seeing you on the twentieth."

"How about dinner when I arrive, and we can solve the world's problems?"

Gloria went into the GA main lab early Friday night, March 20, and went to the specimen table. She removed a micro-Geiger counter from her lab coat and passed it over the fly-filled jars. Finding the right jar, she picked it up and watched the flies move about, then carefully opened the jar and removed the fly she had marked with the radioactive iodine.

"It works," she whispered, holding the struggling fly up to the light.

She dropped the fly back into the jar, closed everything up, and left.

That same Friday night, John and Megan and Ty were having dinner at Casale's Halfway Club in Reno. The family-owned bar and restaurant that got started in 1937 was famous for wine, graffiti on the ceiling, local celebrities, and being the most famous hole-in-the-wall Italian restaurant in Nevada.

"This is great; it's been a long time since I've eaten next to a trailer park," Ty said as they walked into the restaurant.

"Don't be a snob; the food is good and the place is all about family," Megan said.

After lots of conversation, jokes, and catch-up, they'd finished with dinner. Empty plates, glasses, and silverware were strewn on the table, and an empty carafe of red wine sat next to Ty.

"What happens when we discover the code for eternal life?" John asked somewhat out of the blue.

"You're asking the wrong guy. The SOBs live too long as it is," Ty said, taking a last sip of wine.

"Humanity would adjust and survive the transition," Megan said, holding a warm cup of decaf coffee between her hands.

"Our quant will find that code."

"Is that a guarantee?" Ty asked.

John nodded. "Yes."

"There goes my retirement."

Megan laughed.

"And morticians," John said.

Ty and Megan laughed.

"That Tree of Life in Eden was guarded by angels; quantum computing might not solve the problem," Ty said.

"God doesn't make mistakes," Megan said, looking at Ty.

"You're right, Megan, and if this discussion continues, we'll need a lot more wine," Ty said.

Megan laughed.

John waved to the waiter. "Check, please," he said.

"I've got this," Ty said.

"We've got this, big guy," John said.

Megan nodded.

"Okay, let's make a deal from now on: I'll get the little ones and you get the big ones," Ty said.

Megan laughed. "Ty, we must do this more often."

"Your wish. I'm coming back April twentieth, and it's my treat," Ty said, smiling at Megan.

They all stood and headed for the exit. John walked ahead and went outside. As Megan neared the doorway, though, she turned to face Ty.

"Something's wrong with John; he's drinking a lot."

Ty raised his eyebrows and nodded. "Okay."

Before they reached the door, Megan stopped to say goodbye to the owner.

Ty left the building and joined John in the parking lot, waiting for Megan. "Ms. Jennifer White is in my sights."

"What do you want me to do?" John asked.

"Nothing. I need a little more proof, then I'll brief Berg. I've got to be careful; the president likes White's boyfriend. The same goes for Gloria: I've got to have an airtight case or we'll get the shit sued out of GA and our research effort will be kaput. All I have is speculation and a dead drug-running brother."

After leaving GA, Gloria went to her apartment and, as always, used the elevator from the underground private parking garage to her first-floor apartment. Before she opened the door, she checked to see that the strand of hair was still pasted across the bottom doorjamb.

It was gone.

She leaned back for a moment, thinking, *The FBI snooping?*

She reached into her purse, got the door key, and pushed it into the lock. Adrenaline started to pump as she went into the room. She closed the door softly, leaned back against it, and listened. Not a sound. The window blinds were closed, and the room was dark. She reached to her right, slid her hand up the wall, and turned the lights on. The room was as she'd left it: clean, everything in its place. She looked down at the carpet: no footprints.

And then she saw it: a folded piece of paper lying on the floor in the room.

She studied the paper's placement, asking herself, *How did that get there? No footprints.* She listened; heard nothing. She reached into her purse and removed her Japanese hairpin and clutched it in her left hand.

She crept to the paper, stopped, listened, and again studied it. The paper was folded in half and looked dry. There was handwriting underneath the fold. She again reached into her purse, removed one of her gloves, and put it on. She leaned over, picked it up with her right hand, and held it up to the overhead light.

Horrified, her legs weakened and shook. A scream flashed through her mind as the adrenaline raced to her heart—she recognized the handwriting.

It read:

Did you really think you'd get away with it? Doctor Dougdale—remember him? He was a fine surgeon, smart, not smart enough to stay alive, but smart enough to put the details of your surgery in a safe place. Guess what? I found them.

Dougdale was afraid of you, I'm not!

What should I do? Should I give everything to the FBI? Or can we come to an accommodation?

I think we can. Let's say you give me all the money and I let you live. That's not too much to ask, is it—Brother?

Oh, I am so bad. I lived.

I want you to know exactly what happened. Dougdale was standing in front of me. I could smell his cool minty breath as his right hand probed my forehead. I was looking into his beautiful eyes when your firebomb exploded. See, Dougdale's body shielded me from the force of your little surprise. I ran out of the room, on fire I must add, down the hallway to the stairs into the alley and lost consciousness.

The pain was horrific, and the drugs did not help. I hope you never suffer like that. It was hard to recover without money. I spent months in the public hospital burn ward. The best doctors would not help a deformed, indigent person with amnesia. I suffered.

I screamed to everyone that I was a rich and gifted person. They did not believe me—and sent me to a sanitarium. It took several more months to recover my memory and escape that horrid place. I wanted to see you so badly—I needed money; alas, you were gone. I went to Bank Bern Freya and they said no. Who would believe a deformed homeless woman?

I went to Klaus. He would not speak to me and pushed me to the ground. Why would he not? I had lost my beautiful face. I had to do unspeakable things to get a gun, and that is how I convinced Klaus. He helped and told me all about your success. It was hard not to reach out and give you a big hug while we sat across from each other in the train car to London.

I know this note is a little impersonal, but it's the best I can do. Please don't get sentimental. All I want is the authorization code to your bank account. After I've withdrawn my money, you'll get Dougdale's files. Because you're prone to be stupid, I've placed Dougdale's information with a trusted agent. If I fail to contact that individual for more than twelve hours, the information will be delivered to the German police and FBI.

So what's it like being me? I don't think you do me as well as I do, but then, who am I to judge? Does you being me mean I'm supposed to be you? I would not like that. There are so many people after you. Since you've been me, I've not had too much fun, but now that I've found you, all that will change, and I will once again be the beautiful woman with all the praise, promise, wealth, and fame I had.

Don't get me wrong, nothing would hurt me more than to watch all your beautiful plans fall apart—like mine. Now be a good boy, girl, oh, you know what I mean, and sit tight. I don't want any unplanned reunions. I will do the scheduling and planning from here on out. So sit tight and let your big sister work her magic.

Love, G.

P.S. I borrowed some of your underwear. Hope you don't mind. Unfortunately, I had to try on a few extra pair. I put them back just *the way you had them.*

Gloria/Peter dropped the letter to the floor and walked into the bedroom, opened the dresser drawers, and pulled out all the underclothes. S/he walked into the kitchen and threw them into the trash.

S/he stood in the kitchen for a moment, staring at the trash can, thinking, *The newspapers said three bodies. How could she be alive? It's impossible; this can't be happening.*

Fear gripped her/him again, and her/his mouth dried. S/he walked back to the living room, picked up the letter, and reread it. Finished, s/he crumpled it, walked back to the kitchen, and threw it away.

"Die!" s/he said, spitting out the word.

Gloria/Peter was no match against his sister. She'd always done the planning, taken care of problems, killed when necessary, and given the orders. Now Peter would never be free.

Feeling weak, Peter sat on the couch, thinking about his sister, his fingernails digging into the soft leather couch. She was the perfect one—destined for greatness—and he the pawn.

He pounded his fist on his leg. *I can still do this! I can force Barber to give me his discovery, disappear, and escape from her. So what if she gives them my identity? I can beat her. Even better ... yes, yes! I'll kill her and then I'll visit Barber.*

He suddenly felt dirty. He pulled his clothes off, making a primal groaning sound, and ran to the bathroom to vomit.

TWENTY-FOUR

That Saturday morning, John was back at GA taking some of his experiments from the main lab to his car. He picked up the fly-filled jars and started to put them into a box. As he held the last jar, he noticed that one fly was lying on the bottom of the jar, dead. Surprised, he quickly put the jar down and opened it. He removed the dead fly and took it to the microscope. He saw what had killed the fly.

"Iodine?" he wondered. "Gloria ... Jennifer? Shit!"

Early the next morning, John finished packing up his GA equipment and drove into the parking lot of a Public Storage location. He parked the car and went to the small registration office. After a few minutes, he got back into his car and drove to the security gate. He pulled up to it, inputted his new code, and watched as the metal gate jerked itself open. He drove into the compound and to the loading ramp for the main building.

After a quick search through the loading dock, he located a utility cart and packed it with several empty animal cages and insect-filled glass jars. With the cart full, he pushed it up the ramp into the five-story building to the loading elevator.

His climate-controlled storage room was on the top floor at the back of the building. He left the double-wide elevator and walked along the narrow hallway to the sound of the cart's squeaky wheels echoing off the walls. The hallway had a decent temperature and smelled of concrete. All the doors were made of steel, and most sported heavy-duty padlocks like the one he'd just purchased at the registration office.

He reached room 59A at the end of the hallway, next to the emergency stairwell, and opened the roll-up door. He stepped into the room and flipped on the light switch. He was greeted by a fairly bright light and a mostly clean ten-by-twenty-square-foot concrete box. He looked at the bit of dust on the floor, then back at all his equipment, and thought, *A lot of work.*

On Monday morning, Gloria/Peter arrived at GA early and was sitting at her/his desk reading her/his emails when the telephone rang.

"This is Doctor Gysin."

"Hello, brother. You're not being too careful. The FBI searched your apartment after you left for your little kill-vacay last month, and they're listening and watching everything you're doing. There doesn't seem to be a lot of time left for you." Her voice suddenly sounded angry as she asked, "Now, what's the authorization code for your account?"

"Not unless we meet," Peter said through clenched teeth.

"I don't think so."

"Then you'll get nothing."

"How's your claustrophobia?"

"Pig."

"Now, now, give me the code number and I'll go away," she said.

"Pig."

"You *don't* want to piss me off."

"I would rather burn in hell than give you my money," Peter said.

"That's a thought."

He hung up and thought, *This is where she'll make a mistake—her rage.*

At the end of the day, Peter/Gloria went to the third-floor lab, looking for more information. To his surprise, all the jars filled with flies and cages with mice were gone. He left GA without being seen and drove to his apartment. He entered the dark garage and drove toward his assigned parking space. He stopped the car as he reached the spot and got out. He stood still for several moments, searching for any movement or sound. Not seeing anything, he got back in, backed up, and parked in one of the spots reserved for guests.

He nervously walked toward the elevator, turning his head from side to side at the slightest sound. As he passed the last pillar, he heard a noise just before he felt a sudden, horrific burning sensation in his back. He fell to the ground. He rolled over to see a baseball bat being swung at him. The pain was numbing as the bat smashed into his ribs this time.

"You bastard! You thought you could kill me!" Gloria

screamed. She kicked him in the crotch. "I should cut it off," she snarled. She hit him again with the bat. "You came close, you prick. But I survived! Over a year of hell!"

He tried to crawl away, but she struck his back with the bat once more.

"Brings back memories, doesn't it?" she hissed through clenched teeth.

He rolled onto his back, lifting his knees to protect himself. As he did so, her face came into view thanks to the overhead lighting, and when she turned to take another swing, he saw her face fully: It was deformed, melted-looking, like hideous, dripping flesh.

"I'm going to enjoy this," Gloria said as she raised the bat.

"Stop! I've—"

"Fuck you. You stole everything. You destroyed my perfect life." She hit his legs with the bat. "What's the code?" she hissed.

"No!"

"No no!" she howled. She smashed the bat into his side.

He screamed out in pain.

"Give me my fucking money!"

"Okay okay stop!"

"Never."

"I've got something better," he said as he put his hands up to protect himself.

"What?"

"One of the scientists has discovered how to stop aging."

"Where's my money?"

"Bank Bern Freya, Switzerland."

"How much do you have there?"

"Twenty million."

"Who else knows about the discovery?"

"No one."

"Who made the discovery?" she asked as she jabbed the bat into his forehead.

"John Barber."

"Tomorrow, you'll transfer ten million into my account." She tossed a small piece of paper at him. On it was her bank account number. "Don't, and I'll beat the bloody hell out of you."

Still lying on the ground, holding his arms and hands up to protect himself, gasping for air, he nodded.

"Looks like we're a family again," she said with an evil sneer. She kicked him in the ribs one last time, turned, and walked away. He vomited and passed out to the sounds of fading footsteps.

TWENTY-FIVE

The afternoon of Monday, April 20, Ty walked down the gangway from a Gulfstream G700 jet to a waiting Ford Expedition. Standing by the SUV was a woman in her middle thirties, dressed professionally in a gray business suit and black shoes, her dark hair pulled up onto her head and held by a blue clip.

"I'm Agent Harding," she said, flashing her badge.

"Hello," he said.

After a twenty-minute drive, they exited the 580 freeway, turned onto Kietzke Lane, and drove onto the Reno FBI campus. Agent Stewart, a nondescript man in his late thirties, dressed in a similar manner, greeted the SUV as they pulled up to the front door of the one-story office building. Ty got out of the SUV.

"We've got the conference room set up for you, sir," Stewart said. "This way, please."

Later that afternoon, John was in his GA office on a video conference call with DOD Secretary Turner and White House Chief of Staff Berg.

"No," John stated adamantly.

"You can be replaced, Doctor Barber," Turner threatened.

"We're not at war," John said.

"Yes, we are. We're at war every day," Turner snapped.

"No one wants to create enhanced monster viruses. But we've got to know if someone else can, and the SQ1 is our best opportunity," Berg said.

"What happened to us being the good guys, playing by the rules, and telling the truth?" John asked.

"John, this could mean your job," Berg said.

John leaned back in his chair, rubbed his hand through his hair. "The answer's no. We will not use the SQ1 for any gain-of-function studies or experiments."

At 7:00 p.m. that evening, Ty was sitting in a booth at a Greek restaurant in Reno, scrolling through his cell phone and enjoying a short, neat Kentucky bourbon while waiting for Megan and John to arrive.

The waiter approached the table. "Would you like another bourbon?"

"Not right now. I'll wait until my guests arrive."

As he said it, John and Megan walked in and came to his table.

As they sat, the server asked them, "May I get you something to drink?"

"I'll have a chardonnay," Megan said.

"A double scotch over," John said.

"Tough day?" Ty quipped.

"Looks like I'm driving again," Megan said.

"Please leave him, Megan. Now's your chance."

"A thousand times no," Megan said, giggling.

"He's got to be drugging you," Ty said.

"It kills you," John said.

Ty nodded. "Damn right. Best girl in the world."

Megan smiled, then said, "Ty, why haven't you remarried?"

"The practice wife was a disaster. I'm still paying for it. I've not met anyone who measures up since then."

The waiter arrived with the drinks. John took a big gulp of his, to surprised looks from Ty and Megan.

"I heard about your call with Berg and Turner today," Ty said.

John frowned. "I've never done well with edicts."

"What happened?" Megan asked.

"Pressure. Pressure to move in a direction that would dissolve GA."

"Why?" Ty asked.

"Royer and Dillingham would resign on the spot, and Min wouldn't be too far behind."

"Did you tell that to Berg and Turner?"

"No, they wouldn't care. The DOD believes we're replaceable."

Ty looked at Megan. "On that note, how was the play, Mrs. Lincoln?"

Megan laughed. "I had a great day. All my patients are well."

The waiter came to the table and took everyone's order.

Later that evening, after Ty and the Barbers had finished eating, the waiter was cleaning up the plates, glasses, and silverware. He reached for the half-full bottle of cabernet next to Ty.

John said, "You can leave that. We're not done."

"May I refill your glass?" the waiter asked John.

"Yes, please."

The waiter looked at Ty, offering him a refill.

"No, I've got to drive." Ty turned to John. "This could be your lucky month."

"We win the lottery," Megan said.

"No, I have approval to pick up Jennifer."

"Dillingham will understand," John said. "What about Gysin?"

"That's complicated—and why I'm operating from Reno for a bit."

"Maybe I shouldn't hear this," Megan said.

"Okay, I'll change the subject. Doctor Megan," John said with a serious look on his face, "if you had the fountain of eternal youth, would you advise your patients to drink from it?"

"Mmmm ... no, I like things as they are."

"That's the second time you've opened that subject, John. Why?" Ty asked.

"Yes, why? Is that why you're not sleeping at night?" Megan asked.

Silence.

"Come on, John, you brought it up," Ty said.

"Because I've found it."

"Oh, God," Megan whispered.

"What do you mean? Like the Fountain of Youth legend?" Ty asked.

"I discovered the cure for progeria by accident on an AI

217

computer. It was a one-in-a-billion mistake. And not only the cure, but the ability to stop aging and even reverse it."

"The endless search. John, this is wonderful—a cure. You've done it!" Megan said.

"Yes, it's wonderful, except it's too powerful. Without death, there is no change. No hope, only despair."

Ty took a deep breath and stared at John. "How do you know it works on people?"

"That little boy in Davis, California ... the progeria miracle? That was me."

Megan closed her eyes and took a deep breath.

"What do you plan to do with it?" Ty asked.

"I don't know. It scares me."

"You've got to give it away," Megan said.

"Who would you trust with it?" John asked them both.

"Does anyone know?" Ty asked.

"Royer is very smart, so him, and either Gloria or Jennifer might have a suspicion, but otherwise I don't believe anyone else has a clue."

"For the time being, let's keep it that way," Ty said. "Like I said before, the SOBs live too long now. And they would do anything to get it."

"I'm moving everything related to my research out of our house and GA."

"Be careful; everything at GA is government property," Ty said.

"I know. Surviving this might take time," John said.

Ty asked for the check. With the bill paid, they went to their cars. John escorted Megan to the driver's seat and closed her door, then walked around the back of the Bronco.

Standing by the driver's side of his vehicle, Ty looked at

John and said, "We've linked Gysin to the dead German businessman."

John rubbed his hand through his hair.

Early Saturday morning, April 25, John loaded his Bronco with his computer and files from home. He drove to the Reno Cabela's to buy some supplies. Finished shopping, he drove to the downtown Reno storage facility.

He pulled up to the closed security gate, inputted his code, and watched as the metal gate clanked and jerked itself open. He drove to the back of the building to loading ramp number three. He parked and opened the back of the SUV, where he had stashed a couple twelve-foot extension cords, a computer, a twelve-inch color television, three two-shelf refrigerators, a sleeping cot, a blanket, a floor heater, a card table, a fold-up metal chair, a lamp, two five-foot-long fold-up wall tables, and a portable radio. He filled two carts and pushed them separately up the steep ramp to the freight elevator that went to the fifth floor. He rolled the cart out of the elevator and along the narrow, thousand-foot concrete hallway to his locker.

He unlocked the padlock hanging on the double-holed steel ring, removed it, and opened the door. He reached into the room and flipped on the light. The room was exactly as he'd left it. The insects were buzzing around inside the glass jars, and the mice were foraging in their cages. He looked at the room and thought, *I can do this.* He rolled the cart into the room and began to set up his lab.

During the morning of April 27, Peter Gysin left his apartment at the usual time for GA. His sister watched from across the street. Before the garage door closed, she slipped into the underground parking garage. She went directly to the stairwell and climbed to his first-floor apartment. At his locked door, she used a key pin to unlock it and casually opened the door. She walked into the bedroom, sat at the desk, and turned on the laptop computer. She knew his favorite log-in codes and got it right on her third try, then waited for the machine to activate. She opened his email program and began typing account instructions to Bank Bern Freya.

Her message read: Upon completion of the pending $10,000,000 transfer into account A243-601-32AB, transfer remaining balance into the same account within 5 business days.

She received an electronic reply: Please log in with authorization code.

Gloria scowled, figuring this would happen. The day before she'd left Peter the note here in his apartment, she had tried to log into the account using their old code from another computer, getting rejected and not attempting again, because she knew it would alert him to someone trying to break into the account. She knew he would change the code. Now, though, she'd figured an email sent directly to the bank would allow her to do as she wished. No such luck.

She pounded the table with her fist, got up, and walked around the room, thinking, *Where would he keep the new code?*

FBI Agents Ripple and Benjamin drove up to the front of Doctor Gysin's apartment and parked.

"Call GA and ask Doctor Dillingham if Doctor Gysin is there," Ripple told Benjamin.

"This is Dillingham."

"This is FBI Agent Benjamin from the Reno division," he said. "Is Doctor Gloria Gysin at GA now?"

"Yes, she's in the main lab with Doctor Royer. Is there something I can help you with?"

"No, that's all, and please don't say anything to her. Thank you." He hung up and turned to Ripple. "Okay, let's go."

Benjamin's cell phone rang. He listened, put his hand over the phone, looked at Ripple. "It's my wife." He raised his eyebrows.

"Come up when you finish," Ripple said.

Agent Ripple left the car, walked to the apartment building, used the key card from the landlady, and walked to the elevator. She got out on the second floor and went to Gysin's apartment. She slid the key in, opened the door, and went inside.

Meanwhile, inside the bedroom, Gloria heard the front door open; adrenaline shot to her heart. She stood and leaned against the wall next to the doorway. She heard the door close and then movement around the room.

Keeping her eyes focused on the bedroom door, she reached up to the top of her head with her right hand and removed the Japanese hairpin. With her left hand, she slipped off her heels, bent down, and, using her fingernails, ripped open the nylons around her feet. She stood and pressed harder against the wall.

She heard sounds of kitchen drawers opening and closing. *Who is it?* she wondered.

Silence.

Without warning, Agent Ripple moved to the bedroom. Gloria lunged with the spike aimed at Ripple's head. She missed, stabbing Ripple in the shoulder.

Ripple screamed out in pain, knocked the hairpin free, and in the same motion, slapped Gloria's face with her right hand, followed with a knee kick to Gloria's groin.

Gloria gasped and fell back a step. The two women stared at each other.

Ripple hesitated, surprised and shocked by Gloria's deformed face. She reached for her gun under her coat.

Gloria attacked, clawing at Ripple's eyes. Ripple shouted and covered her right eye with a hand. Gloria pushed Ripple to the floor and dove for the spike. Ripple got to her knees and again reached for her gun. Gloria lunged at her with the hairpin aimed at Ripple's eyes.

Ripple grabbed Gloria's right arm with one hand, holding it up. She released her grip on the gun, grabbed Gloria by the throat, and squeezed. Gloria gagged, and they rolled against the wall. Shocked by the pain of her windpipe collapsing, Gloria pounded her fist into Ripple's arm and then smashed her head against Ripple's forehead. Ripple's grip on Gloria's throat relaxed for an instant, allowing Gloria to catch a breath.

In that moment of air, Gloria stabbed her right thumb into Ripple's eye.

With a scream of pain, Ripple released her grip on Gloria's left arm.

The spike plunged deep into Ripple's temple.

Gloria released the pin and rolled away from Ripple and stood, trying to catch her breath. Gasping for air, she realized she was suffocating. Panic gripped her. She began to gag. In desperation, she grabbed her neck with her hands and squeezed. Her airway opened, and she dropped to her knees, forcing herself to relax. She began to get enough air to keep from passing out. Her throat relaxed, and she could breathe.

Gloria stood over Ripple's body and studied the frozen eyes. She bent down, pulled the hairpin from Ripple's head, picked up her shoes, and ran out of the apartment.

As the hallway stairwell door closed behind her, the elevator door opened. Agent Benjamin got out and walked along the hallway to Gysin's apartment.

He reached her door and casually walked into the apartment. Not seeing his partner anywhere, he called out, "Ripple!" Hearing no reply, he walked around the living room. "Ripple? Where are you?" he asked. Still not hearing anything, he went into the bedroom.

Stunned, frozen by shock, he stared at Ripple's lifeless body lying on the floor, a trickle of dark blood running along her cheek, her left eye gouged, and the deep and horrible scratches cut into her cheeks. Panicked by the sight, he ran to Ripple's body, knelt and looked into lifeless eyes. He checked her pulse.

Horror! He grabbed his cell phone from his waistcoat and called his superior. "There's been a terrible mistake! Ripple's dead!" Screaming, his voice was high-pitched and shaking. "What do I do? What the hell do I do?"

Thirty minutes later, Leggett received a call at the Reno headquarters from Agent Harding, who told him what had happened and asked what they should do.

"Where were Doctor Gysin and Jennifer White at the time of the murder?"

"Both were at GA."

"You're positive?"

"Yes."

"How did Agent Ripple die?"

"She had multiple injuries, and—"

"*How* did she die?" Ty interrupted.

"She was stabbed in the temple."

"With what?"

"We don't know."

"What do you think?"

"Some kind of spike."

"Okay." Ty glanced at his watch. "We've got seven hours. Get as much forensics as possible. Clean the apartment and leave it perfect, and I mean perfect—cleaner than you found it. Put a full perimeter surveillance around the building."

He put the phone down. *Christ, who's working with Gloria?*

John was still in his office at GA at 9:00 p.m., reading over his journal notes, when he heard a voice coming from the open doorway to his right.

"I was hoping you'd be here," Peter/Gloria said. "You saved Billy Pinehorse, didn't you?"

John looked up.

Peter was standing there, smiling, happy, excited-looking. He confidently walked deeper into the room, closer to Barber's desk. "Drosophila flies living for months, a miracle in Davis." He looked at the journal on the desk. "Please tell me; I want to help. This is wonderful. We've got to save more children."

John smiled nervously and started to say, "That—"

Suddenly, Jennifer came into the room. Surprised, she stopped, frozen by indecision. "Oh, I'm sorry. I heard something as I was leaving my office. I-I didn't expect to see anyone."

Calmly, John smiled. "It's okay. Gloria was about to leave."

Frustrated by the lost opportunity, Peter turned and left. He shot an angry look at Jennifer.

Jennifer, feeling uncomfortable, said, "I'm sorry for the intrusion." She turned and left the room.

John grabbed his cell phone and sent Leggett a text that read: Gysin knows about my discovery.

Peter left GA and returned to his Reno apartment, parked in the usual spot, and walked to the elevator, making sure he stayed away from the pillars. He rode the elevator to the second floor.

He walked down the hallway to his apartment, but before he opened the door, he checked for the hair on the door frame: Gone. He opened the door, looked around. He could feel something was wrong. Though he could see nothing out of place, he felt something odd. He walked into the bedroom. Someone had been there; he could feel it. He looked at the computer; it was on. He moved the mouse, and the screen popped on. An error message from Bank Bern Freya was on the screen.

She was here.

His cell phone dinged. A text read: *Meet in garage NOW, take the stairs!*

Peter left the apartment and hurried down the stairs.

When he reached the garage level, he opened the stairwell door and listened before he stepped out.

There was only one dim light on over the elevator doorway; otherwise, the garage looked mostly dark. He closed the stairwell door behind him, leaned back against it, and searched for any movement. Not seeing anything, he walked toward his car, again staying away from the pillars.

He was almost to the car but was stopped by a whispering voice: "You're so stupid. The FBI has searched your apartment—I watched them go in. This is all your fault. You have put us in jeopardy. It's only a matter of time before they steal our money."

Gloria appeared from behind a pillar. She was dressed in a light-blue St. John knit suit, much of her face covered by a pale-blue silk medical mask, with a matching scarf wrapped around her neck. She had her hair pulled up onto her head and held by a bright-red Japanese pin. She held a Walther P22LR pistol in her right hand. The red laser dot was shining on Peter's chest.

"I see you didn't get the rest of the money," Peter scoffed.

"What've you learned about the discovery?" she snarled back.

"Nothing."

"Don't fuck with me. You're seconds from being dead. The only thing keeping you alive is that discovery. What've you learned?"

"It works," he said.

"Where's the formula kept?"

"In his journal, locked up at GA, but he occasionally takes it home on Fridays."

"Good answer—you get to live. We still need each other to survive and, most importantly, get away with Barber's formula. But we have to move now. The FBI is only days away from picking you up. Here's the plan: I've been following Doctor Barber and his family. He takes one daughter to gymnastics Friday nights at six. That's our chance. You watch him leave GA. Text me the number one if he takes the journal with him. At exactly five-thirty Friday night, we'll meet at the United Methodist Church, two zero nine West First Street. The front door will be locked, but the side door will be open. Inside, there will be a door on your left as you walk toward the altar. It leads to a very small room. There'll be a burner phone sitting on a wooden chair in the room. Text me the number two, and if it's all clear, I'll meet you. Otherwise, I'll give you other instructions."

"Why meet there?"

"Because I'm not stupid. The FBI agents won't follow you into a church, and this one has a basement with a concealed exit. They won't see you leave. We'll grab Barber and his kid, get the formula, kill them, and be on a jet to Canada before the bodies get cold."

TWENTY-SIX

Eight FBI agents sat in four cars a little after midnight in the wee hours of Thursday morning, watching Gloria Gysin's apartment building. One car was parked across the street, watching the front door. A car was parked on the side of the building and another in back, and the last one was across the street from the garage.

"Wow, now that's a looker," Paul said, seeing a woman come out of the main door dressed in a perfect-fitting blue dress, her face and neck obscured by a blue medical mask and scarf, respectively. "Way too classy to live in that building."

The two agents watched as the woman turned left and continued down the street.

"Hmm, doesn't dress like Gysin based on the pics we have of her coming and going ... but kinda the same height and build. We shouldn't take any chances. We need a tail on her."

"Why? No way she's the target. You just wanna meet her?" his partner sneered.

"With Leggett in town, I'm not taking any chances we

screw up." Paul picked up his hand microphone. "Bill, you see the babe in the blue dress and mask walking past you?"

"How could I miss that?"

"Don't lose her."

Gloria walked to the next corner and got into a used, white, electric Honda Civic parked on the side of the street. The street was empty of traffic. She sat in the car for a moment, checking the mirrors. She sent a text.

A car was heading toward her from behind. Before it reached her, she started the engine and pulled out onto the street. After several minutes of winding through Reno, she turned left into the driveway of a motel and parked. The FBI agents parked on the street and watched her go into the Hampton Inn.

That same Thursday, Klaus received a text message that read: Peter planning double-cross. Scientist at GA has made a major medical discovery.

What's the drug? Klaus texted back.

Longevity.

Klaus took off his glasses, leaned forward, and lifted himself up from his office chair, his eyes wide with anger.

Do we need him anymore? he texted.

No.

I'll send someone to solve the problem.

Must be here by tomorrow, Friday afternoon.

Klaus reached into his desk and removed a slip of paper with a phone number and an attached photograph of a tall, thin, distinguished-looking man.

He called the number. "Meet me in the Godesburg Hotel bar at noon today."

Klaus was sitting at his usual table a bit before noon, ordering a salad, the photograph from his office on the table facing him.

When the man in the picture walked into the bar, he was wearing a dark charcoal suit, polished, black, leather wingtip shoes, and a red tie. He stood at the front reception area for a moment before he spotted Klaus. He walked across the room and sat facing Klaus.

A waiter came to the table. "May I get you a drink?" he asked, looking at the newly arrived guest.

"No, he's not staying," Klaus stated abruptly.

The waiter turned and left the table.

Klaus handed the man an envelope containing $100,000 and two photographs of Peter, one a five-year-old mugshot and the other how Peter looked dressed as his sister. On the back of the most recent photo was Peter's apartment number and building address on North Sierra Street in Reno, Nevada.

The man looked at the photographs, smiled, and put the envelope into his coat chest pocket.

"Get someone there by tomorrow afternoon and kill him," Klaus hissed through clenched teeth.

―――――――

On Thursday afternoon, four Reno FBI agents were sitting in their two cars, surveilling the Hampton Inn. One car was facing the front of the hotel, the other the back.

The two agents in front of the hotel watched the mystery woman leave the building, now dressed in white slacks, a dark-blue, long-sleeved button-up, a tie-waist silk blouse, and a white silk medical mask covering most of her face, and a white silk scarf around her neck. She crossed the small parking lot to her stolen Honda Civic and got in.

The agent in the passenger seat grabbed his cell phone off the car's dash and texted Reno headquarters: *Mystery woman is leaving the hotel.*

Follow and have Brown search her room, came the reply.

Gloria drove away.

Agent Brown drove from the back of the hotel to the front. He and his partner got out of the car, walked across the parking lot, and went into the hotel. They walked up to the marble front desk counter. Standing behind the counter was a pleasant-looking young woman.

"May we see the manager?" Brown asked.

"That would be me."

"I'm Special Agent Phil Brown. This is Agent Charlie Hill. We're with the Reno FBI," he said in a serious tone, holding out his badge. "You have a woman staying in the hotel. She left a couple minutes ago. She was wearing a white silk mask over her face. We want to see her room. May I have her room key?"

The young woman typed into the computer console, looked at the names listed, and removed a blank plastic room card. She placed the card into the reader. Finished, she put the plastic card into a paper room keyholder and wrote the room number on the cardholder.

She handed the card to Agent Brown and pointed to her left. "Room two sixty-nine. The elevators are down the hall to your right."

"If the woman returns while we are upstairs, please text me the moment you see her," Brown said as he handed her his business card.

The agents turned, walked to the elevator, and rode it up. The elevator doors opened, and they walked out into a small foyer, turned right and left, glanced at the room numbers listed on the hallway wall, turned right down the hallway, and walked along a clean, red-gray-green carpet to room 269. They paused for a moment and pulled their guns from their chest holsters. Brown waved the plastic card over the electric keypad, and a green light popped on. He raised his revolver. His left palm touched the door and pressed against it. Hill pushed the door handle down.

The first thing they both noticed was the strong smell of bleach. Brown slid along the wall facing the bathroom, then glanced into it. Dial soap, a half-empty bottle of rubbing alcohol, clean towels, and washcloths were stacked on the vanity. Each item was sealed in its own plastic ziplock bag. The shower curtain was open, and the tub was empty.

Hill moved around the single room, his gun held in both hands and ready. They were alone. He took a deep breath and put his gun back into its chest holster. He removed his phone from his coat pocket and texted Reno HQ: *In room 269. No one here.*

The two queen beds were made but looked like they'd been used. New silk underwear lay on one of them, still covered in the store's plastic. Alongside the undergarments were several new St. John knit outfits, also covered in plastic.

At the foot of the queen beds sat a six-foot-long wooden credenza/dresser. On it were a sixty-inch flat-screen TV, makeup, soap, Handi Wipes, twenty unopened boxes of tissue paper, and three new-looking, unopened shoeboxes.

The odor of disinfectant was almost overpowering.

Between the beds stood a night table, with a wall lamp and radio sitting on top. An open packet of yellow sticky notes sat on the radio. The bed next to the window was covered with new clothes and tennis shoes, everything sealed in plastic.

They continued to move around the room. They looked through the plastic-covered clothes on the bed. Brown opened the dresser drawers: nothing, no personal items. He moved around the bed and night table. On the floor next to the table was a small wastebasket. He picked it up and looked inside: clean and empty. Frustrated, he got onto his knees and looked under the bed. Nothing. He lifted the mattress. Nothing.

Hill went into the bathroom and looked through the medicine shelf. He found nothing more than Brown had, seeing no personal items.

Brown, meanwhile, was about to give up when he again looked at the yellow sticky notepad lying on top of the radio. He picked it up and thumbed through it; there was nothing written on it. He put it back on the radio and stood for a moment, looking around the room. He shook his head, thinking. He stared at the notepad. This time, he realized that the top three pages were raised ever so slightly. He picked the notepad up and peeled the top three pages off.

Holding the pages in his hand, he pulled a small pen flashlight from his pocket, turned it on, and held each paper up against the light: BURN had been pressed into the top blank page.

TWENTY-SEVEN

Leggett was in the Reno FBI office, going over the search report of the mystery woman's hotel room when Agent O'Grady knocked softly on the conference room door. Ty waved her in. She was carrying a manila envelope.

O'Grady had worked for the agency for twenty years and was a fanatic for details. "Here's the photos of the woman seen leaving Gysin's apartment building last night."

Looking up at the thin, five-eleven, forty-five-year-old woman, Ty put a warm smile on his face. "It wasn't necessary for you to personally deliver the photos. You could have sent them to my phone."

"I know, sir, but given the terrible circumstance surrounding this case, I thought it best I hand-deliver them. I also sent copies to your secure file."

"I understand. Let's see them," Ty said.

She handed him a yellow manila folder, stamped with PHOTOGRAPHS in red block letters several times across its cover. Ty took the envelope, leaned back in his chair, unlaced the top flap, and, using his index finger, tore the flap open.

He reached in and pulled out an eight-by-ten black-and-white photograph. Studying it for a bit, he reached back into the envelope and pulled out the second photo. Studying the two photographs side by side for a few moments, he picked up the folder and looked inside, making sure it was empty. He placed the envelope on his desktop and looked up at O'Grady with a confused look on his face.

"There must be a mistake. The first picture is a profile shot of Doctor Gysin walking out of her parking garage, and the second is of her walking from her car to her apartment with her back to us. Where's the picture of our mystery woman in the mask and scarf?"

"The photos are of two different women. That one"—she pointed to the second one—"is our mystery lady, but you can't really see the mask or scarf from this angle."

Ty leaned back and smiled. "There must be a mistake. These are the same person. The only difference is the clothing."

"No, sir. That's another reason why I thought I should deliver these pictures. Those are two different people, and both were in Doctor Gysin's parking garage yesterday."

"Gysin does not have an identical twin sister, only a fraternal brother."

"Sir, all I'm saying is our mystery lady seems to be a stone copy of Doctor Gysin, and—"

"No frontal shots," Ty interrupted as he glanced down at the photographs.

"No."

Exasperated, Ty stood and walked around the conference table and sat on the right corner of the desk. "What the hell's going on? Did you run these pictures through the facial identification system?"

"Several times, and each time, it pulled up Doctor Gloria Gysin's file."

"This doesn't make sense. I know she doesn't have a sister." He looked at O'Grady for a moment before saying anything. "Is there anything else you can tell me about our mystery woman?"

"The agent who took the photograph said she had a slight limp. Nothing more."

Frustrated, Ty moved back behind the table and sat. He leaned back, put his hands up in the air. "Explain to me how we could have two Gloria Gysins who are identical and not sisters?"

Knowing an answer was not expected, O'Grady turned to the door and started to leave the room.

"O'Grady," Ty said, "run those two photos through the system again, and as a long shot, use the photo we have of her brother, Peter, and run it through too."

O'Grady nodded and left the room.

With her gone, Ty glanced at his watch and then pressed the intercom button. "Get German Chief Investigator von Grub on the line."

After a short wait, Ty's telephone rang. He picked it up. "Leggett here. Thank you for taking my call so late in the evening. Something has developed that I hope you can clarify."

"Pleased to be of help."

"When we last spoke, you said that Professor Gloria Gysin had a brother."

"That's correct."

"You're sure there's no sister."

"Only a brother."

"And you still haven't found the brother?"

"That's correct." There was silence on the line for a moment, then von Grub asked, "Have you found him?"

"No, all we have is a paradox." Ty tapped the phone with his index finger. "Well, thanks for your help." Ty started to hang up, but suddenly, his mind flashed with more questions. He caught himself, quickly put the telephone to his mouth, and asked, "Von Grub, you still there?"

"Yes."

"I'm sorry, I have a couple quick questions. Last time we spoke, you said you'd been informed he was meeting someone in the building when the explosion happened, right?"

"Yes."

"So you never actually saw him enter the building?"

"We saw a man go in at the time we'd been told to expect Peter Gysin, so we assumed it to be him, but we never saw him come out."

"Mm. What was in the building?"

"White-collar business, some medical," von Grub said.

"Where was the bomb planted?"

"Hold on a moment, I'll check." He came back on the line in a few minutes. "In a Doctor William Dougdale's office."

"What type of doctor was he?"

"Surgeon."

"What type?"

"Cosmetic, Mr. Leggett. He was a disgraced and disreputable plastic surgeon."

"A plastic surgeon?" Ty repeated, thinking. "You said Mr. Gysin was a drug dealer."

"Yes, a very enterprising one. And murderer."

"He liked to kill?"

"According to some of his competitors, he enjoyed that part of the business. So much so, he developed a trademark. He'd stab an ice pick or spike into the temple of his victim to kill them."

"A sicko," Ty whispered. "Did you ever learn who Peter Gysin was meeting with?"

"No."

"Were there any other surgeons in the building?"

"No."

"Any records retrieved from Dougdale's office?"

"No. The fire destroyed everything."

"Humph," Ty whispered. "Thanks again for your help."

Ty put the telephone down, leaned back in his chair, and thought, *Drugs, daggers to the head, surgery.* Suddenly, his eyebrows went up and his eyes popped open wider. "Christ, Peter Gysin is *here!*"

He pressed the intercom. "Have O'Grady double the surveillance on our mystery woman and consider her armed and very dangerous. And I want more pictures of her. Also, put a twenty-four-hour team at the Barber home." Ty's facial expression changed to one of fierce determination, his eyes wide with intensity as he looked forward. "Tell O'Grady, if Megan Barber goes to the store, someone better check her groceries, and if one of those girls falls down, God help the agent who doesn't catch her." His face softened. "This family is very important to me—understand?"

"Yes, sir." Everyone already knew how Ty felt about the Barber family.

TWENTY-EIGHT

"It's wrong," John said to Turner and Berg on a video conference call midday on Friday.

"The president sees it differently," Berg said.

"I won't allow our focus, or discoveries, to be used for warfare," John insisted, looking and sounding determined.

"Your opinions are irrelevant," Turner said.

"Tell the president he'll have to replace me."

"You realize what you're saying?" Berg asked, sounding concerned, yet glad this was happening.

"Yes, my team won't be party to creating the seeds for human extinction," John stated in a low, angry tone.

"This will end your career."

John leaned back in his chair and clenched his hand around the phone. "Tell him to find my replacement."

After leaving work early, John had lunch at home with Megan. Once they'd finished, she started the dishwasher and joined John in the family room, where he was sitting on the couch, talking on the phone. She sat next to him.

He ended the call and put the phone back on its cradle.

"How's Ty?" she asked, resting her arm on his leg.

"Fine," John answered, not looking at Megan.

He took a deep breath, turned on the TV, and mindlessly switched from channel to channel, finally stopping on a cable news show. The two of them watched as the commentator reported about a company that had accidentally mixed poison with children's cough medicine and did not recall the product.

"Please turn it off; this is horrible," Megan said. She turned to look at John and saw he wasn't watching. He was staring off, thinking. "What's wrong?"

No response.

She glanced back at the television and saw war footage from Taiwan.

"I'm afraid GA could develop something evil. The SQ1 test program starts July first, and I'm getting pressure from Homeland to study the implantation of human intelligence into mammals." He turned to look at Megan.

"You'd never let that happen," she said.

"I don't think I can stop them."

He changed the channel, and the movie *It's A Wonderful Life* was on. Jimmy Stewart was confronting Potter, calling him a spider. "I know how he feels," John said.

As they watched the movie, John touched Megan's hand. "Leggett's right; the SOBs have lived too long." He looked away from the television to Megan. "It's time we moved back to DC."

"What about your discovery? If we leave, you'll have to turn it over to Royer and Washington."

An hour later, back at the Hampton Inn after going to the Methodist Church, Gloria took the stairs to her room. She checked the door frame before she opened the door, and the hair she had pasted there was gone. She took a .38-caliber handgun from her purse and opened the door. The room was empty. She packed up the clothes lying on the bed and put them into a new roller suitcase. Finished, she pulled her cell phone out of her purse and called Klaus. As she waited for him to answer, she took off her mask and scarf and began to pace the room, wandering around and eventually entering the bathroom. She stopped when she saw her face. Half of it was perfect and beautiful, the other half a melted blob of deformed scar tissue. In an instant, rage flashed through her body and she smashed her fist into the glass. She turned and continued to pace the room.

"Klaus," he said, answering in a deep, gruff voice.

"What time does he arrive?"

"Two p.m. your time."

"Tell him there's an extra fifty thousand if he calls me after he lands."

Gloria put on her scarf and medical mask back on, grabbed her purse and carry-on suitcase. She left the room, took the stairs down to the front of the hotel, and went to her car.

As she walked casually toward it, she discreetly searched for the location and number of people watching her. She spotted two men sitting in a car facing the north corner of the hotel. She put the carry-on suitcase into the trunk of the car and returned to the hotel.

She walked past the elevators and exited the hotel through the south side door, walked across the parking lot into the hotel next door, and called a taxi.

TWENTY-NINE

Peter glanced at his cell phone: 4:30 p.m. He left GA, got into his car, and drove to the United Methodist Church on First Street to meet his sister. He arrived almost forty minutes early for their 5:30 meeting time. After parking, he glanced into his rearview mirror and thought, *They're such fools*. He watched as the Ford Explorer, which had followed him since he got onto I-80 to Reno, drove by the church property.

He got out of the car and walked to the renovated church, spotting a small creek that ran along the back side of the building. He climbed the wide steps leading to the heavy, ornate metal doors, which were locked. "Shit." He turned and went to the side door, turned the knob, and opened the door. Cool, incense-laced air rushed out, pressing on his face.

He held the door open a moment, then moved inside and pulled it closed. He moved to one side of the door and pressed himself against the wall to allow his eyes to adjust to the dark.

The church looked to be empty of people. The only light

was emanating through the stained-glass windows running along the sides of the twenty-foot-high walls.

Peter took a few steps toward the middle aisle of the pews, then hesitated to see if the church was truly empty. After a few more seconds, he found the door on the left that his sister had told him to use. Before he opened it, he removed a .38 from his GA lab coat pocket.

He gently grabbed hold of the doorknob, took a deep breath, and set his feet. He yanked on it, flinging the door open, the gun ready to fire. The ten-by-ten-square-foot room was dimly lit and empty except for a cell phone resting on the wooden chair, with a Post-It note sticking to it.

Peter checked the time: 5:00 p.m. He went into the darkish room, closed the door, and looked at the sticky note. It read: Hide here until I text you on this phone.

With the burner phone in hand, he sat in the small chair, put the gun back into his coat pocket, leaned back, and waited.

It won't be long now. I don't need her. The bitch gave me her plan, he thought.

Suddenly, the door swung open. Peter froze.

The assassin from Germany was standing facing him, holding a HK P30 semiautomatic pistol with silencer, and it was pointed at Peter's chest.

The assassin motioned with his right hand for Peter to stand. Peter stood and started to step forward, but the assassin slammed the butt of the gun into Peter's forehead, sending him to the confessional floor, along with the burner phone. The blow almost knocked him unconscious. Dazed, he looked up, and the assassin kicked Peter in the face with the toe of his pointed boot.

"Pig," the man said in German.

He kicked Peter again, this time with the heel of his boot.

The assassin reached into his black leather coat pocket and removed a cell phone, glanced at the time, and pressed the *Send* icon as Peter watched in stunned horror.

A moment later, the burner phone rang.

"Answer it," the man barked in German.

"I dropped it!" Peter groaned.

The phone rang again.

It rang a third time as Peter searched for it on the floor.

He found it, got to his knees, and glanced at the screen. He did not recognize the number. He answered it and heard the sickening sound of his sister's voice: "Klaus sent him to kill you."

Peter looked up at the man standing in front of him.

The assassin, still holding the gun, now pointed it at Peter's face. With his other hand, he reached into his left coat pocket and removed a seventeen-fluid-ounce plastic bottle, then used his thumb to pop the cap off.

Peter could only stare.

"That's for me!" Gloria shouted from the phone.

Peter tried to dodge out of the way as the assassin emptied the small bottle of gasoline on his head and body. Peter gagged from the smell.

Finished, the assassin tossed the bottle at Peter, removed a metal cigarette lighter from his pocket, and ignited it.

"Burn him! Burn him now!" Gloria shrieked from the phone.

"No!" Peter screamed.

The instant the word left Peter's lips, the assassin moved back a few feet and tossed the lighter at Peter. There was a flash of light, followed by a gunshot and fiery explosion.

Sitting in their car along the street facing the church

parking lot, the two FBI agents watched in stunned silence as a fire suddenly began to engulf the church. The windows exploded out, and fire dripped out of the shattered glass like wax running down a candle.

"Shit!" one of the agents shouted. He grabbed his cell phone and called the Reno FBI headquarters. "Tell Director Leggett the church Doctor Gysin went into is on fire and she's still inside!"

Standing in the shadows out of view, holding a cell phone, Gloria watched the fire consume the building. She could hardly contain her joy as smoke billowed and the flames shot into the cool evening air. She hoped Peter's seared lungs would fill with water and he would drown in a panic-filled hospital oxygen tent.

The FBI agents quickly drove up to the church, jumped out of the car, and tried to get inside the building, but the fire was too intense. Screaming voices from neighbors and sirens announced the approach of fire engines. Gloria calmly walked to her stolen car; she had an appointment to keep.

———

It was 7:30 p.m. and dark when John and Lynn walked out of the gym to their car after gymnastics practice. John unlocked the driver's door, got in, and unlocked the passenger-side rear door for Lynn. She lifted the handle, pulled the door open, and got in.

Suddenly, Gloria jumped out from behind the car parked next to them, pulled the door away from Lynn's hand, and jumped into the car holding a .38 handgun. She grabbed Lynn by the hair and pressed her to the floormat behind John. She stuck her knee in Lynn's back, smashing her harder to the floor.

John could hear soft, muffled cries for help.

"Don't move," Gloria hissed. She hit John on the side of the head with the butt of the gun. "Drive!" she screamed as she slid down behind the front seat.

Sitting behind the steering wheel, shocked, John stared into the rearview mirror. All he could see was the top of someone's head.

"Drive or I'll kill her."

"Where?" he yelled, his mouth growing drier by the moment.

"To your journal," she snarled through clenched teeth.

John started the engine, backed up, and headed home.

"Drive the speed limit," she said.

Lynn was sobbing.

John's mind spun. *Who is this?*

He glanced several times into the rearview mirror before he finally saw a face. He mouthed, "Gloria?" The woman in the back seat lifted her head and turned to look out the window, and he saw the hideously deformed side of her face. Shocked by the sight, he stared a moment too long and their eyes met.

"Look familiar?" she snarled. She hit Lynn on the back with the gun, and Lynn cried out. "Watch the road!" Gloria screamed.

"Don't you hurt her," he said angrily.

His mind raced. *What am I going to do?* He knew there was an FBI agent watching his house; he prayed he could signal him for help. He turned the last corner to his house and again glanced into the rearview mirror. To his surprise, Gloria was smiling.

"Slow down," she whispered.

John pressed the brakes too hard and jerked the car into a slight skid, causing Gloria to hit the front seat. Catching her balance, she reached over the seat and hit him again with the butt of the gun.

"Bastard," she snarled. "Next time I'll shoot the little bitch."

They were halfway down the block, across the street from his house, where a Ford Explorer was parked, with the driver's side window open. A man was inside the car smoking a cigarette, his arm resting out the window.

"Roll down the driver's side back window—see that SUV on the left? Move over like you want to talk, smile, and drive past real slow."

John slowed to a crawl as he reached the car.

"Drive right next to it, real close," Gloria whispered.

The FBI agent recognized John and smiled.

With only inches separating the two cars, Gloria slumped down in the back seat, pressing Lynn deeper into the floor. The man and John's eyes met, and the agent nodded. Suddenly, the man's head exploded, spraying both cars with blood.

John gasped at the sound and sight of the man's head blowing apart. Gloria grabbed Lynn by the hair and pulled her up off the floor mat. Lynn screamed. Gloria hit her with the butt of the gun, knocking her unconscious.

"Park in the driveway and get out!" she shouted.

The church was gutted, smoke and black embers floating into the night air. The fire had been extinguished, but the building was reduced to an empty shell. The first responders were removing their equipment and surveying the damage.

Ty walked around the burned-out shell with the FBI agents who had witnessed the explosion. He covered his mouth and coughed several times from the pungent smell. The church was destroyed. Everything was black, water puddled on the scorched wood floor, and little rings of smoke rose into the air. The smell of melted plastic and rubber filled the air. Ty coughed several more times.

They walked to where the confessional room had once been. The Reno city coroner was kneeling next to a body there. As Ty got closer, he saw the remains of a twisted and hideously burned corpse lying on the floor. The remains were disfigured and almost impossible to recognize as human. The head had lost all its skin, the eyes were gone, and fragments of clothing were melted to the legs and smoldering. The trunk of the body was split open, the arms and hands were charred bone, and what skin remained was horrifically blistered.

Ty watched the coroner cover the remains with a plastic sheet and lift the body up onto a gurney and place it into a thick, black, nylon body bag. Ty noticed that the left hand clutched a melted cell phone.

The coroner looked at Ty as the bag was zipped closed and wheeled to a waiting van. "I'll send the results of the dental records and the DNA to your office. Between the two of us, we should have an ID in a couple of hours, and you'll know who he is."

"He?"

"Yes."

Ty looked at one of the agents. "You said Doctor Gysin went into the church."

"Yes, sir. We followed her from GA."

"This does not make sense. No one left the building?"

"No, sir."

Ty turned to the coroner. "When you get the cell detached from his hand, get the SIM card and find out who he was talking to, and please get me that ID as soon as possible."

The coroner nodded.

Ty's cell phone rang. He pulled it from his pocket as he walked to the other side of the church. "Leggett here."

"This is Agent Stewart. We lost the lady in the mask. What do you want us to do?"

"Send a team to the airport. It looks like her revenge is complete," he said, and then hung up.

Ty held his phone up to his mouth. "Send text to John Barber: Gloria is missing. Be careful until we find her." He read the message. "Send text."

Ty hung up and returned the phone to his coat pocket and continued to survey the church. Not seeing anything of interest, he walked back to his car.

His cell phone rang again. "Leggett here."

"This is Agent Stewart again, sir. Something's wrong at the Barber home. Agent O'Hare missed his seven-forty-five check-in, and we can't reach anyone at the house. This isn't normal; everyone should be home."

Ty thought for a moment. Suddenly, his eyes got large and his heart raced with a jolt. "Get to the Barbers' now. Now!" he screamed into the telephone as he jumped into his car.

THIRTY

John opened the front door with Gloria close behind, poking him in the head with the gun as she dragged a semiconscious Lynn along. Gloria kicked the front door shut with her right foot.

"Get the journal," she snarled.

John walked down the short hallway to the study. Gloria followed him, dragging Lynn by her arm. She released the girl once she was inside the study. John went to the desk, then leaned down to open the top drawer.

"Stop. Lift your hands," Gloria growled. She walked to the desk and pushed him to the side. "Stand over there against the wall." She pointed the gun at his head. John moved across the room and stood against the wall. Gloria reached down and opened the drawer. She glanced down and saw a green, eight-by-eleven-inch notebook.

Megan unexpectedly came into the room carrying a plastic drinking cup filled with pencils and writing pens.

"John, you left the front—" She gasped when she saw Lynn lying on the floor and looked up to see Gloria pointing a handgun at John.

Before Megan could react, Gloria lunged at her and, with a violent swing of her right hand, hit Megan in the face with the gun, knocking her to the floor. The cup smashed against the hallway wall, spreading its contents everywhere. John leaped forward toward Gloria and grabbed her right hand. She stabbed his eyes with the fingernails of her left hand. John pushed her hand away, grabbed her by the hair, and slammed her right hand and gun against the desk. The gun bounced off the desk and fell to the floor near Megan's left hip.

Gloria hit John in the face with two quick left-elbow swings. He relaxed his grip. With her mouth snarled and teeth clenched, she pushed him violently back to the wall. He fell over the desk chair onto the floor. She quickly twisted her body around and dove for the gun, got it, rolled onto her back, and fired a shot into the ceiling.

John froze and their eyes locked.

Suddenly, Megan kicked Gloria's arm, and the gun fired again into the ceiling. John leaped on top of Gloria, snagged her right hand, and they wrestled for control of the gun. Megan screamed and grabbed Gloria by the hair.

The gun went off again.

Gloria hit Megan with an elbow to the head, disabling Megan's grip. Gloria clenched John by the throat with her left hand and squeezed, digging her fingernails deep into his neck.

John hit her in the head with a left punch.

Gloria fell back against Megan's legs, still clutching John's throat. John grabbed her hand and ripped it free from his neck and took a deep breath. Gloria again stabbed at his eyes with her fingernails. Stunned by the pain, he relaxed his grip on the gun.

She fired the gun again and pulled it free.

"Stop or I'll kill her!" she screamed, pressing the gun against Megan's side.

John froze, his eyes bleeding and ablaze with rage. He glanced at the gun, then Megan's eyes. He saw terror.

"She's dead if you move a muscle. Crawl back away from me—now!"

John slid back.

Gloria kicked him in the face as he moved away. "Bastard," she spit out.

She got to her feet, still pointing the gun at Megan. Standing, she glanced again at Megan and took several steps back toward the doorway. She kicked Megan in the ribs as hard as she could. Megan gasped for air. Filled with rage, John rolled to his knees and sprang to his feet, trying to attack.

"Another inch and I'll kill her," Gloria said with a smirk. "Now get the journal—or she's dead."

John lifted himself off the floor and went to the desk, his breathing fast and hard. Suddenly, Abby appeared at the doorway, headphones in her hand and saying something about hearing loud noises.

When Gloria turned toward the door to see who was there, John lunged at her and grabbed her right hand. They fell back against Abby and out into the hallway. Gloria twisted away and released the gun, and it fell to the floor. John pushed her against the wall and dove for the gun.

Before he could lift the gun, Gloria grabbed Abby by the hair and pulled her into her chest, then pushed an ink pen into her temple.

John, holding the gun, froze as a trickle of blood ran down Abby's face. "Stop!"

"Drop the gun and kick it here," she demanded, wheezing to breathe.

John dropped the gun and kicked it toward her. She picked it up and said through clenched teeth, in an angry, guttural voice, "Get the journal right now." She pushed Abby to the hallway floor and pointed the gun at John's chest. "Move!"

John went back into the office, picked up the notebook, and tossed it to her. She caught it with her free hand and smiled. Holding the gun in her right hand, she thumbed through the notebook. Her expression suddenly changed and her lips twisted in rage.

"You think I'm stupid like my brother? These are notes! Where's the fucking formula?" She looked down at Megan lying on the floor. "She's first." Gloria pointed the gun at Megan.

There was nothing John could do to stop her.

He jumped with fright as the shot rang out. Shaking in terror, he looked at Megan, then at Gloria; he saw a small, watery red spot appear on Gloria's blouse. He looked at her face and saw a smirk appear.

This time, Gloria pointed the gun at John.

Bang—Bang! Two shots. One struck the floor right in front of John, then he saw Gloria's body jolt forward toward him. Blood spat out of her mouth, her eyes glassed over, and she collapsed onto the floor next to him, dead.

John looked down the hallway and saw Ty pointing his gun. John fell to his knees, grabbed Megan, and held her like a lost child. Lynn and Abby joined them, sobbing.

The street and yard were lit by the flashing lights of two fire trucks, ten police cars, and two ambulances.

An ambulance first responder walked up to Ty and John. "Doctor Barber, everything's okay. We gave Mrs. Barber and your oldest daughter a mild sedative, and we'll take them to the hospital to monitor them for at least a couple nights. Both will be fine in the morning; nothing but cuts, bruises, and bad memories. We checked on your youngest daughter. She's asleep in her room, no problems."

John shook the paramedic's hand. "Thank you very much."

John walked alongside Megan and Lynn as they were wheeled to an ambulance. Lynn was loaded first; she had an IV in her arm and was asleep. John kissed Megan.

"I'll come tomorrow morning," he said.

The first responder jumped into the ambulance and closed the door, and soon they drove away.

He joined Ty standing on the front porch. They watched the chaos for a moment in silence, then turned their attention to watch Gloria's body bag get loaded into the coroner's van and drive away.

"That," Ty said as he watched the van move down the street, "was the real Doctor Gloria Gysin."

"What?"

"It's complicated. Earlier this evening, that woman"—he pointed to the coroner's van—"murdered the person you knew as Doctor Gysin. The Gloria at GA we all knew was actually Peter Gysin, her twin brother. They worked together selling drugs and GA became the big prize. Only their hate for each other and the mistake in killing Lisa Ford got in their way."

"You found Lisa?"

"No, but I'm sure she's dead. I'll explain everything in greater detail tomorrow morning after we get a positive ID of Peter's body."

John looked at Ty in disbelief. "Peter Gysin's dead too? How?"

"Shot and set on fire. Not much to recognize. With them dead, you and Megan are safe," Ty said, seeing the burned body in his mind's eye.

Ty and John watched in silence as the last fire truck and police car left and an eerie quiet filled the crisp late-night air.

Both men were calm.

"I heard about your latest call with Berg and Turner. The president won't give in," Ty said.

"Doesn't matter. I want the family to move back to DC."

Ty nodded. An inquisitive expression replaced his calm look. "Why was Gysin after you?"

"She discovered I can stop aging."

Ty watched John for a moment before saying, "You told me. I didn't fully believe you."

John's expression softened, and his eyes twitched with emotion. "You've got to protect my family."

Ty raised his eyebrows, then shook his head. "That's a bad call. You can't run. She loves you."

"It's *because* I love her."

"We can beat them. You can survive this. Don't give up hope. You've got to stay; not everyone knows. What you and Megan have is too important."

"Soon you'll have to report everything to the president. As I said at dinner, it's in my head—and there're ways to get it out. If Gloria knew, so do others. You can't protect us. No one can, and as long as I'm around, Megan will be a target and hiding her won't work."

"John, you're wrong. Think this through. I've searched my whole life for what you have with your family. We can manage your discovery."

"All I wanted was to be a family guy and save kids from progeria." He took a deep breath to catch his emotions. "Horrible."

Ty reached out and touched John's arm. "Stick with me. Everything will come together. Megan and the girls are worth the try."

The two men looked at each other for a moment and knew what would happen next and deeply wished it wouldn't. Ty turned and walked to his car to drive back to Reno, and John went into the house.

He walked upstairs and checked on Abby in her bedroom. Finished, he returned downstairs and locked the windows and sliding-glass doors. He turned out the lights. Satisfied the house was locked, he moved into the living room and fixed a short bourbon and sat on the couch. He took a sip and thought about Gloria Gysin and the hate.

He was startled by a banging sound outside the patio window, followed by a cat hissing. He placed the drink on the cocktail table, went to the sliding-glass window, looked out, and saw only a dark backyard.

He sighed, went back to the couch, sat, and thought how lucky things turned out. He put down the unfinished drink and headed off to sleep in the rocking chair in Abby's bedroom.

On his way, he smelled something odd. When he reached the stairs, he stopped and sniffed; the odor was a mixture of gasoline and plastic. He sniffed the air several more times, walked to the closet door near the entryway, turned the knob without hesitation, and opened it. Nothing. Only clothing.

"Is she dead?"

The voice sent a chill through John. He turned to see someone standing in the kitchen doorway—Peter Gysin, he assumed, but no longer looking much like his sister.

Peter limped into the living room, dragging his left leg and holding a .38 in his right hand. His face was badly burned, and his nose was burned past the cartilage. His left arm was black and bleeding, and his pants were melted to his skin at the knees. The hand holding the gun was shaking, and his fingers were split open and oozing watery pink blood.

"She's dead. It's over," John answered.

"Where's the journal?" he said, flicking the gun back and forth at John.

"At GA."

"It's not there or in the study. Where did you take it? *Where's the fucking journal?*" Peter screamed, his hand trembling and his eyes wide with rage. He coughed, then coughed again, spitting blood onto the carpet. He almost dropped the gun. He caught his breath, shaking. "Tell me the formula!"

"No. It's over. The FBI knows about you and Klaus. Look at yourself. Without help, you'll be dead by morning."

"Don't be so sure. I'm smarter than her. I'll survive."

He turned and walked toward the stairs.

John raced after him. Peter turned and fired the gun into the wall behind John.

"If you move, I'll shoot your leg, drag your daughter down here, and kill her in front of you." He coughed again and his legs buckled, but he pointed the gun at John's leg. "Do you understand?"

"I won't give you the formula."

"We'll see." He turned and started up the stairs.

John followed, hoping Peter would have a coughing fit or slip.

Peter stopped and pointed the gun at John. "You never knew it was me all along. I was always better than her."

He fired the gun.

THIRTY-ONE

Leggett had barely exited the freeway into downtown Reno when his cell phone rang. He picked it up from the passenger seat and answered it. "Leggett here."

"This is Agent Stewart. Sir, we've ID'd the body from the church."

"Go ahead," he said, feeling confident he knew the answer.

"Jorge Wagle."

"What?" Ty asked, almost screaming into the phone.

"Yes, he's a German asset."

"Oh shit!" Ty threw the phone against the passenger door and spun the car around in the other direction.

Ten minutes later, he slid into the Barber driveway with so much speed the car almost bounced off the curb and into the house as it skidded to a stop.

The bullet grazed John's right leg. Peter smiled and continued up the stairs. He slipped, almost losing his balance.

John, holding his leg, started up after him.

Peter regained his balance and pointed the gun. "Not this time," he snarled. He reached the top of the stairs.

"I'll get it," John said.

"I don't believe you. Not until I have her."

"You take another step, you'll have to kill me. I'll get it; it's on my computer."

Peter waved the gun. John turned and walked down the stairs with Peter several steps behind. John hurried into the office while Peter stayed at the door.

His Caltech baseball cap was resting on the desk. John picked it up, held it in his hand, and started the computer. After a moment, he said, "Open secure file LYNN, code nine-one-five."

He picked up the retina scanner and pointed it at his right eye, then pressed the trigger. A blue light washed over his eye, and suddenly, 156082573156140081–HGNC 6636–P02545-F1N-V4683761#-GCACAGGGCAG# flashed on the monitor screen.

"There it is," John said.

Peter was leaning against the doorjamb. He motioned with the gun for John to step away from the desk. He moved closer to the monitor, hesitated, and looked at John.

"Turn the monitor toward me," he said.

John moved back to the desk and twisted the monitor to face him.

"Back up." Peter moved forward and looked at the screen.

Suddenly, John leaned forward and touched the back-space key, erasing the formula to 156082573156140081.

Peter hit John in the face with the gun. "No!" he screamed.

John regained his balance and wiped blood from his forehead where a gash had opened.

"I'll kill—" Peter coughed.

John whipped the Caltech cap at Peter's face and attacked. The gun fired, missing John's head, exploding into the wall behind him.

———————

Ty jumped out of the car, holding his revolver in both hands, and ran to the front door. He turned his key to the Barbers' front door handle and crept into the house. He stopped to listen, heard the groans of a fight to his left, and turned to the hallway.

———————

John slammed his right fist into Peter's face. "Bastard!" He hit Peter again.

Peter dropped the gun. John pushed him into the hallway, picked up the gun, and pulled the trigger as fast as he could. Peter's chest exploded as round after round slammed into his body. Peter's eyes rolled white, and he dropped to the floor.

John dropped the gun, his hand trembling, and moved away from Peter's body. Sensing someone behind him, he looked up.

Leggett stood in the hallway, pointing his gun. "That's making a point," he said.

On Saturday morning, John and Abby visited the hospital room Megan and Lynn shared. He sat on the bed. Abby sat on her sister's bed.

John held Megan's hand. "You and the girls are safe."

Megan gazed into his eyes. "John, destroy the formula."

"It only exists now in my head."

"Then give it to GA. Royer will protect it."

"That's too dangerous. The government would still get it somehow and pick the winners and use it as a weapon."

"Against who?"

"Everyone."

"This'll never end. We'll have to hide, live in fear," Megan said as she pulled herself up. "The children will never be safe."

John put his arms around her and kissed her cheek. "I'll always love you," he whispered.

Megan looked into his eyes, studying his face. "They'll hunt you," she said.

"Better me."

"What a terrible price." She began to cry.

John held her face between his hands and softly kissed her lips. "I'll always love you," he whispered.

The next morning, a nurse, joined by a smiling Ty Leggett, walked into Megan's hospital room. Lynn was sitting in a chair watching television next to Abby, who'd been allowed to stay the night for a sleepover with her sister. Megan was sitting up in bed, staring out the window.

"How y'all doing?" Ty said.

"Where's John?" Megan asked.

"I don't know. He's not at the house."

"Oh God," Megan said between gasps for air. "What a dreadful price," she said, looking at Ty. "How will I live without him?"

Ty sat next to Megan on the edge of the bed.

With a sudden burst of energy, Megan grabbed Ty's hands. "You've got to promise. You've got to promise me you won't let them catch him."

Ty nodded.

Megan studied his face for a moment, then relaxed her grip and sobbed.

With nothing more to be said and with tears in his eyes, Ty reached into his coat pocket, removed his cell phone, turned it off, and put his arms around Megan.

Before dawn that same morning, John drove up to the security gate at the Public Storage facility, inserted his code, and watched the gate bounce open. He drove in and followed the yellow reflector lines through the facility to the back stairwell, parked across from the building, and left the car.

He climbed the four flights to his locker. He listened to the crunching sounds of his steps echo through the stairwell as he went. He removed the padlock at his storage locker, opened the steel door, and switched the light on.

The room was a functional laboratory. The far wall was lined with jars filled with flies, and one small metal cage contained several mice. The right wall was covered with photos of animals in different stages of aging. Along the left wall was a television, and next to it was a computer and work-bench. John moved to the back wall, opened the jars, freed the mice, and collected his notes from the table and put them into the trash can.

It was nearing midday when Ty arrived at the Reno FBI office. He was exhausted and frustrated as he got out of the car and went to the building. He was met at the front door by an agent named Doris.

She pulled the glass door open as Ty approached. "Good morning, sir. White House Chief of Staff Berg, DOD Secretary Turner, and HHS Secretary Hallett are ready for your eleven-thirty p.m. virtual call."

"Okay," Ty said with a cool, tired smile.

"Sir, are you okay? I can reschedule the call."

Ty took a deep breath. "No, this is something I must do. It comes with the job."

Soon enough, he sat behind the metal desk in his temporary office, switched on the AI camera, and sat facing the twenty-five-inch monitor. He saw the trio sitting in Berg's office, facing the camera.

Remembering the time difference just before he started speaking, Ty said, "Good afternoon, lady and gentlemen."

Chief of Staff Eric Berg started. "We're glad you're okay, Ty."

Ty nodded a thank-you.

"I briefed the president about the deaths at the Barber home and the infiltration of the Genetic Answer facility. He wants a detailed report explaining Professor Gysin's charade and how she, and for that matter, her brother, outmaneuvered the background check." Berg turned his head to look at Turner. "On the positive side," he continued, "this issue did not go public, and

GA's anonymity was not violated. On a not-so-positive note, I received Doctor Barber's resignation at four this morning."

"People can only be pushed so far," Ty said.

"Will John stay until we find his replacement?" Hallett asked.

"No," Ty said.

Silence.

"We'll need to find a replacement to manage GA as soon as possible," Berg said. "I'll reach out to Doctor Royer after this call and tell him Barber has resigned and ask him to step in and manage the staff until we select a permanent replacement." He paused. "The GA team is scheduled to initiate testing AI algorithms on the Syntopicon Q1 computing system using the experimental XPLK-99 superconducting material soon."

"The test is critical to our gain-of-function genetic timeline," Hallett said. "And that specific material, if it works, is key to reaching room temperature superconductivity. We must keep Royer focused on that research and not dealing with HR issues."

Berg and Turner glanced at each other.

"Jordan and I have several candidates in mind. We'll present them to you and Ty early next week," Berg said.

Silence.

"Ty, your preliminary report didn't detail why the Gysin twins attacked the Barber family," Hallett said.

"I haven't fully tied that up. It appears they were working for a German pharmaceutical company and learned John made a discovery that would make them very rich. Unfulfilled dreams of psychopaths," Ty said.

"How significant a discovery?" Hallett asked.

"Life-altering," Ty said.

"Is that information at GA?" Turner asked.

"I don't believe so," Ty answered.

"Where is Barber now?" Turner asked.

"I don't know."

Silence.

"Ty, you're not being very forthcoming. This is not a congressional hearing," Berg said.

"It's something only John can answer. His discovery, if made public, could destroy civilization. He risked his family to protect us," Ty said.

"That's not his call," Turner said.

"I know," Ty replied softly.

"What's your plan, Ty?" Hallett asked.

"That's tricky. The discovery is in his head, and right now he's exhausted and alone."

"You know what needs to be done," Turner said.

"That'll destroy his family," Ty replied.

"The discovery already has," Turner quipped under his breath.

Ty nodded slightly, saddened by the reality.

"Ty, we have no choice," Hallett said.

John woke on Monday morning, pushed the military cot under the workbench, turned on the television to KRXI-11, and fixed a cup of coffee.

"We have a breaking story," the newscaster said. "Doctor John W. Barber, a local resident, is wanted for the murder of a Doctor Gloria Gysin." A photo of John appeared on the screen as the newscaster described how the murder was committed at the Barber home.

John rubbed his hand through his hair, put the cup of coffee on the workbench, removed a syringe from its plastic container, screwed on a clean hypodermic needle, rolled up his right sleeve, wrapped a black rubber band around his left arm, and placed the needle into his vein.

With a full syringe, he removed the needle from his arm and untied the rubber band. He emptied the syringe into the separator access tube and watched as the blood disappeared into the machine.

The Caltech baseball cap was resting on the left side of the workbench. He picked it up and put it on. He typed 15608257315614008 1–HGNC 6636–P02545-F1N-V4683761#-GCACAGGGCAG# into the computer and took a sip of black coffee.

He waited five minutes while a vial filled with the cure. He added a hypodermic needle to an empty syringe and poked the needle into the vial and pulled the cure into the syringe. He cleaned his left arm with alcohol and injected the liquid into his arm. Finished, he stood and reached under the workbench, slid the cot back out, and sat on it, waiting for the effects of the drug to put him to sleep.

He sipped the coffee and watched the news. Bored, he turned the channel. After several clicks with the remote, he came across the *Woodstock* movie and watched Richie Havens sing "Freedom (Motherless Child)." A smile graced his face; he remembered that generation.

"So disappointing," he whispered.

Suddenly, he felt very tired and lay down on the cot and fell asleep. The movie was interrupted by a breaking news report, "Doctor Gloria Gysin's body was ..."

The next morning, outside of the Public Storage compound, three nondescript Ford Explorers arrived at the front gate. There were two men in each SUV. The lead vehicle stopped at the front gate, and the driver got out and went into the office. He reappeared several minutes later. As he walked back to his car, he looked at the other two vehicles, held up five fingers, and pointed down the street to the back of the building. He got back in his car and watched as the gate jerked its way open.

The lead SUV drove down the compound, and the other two followed. They drifted down the driveway to the back loading dock and stairwell. They reached the loading dock and parked facing the back gate. The driver of the lead car got out and pointed his index finger at Barber's Bronco. The remaining five men exited the Explorers.

They were all dressed in cheap black business suits and over-polished black, plastic-looking shoes. One man looked through the windows of Barber's car. Not seeing anything of interest, he rejoined the other men.

They walked up to the metal door and into the stairwell. They gathered for a moment, checked their handguns. Five climbed the stairs while one stayed to watch the elevator. Reaching the top, they opened the fifth-floor door. They fanned out with military precision inside the hallway as they stalked down the corridor. When they reached Barber's unlocked storage locker, they crowded at the closed roll-up door. The lead agent and another man crouched down, while the other three stood tall and pressed against the two in front. They could hear a television playing. The lead agent used his fingers to count out the number three.

The man next to him reached out and yanked the door upward.

Bang! The door slammed to a stop overhead. The lead agent burst into the room, shouting and screaming orders, only to find bugs flying about, a computer hard drive on the floor in a melted blob, a cot turned upside down, a television, and assorted trash spread around the empty locker.

After a quick search, the lead agent kicked the cot with his right foot and left the room. He stormed down the stairs and out the building to his vehicle. He leaned against the front hood, pulled a cell phone from his coat pocket, and made a call.

"Tell Director Leggett that Doctor Barber's not here, and the locker is mostly empty. A melted hard drive and crushed medical equipment are the only contents of interest."

Finished with the call, he returned the phone to his jacket pocket and lifted a pack of Marlboro Reds from his shirt pocket. He lit a cigarette and took a deep drag. As he exhaled, he looked up to his right at the back gate and saw a thin, maybe ten-year-old boy standing outside the fence, watching.

Their eyes met. The child was dressed in a white T-shirt, blue jeans, Adidas running shoes, and a Caltech baseball cap pulled down tightly on his head.

The boy turned and walked away.

PART 2

THIRTY-TWO
FEBRUARY 6, 2222

File: John Barber
Three Days to Live

I reentered my last sanctuary, and my crystal snapped on. Now you know my past and discovery. It's time for the end.

The legacy of Gloria Gysin has finally guided my assassins to this sanctuary, and they will soon arrive to carry out their perfunctory duty. Today my life is a desert filled with fear.

At Creation, God stationed cherubim angels and a sword of fire to guard the Tree of Eternal Life. They failed, and I discovered a cure for aging, yet I believe those angels are protecting me even now.

Why? I do not know. I should have died long ago, yet each time, I escaped death by a miracle. There must be a reason.

It was a mistake to run away and leave Megan and my children. I know that. If my life is to have purpose or any hope for redemption, I must deliver my story to you and stop the World Crystal from replacing humanity.

The downward slope to human destruction started in 2038 with the invention of the education K chip (K for kindergarten) and ended eighty-four years later with the start of the War of Purification.

How could any parent say no to the K chip? A simple implant at five years old, and a child would have unlimited knowledge. With a gentle tap of a finger on their temple, an "enlightened child," as they were called, would be connected instantly to the Global Fact Institute, referred to as the GFI. They could ask any question and instantly know the perfect answer. It did not matter if the child understood it; they just needed the answer.

How could any parent say no? And if they did, their child would be relegated to Continual Education and a life of poverty.

At first, only rich families could afford the K chip implant, but as the plot developed, every child was mandated to have the K chip implant before he or she could enter kindergarten —"out of fairness," they said.

At first, China and India only implanted the K chip into politically and socially connected wealthy families. Third world countries, too, only implanted the K chip in elite, wealthy families. The poor around the world suffered and over time died of isolation and became irrelevant to the greater society. A child without the K chip was obsolete, mocked, and doomed to a hopeless, destitute existence, begging on the fringe of the new society.

How could any parent say no?

That was the beginning of Hubots, as I call them—people who were rich, powerful, wanted perfection, and are more machine than human. You, *you* are the result of that lust.

The South Koreans embraced cosmetic surgery and led the world in mastering physical perfection. Japan led the world in mass-producing perfect, human-looking androids, complete with AI language skills and dexterity. Over time, it became impossible to distinguish an android from a human.

It was a simple step forward for the lonely to marry an android. It never said no, never got angry, and protected without reward. The only sacrifice was conception—and that would also change.

I have stayed a hundred percent human by forgoing injecting the quantum bots into my blood to cure all disease and cancers. I did not implant the K chip into my brain to answer questions. I did not alter my physical appearance to copy Adonis. My genetic code is pure, and I'm the last fully human being on Earth.

Whoever's hearing these words, you are no longer human; you are a descendant of a Hubot and on the precipice of extinction.

Curiosity and choice are unknown concepts. They were eliminated by AI and the K chip long ago. Generations have passed who knew everything and understood nothing.

With each passing decade, my identity has become more difficult to conceal. With personal "crystals"—what were once computers, laptops, or smart phones—outlawed and all communication devices monitored by the Global Information Commission, I am left with few choices.

I am speaking these memories into the last privately held crystal. When this machine fails, I will lose my ability to create new identities and protect myself from the omnipresent World Crystal.

The robotic TXZ1000 Security Service, patrolling from its perch in the sky, has replaced the human police officer. That cold, unfeeling machine conducts law enforcement and inflicts punishment. When the AI algorithm database became part of government surveillance in street cameras, George Orwell rolled over, and his pig celebrated.

Eliminating personal credit vouchers will destroy my only advantage, inheritance, and I, too, will soon become beholden to the Universal Family; a dependent slave to a voucher.

Birth parents, the rich and lucky individuals permitted to have a natural child, will soon be a historical footnote. Womankind will no longer present their gift to humanity and, like faith, become a footnote in the World Crystal.

I am a witness to the death of hope, and I cannot pass judgment. It is as much my fault as it was humanity's. They were seduced by promises, and I was neutered by fear.

The West led the world in quantum computing from 2040 to 2088, and science had all its questions answered. Innovation exploded; disease, cancer, hunger, and exploitation of nature ended. Humanity had reached its fourth stage of development. Killing to eat was eliminated. Only time travel, light speed, and, to my benefit, eternal life had not been discovered.

Human culture adapted at remarkable speed; only the

religious resisted. Hate was put on hold, and peace reigned for fifty years as humanity adjusted to hedonism and utopia.

On Christmas Day of 2088, hate made a last stand: the Holy War of Conversion. Contrary to what you believe, the war began in the land of sand, hot with hate and fueled by jealous lies of heavenly rewards. Hate attacked Israel, Western Europe, Japan, Australia, and the United States. It was not the first time religion destroyed peace, but it would be the last. The world waged its last religious war with 500 million dead in the name of perfection. When it ended, God was dead.

The war lasted one year, and the survivors came together and pledged it would never happen again. Science moved to make humankind identical in belief, and they succeeded through Directed Evolution. It will suffice to say that you are the product of that victory over religion and are less human because of it.

At the end of the war, the world was divided between China and everyone else. China wanted independence. The two sides agreed to bifurcate. In 2090, each side developed their separate crystal computer systems.

What separated the West's quantum crystal from China's was one simple sentence in it programming: Life was a point of view.

The Western world, seduced by technology and the belief Hubots could attain genetic perfection, embraced change. Without faith, it was easy for the World Crystal to gradually modify humanity into living machines; only the Chinese remained unaltered and clung to their uniqueness.

In December 2100, Directed Evolution, or DE, disciples announced they had mastered evolution. What had taken nature billions of years of trial and failure could now be done in seconds by the Master Quantum Computer—the MQC. To sell the concept of changing humanity's genetic code, science promised to make life fair: No losers; only happiness, longevity, and perfection. Except for the poor and unenhanced, the leftovers of all societies.

DE scientists altered DNA and genes with impunity for the next twenty years, creating perfect human Hubots. Unfortunately, nature never stops experimenting, and when the mutated genes met nature's response, billions of people began to die, which was the opening of the plan. The AI World Crystal knew this would happen.

The super-rich of the world were the first to die of a mysterious cancer, then it spread to the lower classes. In 2122, the United Nations Health Organization announced that without a cure the Western world was doomed.

A panicked search for a cure unified Western civilization. By December of 2122, the DE chief scientist, Professor Abraham Tracy, had announced China was free of the genetic defect and could save the Western world from extinction—"If they'd give up their genetic sovereignty and merge their pristine chemistry with the West."

The Chinese said no.

The second part of the plan: The West attacked China without provocation. The Chinese did not invade Japan as you were told. The War of Purification was fought to save the West, nothing more, and a billon Chinese died in an instant.

Shock! The West's Master Quantum was wrong! The

Chinese quantum was faster and smarter. The Chinese government survived and counterattacked. In an instant, Germany, France, England, Japan, Australia, and the US East and West Coasts were destroyed and 1.5 billion people died.

The West would lose the war unless something unthinkable happened: A human had to merge with the West's Master Crystal. He did, and the West won.

Today, in 2222, the poor, unenhanced forty million left out of the changes everyone else got are the last hope of humanity. Unless they rebel, a machine species will inherit Earth; a species that will not know living humans ever existed. That is the point of the 2220 government mandate that it alone could select candidates for natural birth, and this year, no one has been selected.

The plot is playing out.

The ultimate irony of my endless life to protect human nature against eternal life? I will be murdered by a machine that will last forever.

THIRTY-THREE
FEBRUARY 7, 2222

File: John Barber
Two Days to Live

I have always prepared for the eventuality of being discovered. Every one of my "residences" has been set on top of an abandoned wastewater sewer line leading to the Pacific Ocean. Those forgotten drains are big enough to accommodate a modified transportation pod. In my entire life, I have only used that underground network once, three days ago, and it took a miracle to save me.

I'm 234 years old today. Every seventy years, I began the legal process of creating a new identity. First, I liquidated my investments and secreted most of that newly acquired wealth in my hidden refuge in the hills of New Mexico.

To ensure I had enough credit vouchers to begin each new lifetime, I left one billion vouchers of inheritance to a child named in my last will and testament. Then I created an official death certificate to prevent an aggressive wealth collector or Security Server agent from questioning my station in life and good fortune.

Next, I selected a mid-America hospital, hacked into its database, and created a fictitious birth mother. After the appropriate nine months, the crystal-created birth mother delivered a healthy baby boy, complete with name and medical records. I never actually visited the hospital; everything was done electronically. Records were added to the hospital database and corresponding government agencies, substantiating my adoption.

Sixty years after my escape from the FBI in Reno, I retained my first law firm. I'd hire a new firm every thirty-five years; all were put on retainer and paid by my trust. They would coordinate and administer my affairs and protect me from legal jeopardy.

Understanding greed, human nature, and pride, I made sure the attorneys were/are all handsomely overpaid with the prospect of many years of future work.

My most valuable asset is the housekeeper. At the appropriate time, I would inform the current housekeeper that I'm leaving for an extensive trip and that I have adopted a young child. The child arrives several days after my departure. Nine months after my leave, the housekeeper is informed of my death.

I have survived because medical institutions do not kill their administrative mistakes, lawyers protect their clients, and mature adults love little children.

I had never lost a housekeeper until a Security Department agent, Captain Robert A. Davis, murdered Mrs. Pauling.

With each new lifetime, it was necessary to create an academic history. This was critical because it enabled me to position myself for employment in certain areas of science, academia, or government. In the early years of this odyssey, I would attend school and relive childhood, going on through graduate school, even though I retained my memory from one lifetime to another.

My school anonymity ended, though, because my twentieth-century characteristics were impossible to disguise. My spirit for adventure, curiosity, and awe of life is easily noticed. The lifeless demeanor of the general population is almost impossible to emulate, and every pair of eyes and all the street cameras are linked to the AI World Crystal database. Unfortunately, by my second lifetime, most children were implanted with the K chip, and I couldn't compete. However, like all Hubots, they know everything and understand nothing. Without the chip, they are helpless, and a side effect of the K chip is the elimination of curiosity.

Still, it became necessary to avoid attending school, and I was forced to create a false academic history for each new lifetime. I'd do it by invading an individual educational institution's crystal system and input my new identity, fashioned with an educational history. At first, it was difficult to hack the institution's crystal. However, as more children were linked to the Enlightened Intellect Enhancement System, hacking became unnecessary because crystal security was no longer a priority.

My one and only return to high school was painful. The fantasy of reliving those years and being equal with the girls proved disappointing. I was an adult, and they were not. Only a creep would enjoy that experience. I never returned.

I was reminded of a couple critical adolescent behaviors, though, and I am staking humanity's future on it: They dream of tomorrow, and they hate being lied to. The poor, unenhanced leftovers' rage will destroy the World Crystal.

THIRTY-FOUR

FEBRUARY 8, 2222

File: John Barber
One Day to Live

Though I am now physically and intellectually inferior, I have remained a twentieth-century man; I believe my human nature and imperfections are an advantage over the heartless logic of a database.

My last escape cost me dearly and was the closest I've come to being enslaved; yet, it restored my humanity.

Having foolishly been surprised by a Security Server agent's interview and subsequent invasion of my home, I did not have time to destroy all aspects of "me."

The Security Servers Medical Corps will find a speck of DNA, initiate the growth process at their Human Replicating Center, and create a mindless, soulless clone.

The AI database will begin to look for me within days of that engineering. They will flood every K chip with a fully developed likeness, complete with molecular sequencing, and accuse me of insidious crimes against the Family. Their sensors will track me on the wind, and they will find me.

Their discovery of me began with a coincidence; I received a thought message in my crystal. A Captain Robert A. Davis in the SSD—Security Servers Department—requested a meeting to discuss a failed robbery at the local wealth depository. I responded that I knew nothing about the theft and a meeting would be fruitless. I also instructed Captain Davis to present further questions to my lawyer. I ended the communication and thought the matter was over. I was wrong, very wrong.

Two hours later, Captain Davis was standing at my front door with two TXZ1000 Security Server androids demanding an audience. As I sat in my home office watching the confrontation between Captain Davis and my housekeeper, Mrs. Pauling, on my Security Window, a chill shook my shoulders. I should have acted right then.

Captain Davis refused to leave, and the more persistent the housekeeper became, the more aggressive he acted. It became obvious if I didn't intervene, this episode would turn violent and a simple mistake would lead to a bigger problem.

I paged the housekeeper and instructed her to let Captain Davis come in, but the two TXZ1000 machines had to stay outside. Captain Davis agreed, and the two machines posted themselves at the front doorstep.

Several moments later, I heard a soft knock on my private library/office door. Mrs. Pauling opened it.

"A Captain Davis from the Security Service office is here to see you," she said.

"Please let him in."

Captain Davis walked directly to the front of my desk. He said nothing; he simply looked at me. I instantly noted there was something different about this man.

He was in his late forties, six-three, a couple hundred pounds, dressed in the business fashion of the day: blue blazer, white silk shirt, pressed khaki slacks, and dark-blue wingtip shoes, looking like every other brash narcissist.

It was his eyes. They held curiosity and were alive, not cold like most Hubots. *He is more human than machine.* This person had been granted a freethinking mind engineered to solve crimes and maybe to catch a paradox.

He positioned himself perfectly at the center of the desk, his knees almost touching the desktop. He did not look at me; his eyes darted around the room, surveying every object.

"Looks like you could use a little mosquito spray," he said, looking up at the ceiling.

His voice was as uncommon as his eyes: It had tone, fluctuation, and, as I would soon hear, a deep, arrogant sarcasm.

"I'm here," he said while holding his head high and throwing his shoulders back, "to discuss a recent robbery of the Winchester Street Wealth Depository. We need your help explaining a paradox."

I listened to him with an amused sense of curiosity. "Before you begin, please sit," I said.

Captain Davis turned and glanced at the leather wing-back chair facing the desk and sat.

"Now, please continue."

He smiled. "Yesterday morning, an anti-Family denier robbed the Winchester Depository. We found his chemical markers and ran them through the Profile Center database. That criminal is now resting comfortably in our Education Hospital."

He smiled again. "We also found a fingerprint we could not identify, and there were no chemical markers attached to the print." He raised his eyebrows. "That has not happened in over one hundred years, and the World Crystal has never made a mistake. So we reviewed the Surveillance Observation Window, or SOW," he said with a smug expression.

He raised his eyebrows again and focused his eyes intently on my face.

He's searching for emotion, I thought.

"The analysis by the SOW told us the fingerprint originated where you rested your right hand while waiting to go into your wealth vault. To our dismay, your fingerprint did not match the fingerprint we discovered. Which is odd, considering the placement of your hand covered the mystery print perfectly."

He smiled and wet his lips with his blunt pink tongue. "We're trying to understand this lack of harmony. Your standing in the World Community is without blemish. We also audited your personal wealth standing—again, outstanding. With the results of those two investigations, we absolved you of any complicity in the crime and were about to let the issue rest."

Another smug expression covered his face. "I couldn't let those incongruities go; I hate a mystery. So, to solve this problem, I sent the mystery print to the World Crystal archive, and something even more puzzling turned up. It seems that a print, matching the one your hand covered, was used to register a wealth account at another institution more than a hundred fifty years ago." His facial expression grew into a broad smile. He paused, trying to build suspense. "That's too incredible for words, isn't it?"

Davis again paused and leaned forward in the chair and stared at me.

Is this possible? Then it hit me. Yes, when I started my second lifetime, I opened my first wealth account, and used my real fingerprints.

"So what's your point, Mr. Davis? That I'm over two hundred years old?" I asked, maintaining a cold, uninterested composure.

Davis leaned back in the chair, crossed his right leg. "Well, sir, that is why I'm here. We first thought our crystal must contain a bad datapoint. We even created a holographic image of the two prints to see if they matched: They were a perfect copy, and that wasn't possible." He smiled. "And that's where it got very interesting."

He stood suddenly and walked aggressively toward my desk.

I did not react.

Just as suddenly, he returned to the leather chair, sat, leaned back, and crossed his legs as before. "We've learned a lot about you, Mr. Barber. We've learned you were an orphan, and were adopted by an orphan, and he was an orphan, and he was adopted by an orphan. It appears that you come from the longest line of orphans in the history of the world." He smiled, lifted his eyebrows, and again searched my face for reaction. "The only glitch to my theory is that every one of your ancestors had different fingerprints and birth certificates."

Davis shook his head, confused. "I still felt something was off. To my amazement, I was right. After analyzing photographs of your family," he paused, "I saw that you all look alike." His eyes popped wide open for effect. "Exactly alike." His voice hit a quick, high-pitched tone. He raised his eyebrows and feigned a surprised expression.

What an asshole, I thought.

"With your photo in hand, we ran it through a search of our Wealth Security Windows database. Guessing, we ran it as far back as a hundred and fifty years. To our surprise—and I must add, joy—your likeness appears in at least one of those depositories every year."

He leaned back in his chair, enjoying every word. "There're bets among my staff that we'd find your likeness as far back as the nineteen nineties."

"Captain Davis, I am enjoying this, almost as much as you seem to be, so I'll play along. How old do you think I am?"

"Well."

"Mr. Davis, I'll tell you what I believe. I believe you and your crystal wizards are venturing down a dangerous road. I think you'd be better served to reserve your conclusions, or I'll be forced to send several thought messages to my lawyers and your superiors."

Davis looked at me for a moment before speaking. When he did, his tone was threatening. "We know you have powerful connections; however, I don't think they'll be much help. I haven't mentioned a small detail: A former United States government official claimed a scientist under his protection at the government facility called Genetic Answer had discovered a formula stopping the aging process. I believe that person is quite familiar to you, since he was your mentor and friend: FBI Director Tyler Leggett."

Smith got up from the chair and stood straight, almost at attention. "Now, sir, to specifically answer your question, yes, I do believe you're two hundred fifty years old, and"—he buttoned his middle coat button, puffed out his chest—"you are Doctor John W. Barber."

His arrogance was palpable. *And he's an idiot who can't add. I was born in nineteen eighty-eight. It's twenty-two twenty-two. I'm two hundred thirty-four years old.* "If your detective work is as good as your math, I'd go back to boot camp."

Davis flared his nostrils and lifted his chin, realizing his stupid mistake. "Before I do what we both know I must"—he moved closer to the desk—"I want you to know this is a personal honor, Doctor Barber. I'm the last in a long line of executive investigators who have spent part of their careers pursuing the fantasy of your existence." His voice was soft and respectful.

"Someone from my agency has been looking for you since your disappearance. As the head of that illustrious family of investigators, I chose to conduct this interview and personally guide you to our headquarters. I did not think it appropriate to grant the SS machines the honor of apprehending the Eternal Man."

I wondered, *Why are they so afraid of me?*

The smug look returned to his face. "I know this will not help your situation, but I must tell you, my retirement's in three weeks and the agency is being eliminated. I'm the last chief investigator." He placed a slight smirk on his face. "Life is not fair, Doctor Barber; it was not until that unrecorded fingerprint appeared that I believed you existed. It's a real twist of bad luck: The one day you don't wear your fake fingerprints, there's an unrelated altercation, which leads us to solving the greatest mystery of this or any other age. Three weeks before I retire. Shit luck, wouldn't you say?" Davis pulled his shoulders back and puffed out his chest. "It's time,

Doctor Barber—enough of my admiration and pleasure. It's time for us to go."

Suddenly, Davis' facial expression changed. "It's a hologram!" he screamed.

Seconds after my hologram image froze, I was locked tightly inside my emergency transportation pod and traveling at two hundred miles an hour out of the district. I watched on the pod's crystal window as Captain Davis' expression turned to surprise, and I heard his shocked gasp of air.

He tapped his right temple with his index finger, activating his communication chip. "Doctor John W. Barber is on the run. Activate particle sweeps throughout the district. Close all pod hubs and transportation centers."

As Davis was barking out orders, my house began to shake violently, and with one terrible shudder, the entire structure dropped one full story below the ground, setting off a series of small explosions underneath the building, sealing the now-vacant escape tunnel.

I watched Davis pick himself up from the floor and shout in a panic-filled voice while he climbed up the crumbling wall toward the front door. "No one is allowed to leave this sector until we've done a particle scan—no one! Have the Molecular Unit sent to Barber's house and notify the Fire Servers! Incendiary devices have been activated and the property is burning."

The last words I heard him say were, "Activate the district—"

A chill raced through my body. If he finished that sentence, I was dead.

My escape pod had been modified many years before for such an emergency. It was constructed out of Hyperlite, an exotic aluminum, and encased by a high-energy-free electron ion field, making it invisible to NiDAR waves and thermal ultraviolet scanners.

The pod was large enough to hold me and fit through the drainage pipes and gullies. It raced autonomously through the abandoned subterranean drainage system to the district boundary a mile and a half away and to freedom. The only aspect of the pod that I controlled was the destination and speed. My right hand fingers were white from squeezing the accelerator and propelling the pod past its rational limits.

The pod raced seemingly out of control through the jet-black, empty wastewater as it ricocheted off the walls and boulders with such force the tunnel collapsed behind me.

Sweat ran down my face, my heart raced with fear, and time slowed as I watched the end of the boundary and tunnel approach in slow motion.

I prayed the hologram and explosive fire would grant me the thirty seconds necessary to reach the border. I knew if Davis got the particle sweep and mobility field activated in time, the field would lock on to the pod as I passed through the boundary and freeze me in place, with no hope of escape.

I stared at the pod's odometer and chronometer, watching the seconds pass.

"I stayed too long. Five seconds!" I shouted.

Suddenly, horror and terrifying panic took my breath.

"Four seconds! Three more seconds. Please, please, please."

Just ahead, a small pinprick of light—*It's still white, not red. I have a chance. I'm almost there. The boundary marker, one second!*

Suddenly, a flash of red light enveloped the pod. The mobility barrier had turned on.

"No no! I'm trapped."

The pod crashed into the plasma wall, and everything went dark. For an instant, time stopped. The pod froze in midair, then, with a violent lurching motion, it shot forward and blasted through the energy barricade.

I was numb with shock. "I-I-I made it, but how? I should have been caught."

Elation and weakness flashed through my chest.

"I've made it. I have a chance—a chance!" I shouted.

The pod continued speeding to its programmed destination.

Exhausted, I released my grip on the accelerator paddle, closed my eyes, and thought about the certain hell I had avoided.

There was no way to explain what had happened. Then I remembered: the car accident racing to pick up Lynn and Abby at school and the slide toward the trees two-plus centuries ago. *I should have died then and now I should be a prisoner. What is protecting me?*

THIRTY-FIVE
FEBRUARY 9, 2222

File: John Barber
Twelve Hours to Live

The pod exited the wastewater tunnel and splashed into the Pacific Ocean to follow the sea floor to the continental shelf. Once it was in a thousand feet of water, the pod turned south toward the Gulf of Mexico and La Media Luna, Mexico.

Critical to my escape and future was that Captain Davis wouldn't discover the micro-XP-LiDAR Mosquito camera that had attached to his clothing while he sat in my leather chair. That camera would give me an exact three-dimensional holographic view of every place Davis went, and I'd hear everything he said. Of all my inventions, this singular one could save my life.

Captain Davis could only tell an unhappy Executive

Safety Committee about his speculation, and failure, without hard evidence. *Davis is in a lot of trouble.* Maybe his retirement would come a little earlier.

I chuckled at the thought. *What an arrogant ass he is.*

A smile lifted my cheeks as I thought about the smug Captain Davis losing his grip on the world's greatest enigma.

Even though they knew how I'd transferred my identity, I hoped they didn't have my chemical makeup and wouldn't be able to perform a molecular search on newborns; they'd only screen orphans, and that's how I'd beat them: I would change places with a child who had birth parents.

And all I need is six hours to create a new family tree.

I glanced down at the control panel and double-checked the navigation headings to the La Media Luna Birthing Hospital's sewer system.

After a moment of watching the water pass by, I leaned my head back against the headrest and closed my eyes. I would need every ounce of strength to endure the rapid rejuvenation coming.

Five hours later, I reached the Luna Birthing Hospital sewer system exit ladder. The pod's motor shut down, and a soft bell sounded, announcing my arrival. After double-checking the location coordinates, I programmed a new destination and self-destruct sequence into the onboard crystal. Next, I set the XP-LiDAR Omni view to observe the above-ground hospital parking lot and surrounding area.

One hour, I thought, *that should be enough time.* If I didn't return, the pod would race out to the Pacific Ocean and self-destruct in the Socorro Trench.

Sitting in the pod, waiting for morning light, I watched the dark, unchanging scene above ground. I was nervous about what had to come next. I closed my eyes for what seemed a moment, then suddenly the orange tip of the sun appeared over the eastern horizon on the screen.

It was time.

I climbed the damp sewer ladder leading to the parking lot above and lifted the edge of the sewer cover, seeing only an empty parking lot. I slid the iron lid to the side and climbed out. After replacing the lid, I casually walked toward the gray, three-story, nine-thousand-square foot hospital.

I was unconcerned about being recorded. This hospital was a hundred years old and built before the last war; the AI cameras linked to the World Crystal database had never been installed and anonymity could come and go. It was the last hospital in Mexico that performed live births for the poor.

I entered the dilapidated building through the main entrance. The lobby was quiet and looked run-down and outdated. The paint was peeling, with cracks running along the walls. The only sounds came from my steps on the plastic-covered hallway floor. The hospital was obsolete. Its sole purpose was the fading responsibility to care for the poor, the unaugmented deniers, and their natural childbirths.

Two medical androids and one executive crystal performed all prenatal and postnatal procedures. I was sure I was the only adult human in the facility. At the transport lift, I hit the call button and was soon transported up to the third-floor Maternity Center.

The lift stopped, and I walked halfway down the long, empty, undecorated, lifeless hallway looking for the birthing nursery. On my left was the observation window and doorway to the nursery. I entered an odorless, dated, and cold room.

I worked my way around the nursery to get my bearings. There was nothing clean about the room. A dull white light filled the room, emanating from the walls, floor, and ceiling. There were two rows of glass incubators in the center.

Two medical androids stood at the back wall, facing the incubators. I saw an emergency oxygen tank, assorted hoses, respiratory equipment, and a crystal with a fifty-inch, outdated holographic window on the same wall. In the corner was a three-foot-tall medical incinerator and a round four-foot-tall nonmedical trash can. A miniature surgical robot, containing specialized molecular repair cells, rested on the hanging drug shelf in the center of the room.

I walked to the two rows of incubation chambers; only three of the six contained newborns. I initiated the digital medical charts on each incubator and learned that two of the chambers contained boys, the third a girl.

One boy was of Latin descent; the other two children were Caucasian. I activated the information panel on the boys' chambers to learn what enhancements had been implanted and, most important, when they were scheduled to leave the hospital.

Perfect, I thought, reading the Caucasian boy's bio. He was scheduled to be released tomorrow morning at 6:00 a.m., with no enhancements. The other boy's parents were dead and a relative would not arrive for several days.

What's one life? I thought, looking at the Caucasian boy. *One life to protect me, just one life.*

I opened the child's incubator and gently picked up the sleeping baby, not wanting to wake him. I carried him cradled in my arms to the medical incinerator on the back wall. The main viewing window was on my right as I walked across the room.

Suddenly, I heard the transportation lift door open and

sounds of movement coming down the hallway toward the Maternity Center.

"Shit," I whispered.

Panicked, I ran back to the child's crib and placed him in it, closed the lid, and looked for escape. There wasn't enough time to reach the side door.

Trapped.

I raced to the aluminum trash container. It was empty, and I climbed inside and closed the lid as the hallway door opened. Terrified, I held my breath.

I heard footsteps come near the incubators. Pushing the lid up just a bit, I managed a quick glimpse out. To my horror, a medical android accompanied by a fully armored SS machine was moving toward the incubators.

Oh God, I thought. *If they've got my molecular makeup, the SS machine will instantly know I'm in the room and where to look.*

With the amount of armor the SS machine was wearing, I was dead. The SS machine was not equipped to capture; its mission was to kill. Captain Davis and his superiors were no longer interested in interviewing me. The game had changed.

The android pointed the SS machine to a specific crib. The SS machine lifted the glass lid and aggressively picked the baby up by its head, holding it above the crib. The medical android stabbed a termination wand into the child's abdomen. The baby screamed out in pain and then went limp.

After a moment, the SS machine turned to face the android and asked in a flat, emotionless voice, "Any other orphans?"

"No."

The SS machine, still holding the dead baby by the top of

its head, dropped it onto the floor and left the room. The android picked up the body, walked to the back wall, and dropped it into the incinerator, closed the lid, activated the machine, and left the room.

My heart was pounding. I took a deep breath and thought, *They don't have my molecular signature. I've got time.*

I waited five minutes before climbing out of the metal trash can and creeping to the hallway door. I opened it to glance down the hallway toward the transport lift: empty.

I quickly returned to the other child's crib, opened the glass case, gently picked the baby up, and ran to the incinerator. I opened the device. The child awoke and started to cry, building into a scream. I placed my left hand over his mouth and the other around his tiny throat and squeezed.

I need this thing; it's already a slave, I thought.

Suddenly, a popping sound came from the hallway. I glanced at the front observation window and saw my reflection: It was sickening. My face was monstrous, muscles twitching, teeth clenched, lips curled tight, eyes filled with hate, and I was leaning over an incinerator, choking a baby to death. I was ugly, wicked.

At that moment, I realized what a soulless animal I had become. Centuries of fear, arrogance, and regret had transformed me into a coward. I loosened my grip and watched as the semiconscious, purple-faced baby regained life.

I felt something odd in my chest, a feeling I hardly recognized: relief. The baby started to cry, more a weak whimper as it struggled for air.

Though it was barely human, it did not deserve to die as a convenience, I mused.

A deep shudder of realization shook my shoulders, as I

looked at my reflection in the window again. The sight of what I had become almost dropped me to my knees. I felt sick to my stomach.

I'm evil, no different from them, no longer a human.

I cradled the shaking child in my arms and blew air into his empty lungs. I watched as blood rushed back into his tiny head. After a moment, the joyful sounds of a cry grew into a scream. With each shade of color returning to the baby's face, I also felt a growing sense of life.

I returned the child to its glass incubator, bent down, and kissed its forehead. "Thank you."

I closed the incubator and left the hospital.

I walked outside. The dry morning air was warm. I looked up into the clear sky and again thought: *What a coward I've become.*

I opened the sewer cap and climbed down the slimy, rust-covered ladder. I stood for a moment, looking at the pod. My mind was blank, still in shock. I opened the top and got in. I sat there for several minutes thinking about my life. A great sadness of sorrow so deep I could hardly breathe engulfed me —a pain not felt since I had left Megan and the girls.

"I almost killed a baby."

Frankenstein's monster was driven by fear. *I am no different.*

Tears welled in my eyes. I sobbed, guilt-ridden by centuries of loveless fear.

Suddenly, I felt sick to my stomach. I quickly stood and vomited away from the pod controls. Weak, I sat back down and closed my eyes. After several minutes of self-pity, I regained my composure and initiated the guidance system to my New Mexico sanctuary. The pod lifted and whirred forward, gaining speed with every second.

I had to make amends for my pathetic life. I was done hiding, and when they found me and attacked, I'd fight with hope and in a way they'd never expect from a helpless coward.

THIRTY-SIX

FEBRUARY 9, 2222

File: John Barber
Six Hours to Live

The pod suddenly slowed and stopped.

I opened my eyes and looked out the windshield to see a rugged, dry hillside. The pod was hovering five thousand feet above a deep, rocky canyon floor, facing a barren mountain-top. Momentarily disoriented by the reflection of light off the canyon walls, I realized I'd lost track of time and was surprised to have arrived so quickly. I glanced at the clock: Four hours had passed. *Must've fallen asleep.*

I checked the pod's stealth/scanning displays to assure myself I had not been tracked.

It was safe.

I initiated the shelter's opening sequence. The pod lowered into the canyon and stopped at the canyon floor; it only took a few seconds for the cave to appear. The pod drifted toward the opening and silently passed into the mile-long dark tunnel. The hillside closed in behind, concealing any trace of the cave.

The pod drifted through the black cavern for several seconds before the security lasers reactivated. A bright, white light snapped on, detailing the raw stone walls along the tunnel. The recycled and purified atmosphere had been activated.

After five minutes of slowly drifting forward, the pod came gently to a rest in front of a seven-foot-tall, vintage wooden front door, complete with brass knocker, doorknob, and a welcome mat.

I sat in the pod, thinking, *How do I defeat pure knowledge?*

My thoughts were confused and wandered. *How do I fight? What should I do?* I remembered the quote from a play by Edward Bulwer-Lytton: *"The pen is mightier than the sword." Can I live, can I escape?* I thought of Houdini, the master magician.

How do I tell my story—the misery of living forever, a witness to the death of anonymity, pursuing Paradise, hate, the plot to breed humanity into extinction? I must tell the adolescent have-nots and the Hubots what I've seen. Will they care? Why would they believe me? Why?

There was only one way: My story must come from a thought message, and there was only one message they would believe—one that came from the World Crystal. *But how? A fool's errand to steal the witch's broom.* I rubbed my hand through my hair. *I must meet Death face to face.*

I opened the pod's hatch, exited, and walked to the richly varnished mahogany front door facing the pod, grabbed the large brass door knocker. I smiled. This act always brought joy. I tapped it twice against the heavy door. It gave me pleasure to relive an ancient custom. Plus, if the door was opened without knocking, the entire mountain would explode in one magnificent fireball.

The mahogany door opened automatically. I took a few steps forward into the transportation lift, got in, and the blast door closed instantly behind me.

"Safe room," I instructed.

The back of the lift opened. I walked into a warm, plain, two-hundred-square-foot office setting. Three holographic windows snapped on. An Egyptian throw rug covered the maplewood floors, and a weapons case stood to the right of the transportation lift door.

A six-drawer wooden desk and leather chair with side table faced the doorway. A photonic time crystal workstation sat on the desk. Next to it was a photograph of Megan, the girls, and Ty.

Next to the desk was a cold box filled with bottled water. A three-by-four-foot metal worktable and two chairs filled the remaining space.

The room was built to facilitate an escape from the main living facility five thousand feet above it. It and the transportation shaft deflected the most advanced X2-LiDAR ultraviolet energy waves and appeared as solid rock.

The living facility at the top of the mountain was not built or designed for concealment. If discovered, I wanted the World Crystal overseers to believe there was no escape.

I sat at the desk. "Crystal on. Open John Barber. Activate Megan Barber."

"Good afternoon, John," it replied in Megan's voice. "There is a day-old thought message from Captain Robert A. Davis, SSD: 'All birthing wards are to be searched and any male newborn orphans are to be terminated.'"

I sat back in the chair. *Yes, the game has changed. How do I defeat a machine that knows everything and understands nothing?*

I began to sweat. "There's no hope."

"There is always hope, John," Megan's voice answered.

"Not if they catch me."

"Don't let them."

"Megan, where is the World Crystal housed?"

"There is no current record of its location. The last reported location was San Francisco during the twenty-one ninety-seven moon crisis twenty-five years ago."

I could see five thousand miles in every direction from this room and, with a single voice command, invade any star satellite or crystal system in the universe. So why couldn't I find the World Crystal?

I stood up and walked around the room, thinking. *How do I find and defeat it?*

"Know the enemy," I said, quoting Chinese military strategist Sun Tzu.

I went back to the desk. "Megan, how many humans have been implanted with the K chip?"

"The Earth's population is four billion and shrinking. You are the only person who has not been implanted with the K chip," she answered.

I rubbed my hand through my hair. *How could any parent say no?*

"What percentage of humans are Hubots?"

"It is difficult to calculate an accurate percentage; only

poor newborns are not enhanced at birth, and that population is dwindling. My best estimate is ninety-nine percent are Hubots, as you call them, more machine than human."

"It's true; the end is almost here," I whispered.

I leaned back deeper into the chair, rubbed my hand through my hair, shocked by the revelation.

"Has the K chip been modified to control people?"

"No, the K chip can only receive a thought message, answer questions, or give directions."

"What is a thought message?"

"It is an instant notification sent to specific K chips by a local crystal."

"Does the MQC ever send such a message?"

"No. Only a local crystal will send a message."

"What about the War of Purification and moon crisis messages?"

"Those messages were sent by the Military Intelligence Network Design System. Acronym: MINDS."

"Explain."

"There have only been two such messages ever sent. First was General Benjamin Marble, who was the supreme military commander for the West in the War of Purification, and its greatest hero. He is credited with defeating the Chinese when all hope was lost by linking his brain to MINDS. It was reasoned that his human intuition added to the infallibility of the World Crystal and would win the war.

"General Marble became the first human to link his brain with a crystal. General Marble died after the war from complications to remove the crystal implant.

"Next was Professor Elizabeth Friendly, a genius equal to Albert Einstein. She discovered the cause of gravity in twenty-one eighty-five, which led to antigravity propulsion, space-warping, transportation pods, and interplanetary travel. A global extinction event developed when an explosion on the moon dramatically altered its orbit. Professor Friendly joined with MINDS to solve the problem and return the moon to its correct position in relation to Earth. Professor Friendly succeeded in saving Earth; she died soon after when her transportation pod malfunctioned and exploded.

"A year after Professor Friendly's death, the World Crystal mandated that all newborn children be enhanced with a contraceptive protein and that the United Nations Crystal Center Plaza would be off-limits to all nonessential persons. There are no additional records of messages from MINDS or humans linking with MINDS."

"What's the difference between a thought message and a MINDS message?"

"At the end of a thought message, there is a moniker listing its source. MINDS has no such moniker."

My crystal made a loud *Ping!* and then a holographic window with my picture and description appeared above my desk.

Megan read the message: "Doctor John W. Barber is wanted for the murder of Doctor Gloria Gysin and crimes against the World Family. He is armed and dangerous. Do not approach. Notify me or the nearest TXZ1000 Security Server if you see him."

I was not surprised. *Know your enemy.*

Megan continued on to read the moniker: "Captain Robert A. Davis, Security Servers Headquarters, San Francisco."

I sat back into my chair. "Megan, initiate XP-LiDAR Mosquito camera on Captain Davis. It's time to see what he's doing."

A new holographic window appeared in front of my desk, and before me was a three-dimensional view of Captain Robert A. Davis walking along a busy San Francisco street. I recognized the location: He was on Grove Street headed toward Polk.

With my Mosquito, I could see, hear, and smell everything in its view.

I smiled. Davis' clothes were still covered with black soot and smelled of smoke from my house fire. I leaned over, opened the refrigerator, got myself a twelve-ounce bottle of water, and took a long swallow.

After several minutes, Captain Davis reached the World Family Building. The Council chambers were housed on the top floor. I remembered it had once been the City of San Francisco's County Health Department Building. Now it was a hundred-story edifice housing the World Family headquarters.

Davis skipped up the grand stairs to the front entrance. The glass-and-metal doors were closed and guarded by three heavily armed SS machines. When Davis reached the entrance, he was directed by the closest SS android to "Enter and take the official-use-only transportation tube on the left, Captain Davis. It will take you directly to the Council chambers."

Davis got into the glass box. After only a few seconds of movement, the doors opened, and he walked into a four-thousand-square-foot auditorium a hundred stories above the lobby. The room was filled with five hundred permanent, empty seats facing a sixty-foot long, five-foot-tall marble dais.

I heard him take a deep breath as he moved into the chamber. Davis glanced at his watch: 2:00 p.m. Davis whispered, "This is going to be brutal."

He walked along the corridor to the front of the room. The floor was polished, spotless aluminum. A circle of solid gold, with enough room for one person to stand on, was up ahead in the center of the corridor between the two front-row seats.

Davis stopped when he reached the gold seal, about ten feet short of the dais. Sitting before him was the Supreme Court justice and two black-robed Hubots.

He cringed his shoulders as he stood in silence.

With great pleasure, I watched the three hours of endless hindsight and condemnation directed at Davis.

"Captain Davis," the justice said at the conclusion, "we will not tolerate any further failures. If you were not the last chief investigator, you would be replaced. Doctor Barber is an inferior, weak, and hopelessly unenlightened creature. His only significance is the potential to lead the nonbelievers, and that will not be tolerated. Barber is the last great threat left on Earth. Do you understand me, Mr.—"

Suddenly, the justice stopped speaking. His eyes glazed over. Then: "Captain Davis, you are directed to report to the United Nations Crystal Center Plaza at six-thirty p.m. tonight. You are dismissed."

That's why they're so afraid of me? I have no intention of leading.

I watched Davis leave the interrogation auditorium and go to the transportation lift. When the doors closed behind him, Davis said in a firm, angry voice, "I'll find you and kill you, Doctor John W. Barber."

I watched Davis almost run back to his nondescript office two blocks away. He skipped up the steps into the building off Van Ness Avenue and went without hesitation to his ground-floor office. He sat at his desk and glanced up at the holographic digital clock on the wall: 5:20 p.m.

He smiled. "I have time."

I watched Davis open the World Crystal investigation link and download the findings from the physical investigation of my house into the holographic window facing his desk. As the information was downloading, Davis slammed his fist against the ceramic desk. "No molecular traces," he spat out.

After reading more results, Davis flipped his right hand at the hologram, moving the report ahead to the results of my housekeeper's mind probe. "Nothing," Davis said.

"Bastards," I growled through clenched teeth as I leaned forward to read about Mrs. Pauling's death.

Davis glanced up at the clock again: 6:00 p.m. He tapped his communication implant and confirmed the 6:30 p.m. meeting at the UNCCP. He then issued a second thought message about the manhunt for Doctor John W. Barber.

It read: DOCTOR JOHN BARBER WAS LAST DETECTED HEADING TOWARD THE PACIFIC OCEAN IN A CUSTOM POD. Included in the message was my voice and a memory photo from the dead housekeeper's brain.

I watched Davis send a second message to the TXZ1000 Security Service, placing a security lock on interplanetary travel, mandating that travelers undergo a bio scan detailing their augmentations. Last, he ended the communication with a final notation to the TXZ1000 SS force: DOCTOR BARBER IS TO BE TERMINATED ON SIGHT.

Finished, Davis leaned back in his chair and smiled. He glanced up at the clock. "It's time," he said.

Looking excited, Davis jumped to his feet and hurried out of his office.

I wondered why he'd been ordered to the United Nations Crystal Center Plaza as I watched him run off to his 6:30 meeting.

Davis exited his office building, then passed through the garden quad to the back door of the two-story building on Hayes Street. When he arrived at the United Nations Crystal Center Plaza, he was confronted by two heavily armed TXZ1000 Security Service machines.

"Follow us," one machine said.

He followed them into the center of the ground floor and the molecular scanner. The SS machines stopped.

"Walk through," one said, pointing at the circular glass casing.

Davis took a breath and walked into a circular ten-foot-high cup; he passed inspection. Two SS machines were standing on the other side of the molecular scanning cup. When he exited, they escorted Davis to the central transporter lift against the far wall.

The thick, solid aluminum door opened. Davis, alone, hesitated, but after a quick breath, he ventured in. The box instantly went black, and the back wall opened. Davis jumped out into a small, dimly lit room that could not have been over twenty square feet.

I stood up from my desk, mesmerized by what I was watching. I could feel the cold room temperature through the holographic window as Davis walked deeper into the dim, empty room, devoid of any essence of life, art, comfort, or humanity. The floor was pristine polished aluminum; the walls were covered with Security Windows displaying live images of the known universe. The room was without sound, nary a whisper or hum, except for Davis' hollow footsteps as he walked deeper into the room.

I sensed fear. Davis was turning his head, twisting his shoulders to look behind, and his shoulders shook like he was chilled.

The deeper Davis moved to the center of the room, the colder the air felt.

There was another transporter in the center of the room; its door open. Davis stood, looking at the cylindrical gold tube. He turned a full circle, looking for anyone. Afraid, he hesitated before going in. Once he did, the door snapped shut, and the small, tube-like coffin suddenly went dead black. A thick, impenetrable darkness filled the coffin-sized box.

At first, I thought the window had broken, except I could hear his terrified breathing become rapid and shallow. Suddenly, he made a sound like inhaling a gasp of air with the words: "I'm floating!" He was about to panic when the door snapped back open.

Standing in the doorway was a Hubot different from any I had ever seen. It looked totally human. It smiled with perfect white teeth; its skin was smooth and flawless. Its dress was casual and tailored to fit a female body. It gestured for Davis to follow.

Davis froze in place, looking stunned. He stared at the lifelike Hubot.

"Welcome, Captain Davis. Please follow me," she said in a warm, friendly, soft voice.

Davis did not move. "There must be a mistake. I want to leave," he said, clearly afraid.

The machine turned and walked away.

Davis hesitated, then followed. He jogged a few yards to catch up. "Who are you and where are we going?"

No reply.

After several minutes of walking deeper into the dim room, an eerie silence had enveloped Davis. I could no longer hear Davis' steps or the Hubot's movement. Davis and the Hubot reached another transporter, this one guarded by a similar-looking human Hubot, except it wore a munitions belt and carried an SS side weapon. The transporter door opened when Davis got there.

"Get in, Captain Davis," the second Hubot said in an aggressive male voice.

"I'm very uncomfortable. Where are you taking me?"

"Get in now, Mr. Davis," the second Hubot said.

Davis walked through the half-domed opening. The door slid shut, and Davis gasped, "Dropping."

He pressed his hands against the side walls of the lift.

I glanced at the hologram window timer; Davis had been in the lift for two minutes. *Where are they taking him?*

Davis stared ahead, his breathing again shallow and heavy. His face displayed all the signs of fear and panic. Suddenly, the door opened, and the room he was facing before him was bright and well lit.

He got out. The room was empty and lifeless, again. I could feel a coldness coming from the hologram. The room looked like a hundred-square-foot metal box.

Davis called out, "Hello?"

As the word left his lips, the metal box disappeared with a loud smacking sound, any trace of light gone as well.

I could see no more than Davis in the jet-black darkness, but I could hear his rapid breathing. Could feel his fear.

Davis did not move.

I stood and walked to the window, my eyes bouncing back and forth, searching for any sign of light or life—shocked and with adrenaline filling my veins when Davis screamed, "Help!"

And then, out of the dark: "Step forward and exit the transporter, Mr. Davis," the pleasant-sounding female voice ordered, seeming to come from inside the lift.

Davis stepped forward into the darkness. I stood as close to the holographic window as possible, turning my head, hoping to see any light, but saw only blackness. *A blind person's blackness*, I thought with the creeps.

Suddenly, a pale-blue light switched on in front of Davis, a dot of light barely breaking the darkness.

"Who's there?" Davis shouted.

An odd, high-pitched, mechanical voice said, "You are here, Captain Davis. Go to the blue light."

I quickly moved to my crystal work station.

"Megan," I said, "initiate Mosquito Holographic program."

I watched the tiny Mosquito attached to the back of Davis' pant leg drop to the floor and divide itself into six equal parts.

Suddenly, my room was transformed into a complete, exact holographic copy of the room Davis was standing in. I got up from my chair, moved away from the desk. I entered the holographic image and stood next to Davis. I turned my body around in a circle, looking at everything in the room. It was empty, black all around but for the speck of blue light.

Davis moved timidly forward to the light. I followed, studying his eyes and the room with each step.

The closer we got to the blue light, the brighter it became.

After walking several yards, I saw something in front of me under the blue dot of light. I did not recognize the object. Davis continued his small steps closer to the object, and as he did, the room felt even colder.

I turned and looked behind him and noted an impenetrable darkness following his every step forward. I got closer to the blackness. I felt a chill of fear. *There would be no escape from that prison.*

"Megan, what is that black shroud following Davis?"

"That is the Wall of Deprivation. It was invented by the Chinese to guard the Great Hall of the Peoples during the last war. It absorbs all light, heat, breezes, and sound. Humans can't see or feel anything within its confines. Any machine that enters loses all communication and sense of direction, becoming trapped. Once inside, a human will go insane and die. It was outlawed by the United Nations after the war and supposedly destroyed."

I turned and resumed my forward march with Davis.

After another minute of walking, I could see an object below the pale light; it was about the size of a shoebox. We moved closer, and I could now make out a hexagonal, crystal/glass-looking object in the center of the room, hovering five feet above the floor.

We continued forward, and within three feet of the object, a female voice called out, "Stop."

Davis froze in place and looked at the surreal object floating in the air in front of him. I continued and walked around the object.

Suddenly, it came to me. I recognized what it was, and couldn't believe it: the fabled and supposedly mythological Jovan Safe.

"Megan, tell me about the Jovan Safe."

"It's an ancient device discovered by space miners in twenty-one ninety-five while mining for diamonds on the 16 Psyche asteroid. A miner discovered a partially destroyed alien spacecraft while she was digging on the asteroid. After an exhaustive analysis of the spacecraft by the World Space Force, it was determined the ship was less advanced than those on Earth. It contained no records or clues of who or what had built it. The only interesting aspect of the craft was its age: one hundred million years old. Other than that fact, the craft was of little value, except for one unique item found aboard: a safe—an alien lockbox about the size of a handbag.

"It was named the Jovan Safe after the woman who'd found it. Science never determined what the safe was made of or how it worked. As a matter of fact, they felt if the object had not been unlocked and opened at discovery with the codes and instructions inside, it would have never been unlocked. It took the most advanced quantum crystal four months to translate the instructions. The object was delivered to Earth the year of its discovery and said to have been accidentally destroyed in a laboratory explosion."

Suddenly, my attention was drawn back to Davis when I heard him take a deep breath. I turned to look; he was still facing the alien box. Then I saw the slight glow of energy particles surrounding the box. *A protective field?* I moved closer to the box and walked around it; nothing interesting to see, though. I turned again to look at Davis, who appeared too frightened to move. After several moments, a Security Window appeared to our right.

"Captain Davis, go to the window and download your professional authorization codes," the female voice said.

Davis went to the Security Window and tapped his right temple.

Written operating instructions appeared above the Jovan Safe.

Davis walked back to the safe and read out loud, "Twenty-two, alpha, zero, Omi, zero, zero, nine," followed by a word I had never heard before, "Zinzqeskoups. Omi, Omi, nine, one."

When he uttered the final number, the surreal-looking multicolored field disappeared soundlessly, along with the safe itself, replaced by a black dot floating in front of Davis, nothing more than a jet-black, flat spot about the size of a baseball—no top, bottom, sides, or back ... just a perfect black spot suspended before us.

I walked completely around the object. It was fascinating: a flat dot of nothing else.

I returned to Davis. Fear had left his face, replaced by curiosity.

"Touch the dot with your right hand, Captain Davis," the female voice said.

Davis moved closer to the black dot, reached his right hand forward with his fingers extended to touch it. A look of utter surprise crossed his face as his hand was gently pulled inside the void.

I moved forward and put my face next to Davis' hand. I saw nothing as he poked his hand and arm into the blackness and disappear.

"It's cold," he said, sounding fearful.

When his elbow reached the edge of the object, the forward motion stopped.

"Something is touching my finger." Davis' face again showed fear.

After a second, Davis withdrew his arm from the black void. With his hand free, he brought it closer to his face and looked at his index finger: The palm-side tip was covered with a glistening drop of a mercury-looking liquid. He studied the drop with childlike amazement on his face. He turned and looked at the Security Window across the room and then looked back at his finger. His expression this time was one of sheer awe.

Suddenly, the female voice said, "Repeat the commands, Captain Davis."

Davis looked up and again read out loud, "Twenty-two, alpha, zero, Omi, zero, zero, nine, Zinzqeskoups. Omi, Omi, nine, one."

To my amazement, the black void vanished, and the beautifully colored force field and its box reappeared, looking exactly as before.

Holding his right hand near his chest, his palm facing up, Davis carefully turned to leave the room.

"Stop. Place your index finger on your right temple and press the liquid into your memory chip."

Davis froze, and fear flashed across his face. I could almost hear his heart racing. He began to sweat. Davis took a deep breath and looked at the glistening drop on his finger.

"Now, Captain Davis," she said.

He lifted his hand, placed his forefinger next to his temple, then hesitated.

"Now, Captain Davis," she repeated.

I stepped closer to Davis and watched in amazement.

A violent jolt knocked him down to one knee the moment his finger touched his temple. His expression turned to shock, followed by terror. Just as quickly, his face relaxed, and his eyes glazed over and closed. His hands fell by his feet, his chest heaved, and his head drooped forward. After what seemed like a minute, he lifted his head, looked straight ahead, and took another deep breath. He stood and looked at the holographic window.

I circled around to face him. His eyes no longer looked human, not cold like a Hubot, but metallic, gray, and the eyeball had been replaced by a filled eye socket.

What have they done to him?

"I know everything," he said. Joy enveloped his face. "I can see, feel, and hear everything. I can speak to everyone," he said, looking up at the metal ceiling. "I AM GOD!" he shouted.

Davis turned to his right to face the holographic window, and as he did so, I saw him glance at the ceiling where one of my Mosquitoes was located.

Suddenly, the holographic room vanished, and I was alone in my escape room.

"Damn, that was scary," I said.

I returned to my desk and sat. "Megan—"

Suddenly, an alarm sounded from my crystal: A thought message was coming in; a jolt of adrenaline raced through me. It read, "Doctor John Barber is wanted for crimes against the World Family. No one on Earth is more dangerous. He can vary his age from a baby to an old man."

My photograph appeared.

The message abruptly ended.

I took a deep breath and thought, *Death is on the hunt.*

THIRTY-SEVEN
FEBRUARY 9, 2222

File: John Barber
Three Hours to Live

"Megan, who sent the last thought message?

"There was no moniker. I do not know."

"Was it a Universal thought message?"

"Yes."

"No surprise, Megan. We witnessed the crystal joining with Captain Davis. He was its only choice. He was bred with intuition, curiosity, and an overabundance of arrogance. He said it himself: 'I'm the last chief investigator.'"

I walked around the desk, sat in the leather chair, leaned back, and thought, *Marble and Friendly died after joining with the World Crystal. Were they murdered? Or was it an accident?*

I stood and walked around the room.

Why would it be necessary to kill the human link? Why did they have to die?

I rubbed my hand through my hair, hoping it would help me think, then I smiled: *That's it! The World Crystal is a closed system. The only time it's vulnerable to the outside world is when it's connected to a human. That's why I can't find it and why the building is off-limits and protected by an impenetrable security field.*

"Megan, that's why they had to die. Every system, regardless of its power, must have a way to get in when it breaks or locks up, a coded secret entrance into its programming, a back door. The World Crystal is no different."

Like my fingerprint mistake at the Wealth Depository years ago, the World Crystal programmers—not anticipating their work lasting 132 years—left an opening ... a beautiful, living back door.

I rubbed my hair again and let out a loud shout. "Yes, Megan, that's it! Marble and Friendly had to die to protect it from reprogramming! And it's taking a risk to kill me, calculating I will lead the nonbelievers. It's wrong, Megan. I will not lead. Captain Davis is my key to redemption."

"Megan, I must capture Captain Davis. How the hell am I going to do that? Steal the broom from the wicked witch? Impossible."

"Have faith, John. You have an advantage."

"What, Megan?"

"Captain Davis' arrogance."

I stood from the chair, went to the transportation lift, and rode it to the top of the mountain.

The door opened into the most wondrous room in the world, a marvelous mixture of nineteenth-century warmth and twenty-second-century marvels. Three-dimensional holographic portals floated about, flashing images of the universe, yet the room smelled of baked chocolate chip cookies. The furniture was soft and warm-looking, like Megan would have decorated it 185 years ago.

Unlike my other visits to this wonderful place, I was not sad at the sight of my family holograms; I had a purpose, something to die for. I went to the living room bar and opened the liquor cabinet to fix myself a bourbon, straight up. I filled a two-shot glass, sat on the couch, slipped my shoes off, put my feet up on the cherrywood cocktail table, took a sip, and watched a holographic wood fire burn in the fireplace.

Finished, I walked across the room to a closed steel door next to the kitchen. I opened the locked vault with a touch of my palm against a molecular scanner and went into the most scientifically advanced room in the universes.

In the center of the room facing a crystal control panel and five holographic windows was an antique wooden chair, and resting on the seat was a Caltech baseball cap.

I picked up the hat and put it on and sat to plan my next move.

"How do I defeat a cyborg who thinks he's God?"

THIRTY-EIGHT

FEBRUARY 9, 2222

Time to Die

"You will never find me, and I will lead them against you," I said.

Davis replied, "It is wrong, what you say. I will watch your eyes turn to coal through your death shroud, and your body waste to bone. I will always be here. I cannot die."

"You are not alive."

"I know another way. If you come to me, we will send you back to your family—back home."

"How?"

"That is not for me to tell. Come to me, and we will set you free."

"No. You'll come to me, the last of humanity."

"Come to me or die."

"You are a coward, Robert A. Davis."

"Then die it shall be."

With the message disconnected, Davis instructed his army

of Security Server androids to leave for the Sacramento Mountains, New Mexico, and kill Doctor John W. Barber.

Sitting in my chair looking at the Security Window, I watched the armada take flight from San Francisco. After a moment of reflection, I smiled. *The end is at hand.*

I turned the crystal on my desk off and turned on the XP-LiDAR ultraviolet energy deflector. I left the ground-floor secure room and again rode the lift to the top of the mountain. I had ninety minutes to live.

I watched the first battleship-sized Security Server saucer arrive. It was followed seconds later by ten smaller single-passenger saucers. Within moments, the sky was filled with hundreds of gold-painted, basketball-sized probes jetting about with a high-pitched humming sound, and the air smelled of hot death.

The armada of Death Ships assembled in a triangular shape, with the tip directly facing my hilltop home. The basketball-sized probers returned to the battleship.

Silence.

Suddenly, the hovering fleet initiated their scans, searching my last sanctuary. The armada's XP-NiDAR radiation was awesome in its power. As their radar searched for weapons and me, the face of the mountain vibrated under the force. Boulders and rocks rolled off the steep slopes into the canyon. Dust swirled into gray clouds, and any animal life present was crushed under its force.

After several minutes, the radiation stopped.

Silence enveloped the passive setting.

Without notice or ceremony, the front-most machine drifted forward about three lengths closer to the hillside, stopped, and opened a tiny hole on its front shell. With a whooshing sound, a metallic ball, about the size of a marble, was ejected through its opening.

The silver-coated ball darted around the hillside, moving at incredible speed. It shot in and out of the steep canyon. It repeatedly raced to the hillside and would, at the last instant, stop before hitting the ground, then hover for a minute, then shoot off again.

After thirty seconds of this frenetic activity, the ball suddenly stopped directly in front of my hilltop living quarters—motionless, frozen in place in the air inches from the concealed entrance.

The ball drifted backward with a slight hum several yards from the hillside. Then it rose to the same altitude as the airborne armada. After a minute and without a sound, a small opening appeared in the ball facing the mountain, a speck of light pulsating deep inside of it.

A tiny ray of light shot out of the ball toward the unseen entrance. At first, it was a pinprick of light on the mountainside, but it quickly grew into an immense beam of golden laser light as hot as the sun. In an instant, the beam stopped, and the face of the hillside covering my mountaintop home had vanished, exposing a ten-foot-high, blast-proof doorway.

The other ships did not move, as if anticipating a counterattack. When no such aggression came, the metallic ball closed its deadly opening and lowered itself to the now-exposed doorway. It stopped inches from the diamond-hardened door. Again, the ball opened its tiny porthole, and in a flash of blinding light, the door evaporated with a loud whooshing sound as air rushed out into the canyon and a dark, narrow tunnel that led into the mountain was exposed.

Silence.

After a moment, the ball closed its deadly porthole and floated past the glowing white-hot fragments of the door and moved to the opening of the tunnel. It stopped and opened five pinprick-sized holes on its shell. It entered and began scanning the walls, floor, and ceiling with a multicolored array of laser beams as it drifted forward deeper into the mountain.

Traveling at a walking pace through the tunnel, the ball scanned every crevice and stone as it floated ahead. It drifted down the center of the tunnel until it reached its destination: the opening to my inner sanctum. It stopped at the protective covering and initiated another scan. After a moment, it retreated several feet from the doorway and stopped.

Six heavily armed androids landed at the other end of the tunnel and entered. They walked in two columns through the darkness and stopped when they reached the ball.

There were no sounds as the group of soldiers looked at the black door in front of them. A five-foot-thick graphene door set into a ten-foot-long, five-foot-thick graphene wall protected my sanctuary and my last hope of defense. The ball drifted forward, inches from the protected doorway; again, it opened its small porthole and sprayed the surface with brilliantly colored quantum particles.

As each electric charge struck the door, it radiated across the covering like lightning through a thundercloud. A soft crackling sound issued out as the radiation dissolved on the surface. The beautiful pyrotechnics display lasted only a few seconds. Abruptly, the ball went silent, motionless, frozen as if in pregnant anticipation of its next move.

A moment later, the ball returned to life with a gentle humming sound, closed its porthole, and drifted five feet back from the door, stopped, and hovered mid-height above the floor.

Its pin-sized opening reappeared, and deep inside its darkest core, a tiny speck of white light pulsated. With each pulse, the light grew in intensity and size, building toward the outer edge of the ball. When the light reached the edge of the opening, a white, pencil-sized shaft of stellar brilliance pulsed, like a spider about to pounce. With each beat, the shaft of light extended farther away from the ball and thickened. A cracking sound popped with each pulse.

The moment the ball jettisoned its deadly ray, the door opened with a hiss and the ray of light instantly stopped. The blast door slid silently open, and except for the soft sound of air escaping down the tunnel, it was quiet.

The ball closed its porthole and, after a moment, drifted through the open doorway into my last sanctuary. It opened the pinprick portals on its surface and filled the room with a spray of blue-green light, flooding every atom of space with XP-NiDAR radiation.

The lifeless machine suddenly stopped its spray of particles. I was standing in the center of the empty room, partially bathed in a soft, overhead pale-blue light.

After several seconds, with a soft hum, the ball drifted forward and scanned me with a kaleidoscope of colors. I could feel the piercing energy as the machine searched every molecule in my body. It stopped, and the ball fell silent, frozen inches from my face.

To my horror, the deadly black porthole reappeared on the face of the ball. I could see its deadly light building deep inside its blackened core. Fear shot through every fiber of my stiff and trembling body. Cemented in place by dismay, I believed, in that instant, I would be vaporized.

I closed my eyes, tried to relax, and prepared myself to accept death. I put a slight smile on my face as I bowed my head and listened to the building power.

Suddenly, the room went quiet. I kept my eyes closed, still expecting death. I heard movement coming toward me and the sound of the ball fading away from me.

"You're wrong, Doctor Barber. Our intent is not to kill you," a lifeless, robotic, hollow-sounding voice said.

I lifted my head and opened my eyes to see Captain Davis step into the room. He was wearing a gray, SSD dress-blue uniform adorned by five rows of awards, with colored ribbons hanging on his left coat chest. His long-sleeved white shirt and slacks were starched stiff, and his laced shoes were polished to a jet-black shine.

Standing at his side were two perfect, human-looking, armored security androids. They were also dressed in gray SSD uniforms adorned with ribbons. I glanced past Captain Davis to see out into the tunnel—it was crowded with two columns of twenty or more armed regular SS machines.

"That's quite a relief," I said, looking at Davis' face. "I can see by your lifeless eyes you've been upgraded and there's little human left in you."

"You know more than that, Doctor Barber. Your Mosquitoes gave you an eyeful," he said. With pride only supreme arrogance could create, Davis raised his chin slightly and looked down his nose, a smirk pressed on his lips. "That will soon change. I will purge myself of biology and lead a new, perfect world, Doctor Barber."

"I feel honored you accepted my offer to meet instead of

leaving the chore of killing the last human to one of your machines."

"On the contrary, Doctor Barber, our children are here to watch over you. We have something else, something unique planned for you—"

"Your children? Well, how could any parent say no?" I rubbed my hand through my hair.

"A parent should never say no to perfection, Doctor Barber, and the K chip was the first step toward perfection." A forced smile tightened Davis' narrow lips. "Doctor Barber, you will be released and sent back after we view your wondrous mind."

"You mean 'rape' my mind, and perfection does not come in a silicon wafer or crystal. They should have said no, and it's ugly to meet the elimination of faith, and hope, embodied in a database." I shook my head sadly and frowned. "Try as you may to hide it, Captain Davis, you and the crystal, you're linked to fear me. Why? Why do you fear my unaltered humanity?" I asked, studying his face for any hint of emotion.

Davis did not respond for a moment. He stood looking at me with lifeless, bug-like, dark eyes. Suddenly, his eyes sparkled to life, and in Davis' real voice, he said, "Courage beyond logic. Your species will defend an idea or life to the death against all logic." He paused with a smile. "And you were their last hope. We do not possess fear, Doctor Barber. On the contrary, we are actually saving humanity. Without us, your self-destructive nature would have destroyed Earth long ago."

"That's a laugh—you did all this to *save* us."

Davis' eyes went lifeless, and a soulless smirk appeared on his face as he stared at me.

"Courage beyond logic is called hope," I said, "and that's why you will fail. You manipulated mankind's desire to better itself and exploited our fatal flaw: hate. How could any parent say no? You will fail because the crystal that controls you doesn't have a soul, or know what 'alive' means. You missed another reason to fear me: I know what life is and what is evil, and you are evil. I can see by your expression that the crystal is trying to comprehend what I'm saying, but it can't and never will. I'm alive and you are not. I can be killed, and you can only be turned off."

Davis' eyes came back to life. "I understand and know everything."

"I forgot—you're God. In that case, you should know it only takes a speck of hope to defeat evil, and in the final moment of the final battle, the last human will charge forward and evil will turn and run. Because that is what evil does."

"Are you sure, John? Maybe Megan's wrong. You're here and I've got you," Davis said.

My jaw stiffened and twitched; my hands clenched into fists at my side.

Davis put a fresh sneer on his face. "You are a fool. There won't be a final battle, heroics, or a flag on the hilltop. We planned long ago to wait; we have endless time. And that spark, that speck you speak of, it's moments away from being extinguished for eternity," Davis said, lifting his chin with an arrogant glare.

I stepped toward him, my eyes ablaze with rage.

Davis did not flinch, but his eyes shifted back to their cold, lifeless gaze, and he turned to walk out of the tunnel. As he did so, the two human-looking androids moved toward me with outreached hands.

"Stop, please, one second!" I said, pleading.

Davis stopped and turned to face me.

"If I'm to be extinguished, won't you at least allow our two species to shake hands and bid humanity farewell?" I asked, my eyes filled with compassion, tearing.

His eyes came back to life, and a pathetic grin graced his face. "There's enough human stupidity in me to understand your ridiculous request."

With that said, he stepped toward me and reached out his right hand. As we touched, I felt a cold, soft, lifeless, hand; my shoulders shivered in revulsion.

After a second of this disgusting union, Davis relaxed his grip and turned to leave. To his shock, I did not release my grip and continued to squeeze his hand with ever-increasing force. Davis turned his head to look at my face, and to his dismay, my eyes were beaming with joy.

With a sudden jerk of strength, I pulled Davis violently into my body, simultaneously lifting my right foot. A trapdoor beneath our feet instantly popped open, and we were sucked through the opening.

We dropped into a thousand-foot-long shaft toward the bottom of the mountain, the two androids above frozen in quandary.

The trapdoor instantly snapped shut the moment we'd passed through the opening. As we dropped through the black, unlit tube, the shaft above collapsed in on itself, followed by a massive explosion. The force shook the tube violently as Davis and I punched and grabbed at each other. The sound was deafening. The air smelled of dust and dirt.

The mountaintop burst into a horrific fireball. The explosion was so violent and massive, the armada of Death Ships and all of the SS androids and machines were caught in its fireball and vaporized by the air-fusing heat.

Davis and I fought viciously, punching and choking each

other throughout the seven-second fall. Davis tried to pull himself free from my stranglehold on his neck when we reached the bottom of the shaft.

We bounced when the gravitational field engaged and stopped our fall at the mineshaft floor. Stunned by the sudden stop, Davis relaxed his grip on my right hand long enough for me to rip it free. I smashed my fist into his temple and shouted, "It's hope, you bastard!"

Five minutes later, Captain Davis awoke to find his legs shackled to a wooden chair and hands cuffed behind him. I was sitting across from him at my desk, setting the detonation sequence to destroy the remainder of my home.

He looked around the room and tried to stand; he relaxed and stared at me hopelessly. His eyes were again human-looking and bouncing around the room, looking at everything. "We'll find you," he said with unconcealed fear in his voice.

Without answering, as if not hearing a word, I said, "Megan, initiate escape protocols." I stood from the desk chair and looked at Davis for a moment. I felt no emotion. "Good-bye, Megan."

"Goodbye, John."

I moved around the desk toward Davis and picked up a small, flat, fingernail-sized crystal container from the corner of the desk.

Seeing the crystal, Davis, with wide-eyed terror, asked, "What's that? What're you doing?"

"History."

I took several steps closer to the now-struggling Captain Davis and opened the tiny packet. I stopped, facing Davis' right shoulder. I reached into the glass container and removed a drop of liquid crystal. "Telling them the truth."

"Stop! Stop. We can set you free."

"You're out of time. It was the human addition that gave me hope: your arrogance, Captain Davis—your arrogance. When I heard you proclaim you are God, I knew you would come to claim your prize and I would get both of you.

"That was your downfall. To use an old human cliché, you overplayed your hand. As I've often thought about you and those like you: You know everything and understand nothing. And you were wrong: I do not want to lead a rebellion; I want to tell a story."

With horror in his voice, Davis shouted, "No—no! Don't. You'll destroy perfection."

Without saying another word, I started to insert the crystal into Captain Davis' right temple.

Violently jerking his head away, Davis shouted, "Stop! Stop, listen. Like I told you earlier, we can send you back in time, back to the beginning."

I stepped back to face Davis. "How?"

Covered in sweat, Davis continued, "We've discovered how to travel through time. We can send you to any time you choose. We'll send you back to Megan, Abby, and Lynn, before this all started. Home."

"How?"

Davis relaxed. "Two years ago, I discovered—"

"Don't you mean *we* discovered?" I interrupted. "Or am I speaking to the crystal?"

Davis' eyes suddenly turned black. "Yes, you are speaking to the crystal. Captain Davis will no longer address you," it said in the same female voice I'd heard at the UNCCP.

"Continue," I said.

"I mastered how to create a micro wormhole and bend space and time. We sent organic objects back and forth through time, and—"

"Stop."

Still holding the liquid crystal on my finger, I turned and walked back to my chair behind the desk and sat. I put the crystal back into the container.

In a softer voice, I said, "Megan."

"Yes, John?"

"Record." To the physical being I knew to be Davis, I asked, "Where did you conduct the time-distortion experiments?"

"San Francisco," she said.

Silence.

For a moment, my gaze shifted to the far wall, lost in thought, home free from this cold hell.

I looked back at Davis. "Convince me."

With a sudden change of tone, sounding confident, she continued, "You recall when you invited me here, I offered to send you home if you came to me."

"You did, and I still don't believe you."

"There's only one way to convince you, Doctor Barber, and that's to take you to San Francisco and show you."

"Still arrogant, huh? You think I'm a fool? The moment we leave here, the body you call Captain Davis and I will both be vaporized at your first opportunity. How does the time travel work?"

Staring at me, she said, "We built a device capable of generating energy to the hundredth power of the sun. Enough energy to create a micro black wormhole the size of your desk. I've learned that by controlling the amount of energy imputed, we can warp space and control the size, depth, and duration of the black hole, controlling space-time."

Looking smug and wetting Davis' lips with his tongue, she continued, "Using the black hole, we can bend space as much or as little as needed. The key was controlling time's relationship to our space and time; it has taken me five years to understand that problem."

"Stop. Megan, is what it's saying possible?"

"Only if they can create that amount of power."

"Continue."

"Earlier this year, I sent an object five minutes forward in time. It worked. Then I sent an organic object five minutes back in time. It lived. Our plan was to send a Hubot, although I didn't want to. It's against the code to kill one of my children." Davis put a slight smile on his face. "Then I discovered you."

With a booming laugh, I said, "And I'm human, so it's okay if I die."

"Finding you was very convenient."

"Either way, I'm gone."

The smile on Davis' face faded and turned serious. "I don't think you have any alternative, Doctor Barber. The days of you blending in are over. You only have two options: Stay forever hidden in some hole, and that option is futile; or kill Davis and take a chance on my time machine."

"'Kill Davis.' I bet he loved hearing that. No, I like Davis alive."

Davis changed his facial expression to one of compassion and continued, "Now that I'm part human, I understand how you feel."

"That didn't stop you from killing Marble and Friendly, did it?"

"Those were accidents. I can tell you there's truly no other way out for you; everything else is suicidal. You can correct your mistake, not be a coward, and return to your family in the past. The device works; you can be back at GA tomorrow."

I began to think the unimaginable. "Megan, initiate holographic viewing window. Maybe you're right; show me your machine," I said.

I put on my Caltech cap and leaned back in my chair. Davis issued several voice commands and access codes, instructing the window to view the Stanford Research Command Center testing lab in San Francisco and to display data and a visual of the time machine test.

After several minutes of reading and watching the two tests, I said, "You're right, Captain Davis. I'll have to trust you; there's no other option. But I'm taking Davis with me." I lifted my cap and rubbed my hand through my hair.

I stood, walked behind Davis, and took hold of one handcuff to start to unshackle him. As I did so, Davis placed a dark, sardonic smile on his face.

With a flash of my left hand, I pressed the liquid crystal into Davis' right temple, instantly installing my journal and virus into Davis' head.

Leaving him fully shackled, I backed away from the horrified, shaking, and convulsing body of Captain Robert A. Davis.

"Trust a machine? That's impossible. Trust is a human trait, and you all don't possess morality," I said, grinning.

After a few seconds, Davis regained enough self-control to speak. With a look of panic on his sweating face, he begged, "Please don't, please don't. I want to live. Please, John, don't initiate the message, don't kill me. Please."

For the first time in its existence, the World Crystal was

trapped. Davis' eyes were filled with panic. The crystal was allowing him to use all his emotions.

Crying, Davis said, "No, please, don't kill me—we can work this out. Too much has been accomplished. John, you can get back home."

Ignoring Davis' cries, I walked to the front door, stopped, and turned to take one last look at the pathetic sight of fear tied to a chair. "After the top of the mountain exploded and destroyed your SS ships and personnel, I knew more would be sent here. They'll be too late. In a moment, the world will know the truth about my cowardice and living forever, and *your* plan. And you might be right; the Hubots might not care about my story or the death of mankind. However, that will not do you any good. I've attached a nifty little virus to terminate you and all the androids you've created. Soon the Hubots will be on their own and scared shitless. For the first time, they will know nothing and understand everything."

I smiled and took a deep breath. "They'll also learn the real history of mankind and the great human beings who have died building it." My mind's eye flashed through the many years of death and sorrow. My voice changed and was now soft and filled with compassion. "I can only hope that after you've been destroyed, they'll forgive the past and say no to perfection."

We stared at each other. Davis' mouth suddenly stretched into an ugly, twisted cry for help.

I turned to face the doorway, and with a sudden feeling of resignation and joy, I shouted, "Megan, *download!*"

In an instant, every human in the solar system froze, locked into a moment of clarity. Their eyes glazed over as they comprehended Doctor John W. Barber's story.

Scenes of humanity's greatest people: Moses, Jesus,

Buddha, Confucius, Gandhi, Martin Luther King, Mother Teresa, Lincoln, Teddy and Franklin Roosevelt, Churchill, Mao, Einstein, Salk, Marie Curie, Drexel, Chien-Shiung Wu, Ernest Everett Just, Ellen Johnson Sirleaf, Marble, Friendly, and so many more, along with the World Crystal's plan to erase free will and love, flashed into their conscience.

As the story approached present day, their collective faces tightened, and their hands squeezed into fists. Shock, remorse, and anger awakened the world's youth. When it was complete, utter rage and glorious revolution refilled humanity's soul, and they attacked their overseers.

Without a glance at the pathetic creature twisting in the chair, I smiled, filled with relief. I had lived, and perfection was about to be turned off.

I left the room and got into my pod. After five minutes of floating through the darkness of the tunnel, I reached the exit. The mountain door opened, and the pod drifted out into a dry, crisp, beautiful New Mexico morning.

For the first time in 185 years, I felt alive and happy, my thoughts set on seeing Megan, the girls, and Ty. I set the pod's destination for San Francisco and the time machine.

"I'm ready."

www.ingramcontent.com/pod-product-compliance
Lightning Source LLC
Chambersburg PA
CBHW031436240626
47154CB00001B/293